To V

Enjoy!

LINE IN THE SAND

WHAT READERS ARE SAYING

Praise for *Line in the Sand*

"Readers are treated to a fast-paced action story that moves from Mexico into the classroom and on a flight to freedom that includes a cover-up, confrontations with determined drug lords armed with powerful tracking abilities… a memorable, highly recommended story of killers, cartels, and innocents changed by a series of deadly encounters."
—*Midwest Book Review*

"A cartel is about to take revenge on a family, and two refugee kids find themselves under the protection of a school teacher and a janitor of a Phoenix elementary school. They are 'immigrant kids in a dicey situation,' brought to the US by their mother and left with relatives. Will the untrained teacher and janitor stand a chance against contract killers and a ruthless cartel? It's a ride any reader will want to take, a journey with surprising outcomes."
—*Readers' Favorite*

"The new novel *A Line in the Sand* by author Fred Andersen is an ambitious and successful attempt to relate the reality of how things happen along the US southern border. It is a story in which the characters are never sure who to believe, who to trust. In this it instills great suspense and that knot in your stomach that always comes when you're sure something terrible is about to happen.... I was impressed both with the subplots and the believable dialogue. I recommend it to any reader who loves suspense, action, and a feeling of 'reality' in the books they read."
—Amazon reader review

Praise for *Lily Torrence*

"The author has a real talent for bringing everything together, but still managing to surprise you. If you're looking for an interesting, and unique old fashioned mystery this book is a must read!"
—Amazon reader review

"Well written, punchy dialogue, interesting characters, sharp descriptions, great story."
—Goodreads reader review

"This is not a genre that I typically read, but once I picked it up, I couldn't put it down. It is a fascinating tale with great character development and unexpected twists and turns.... I highly recommend it."
—Amazon reader review

ALSO BY FRED ANDERSEN

Lily Torrence

LINE IN THE SAND

FRED ANDERSEN

Palavr Publ

United States of America

Copyright © 2018 by Fred Andersen

All rights reserved.

ISBN: 9780578422718

All rights reserved. No part of this book may be reproduced or transmitted in any manner whatsoever, including digital, electronic or mechanical without written permission from Fred Andersen.

The characters and events portrayed in this book are fictitious. Any similarity to real persons living or dead is coincidental.

fxandersen.com

Cover design: J.T. Lindroos
jtlindroos.carbonmade.com

Cover art © 2018 Palavr Publ

Editing: Sophia Dembling
sophiadembling.com

Print Formatting: By Your Side Self-Publishing
ByYourSideSelfPub.com

Also by Fred Andersen

Lily Torrence
2016 MuseItUp Publishing
museituppublishing.com

Palavr Publ

First Edition 2019

for the Teacher

Chapter 1
FRANK

Grand Avenue School is an old brick building with high ceilings and wood floors. When it was built, almost ninety years ago, it stood in lettuce and alfalfa fields. Now it's in a ragged part of downtown. A lot of souls have passed through here. Children. Teachers. And janitors. At night, when everyone's gone but me, making my last go-round, there's a sound, a low moan, so soft you can't be sure it's even real. But all the HVAC is off, all the water pipes are still, the traffic on Grand Ave has quieted down, and still there's that whisper, that murmur, that moan. After I started hearing it I ignored it for a while, then I denied it was there. When I couldn't deny it anymore, I looked for the source. I know this place better than anyone. I'm the plant manager—what they used to call the custodian, or the janitor. I never could find a source of the moan, and I came to think of it as the life force, the leftover energy of the day, of students and teachers and everyone else, molecules of hopes and dreams and learning, seeping away through the dried-up window frames, and the worn-out weather stripping. By morning, when I open up, the moan is gone. Then another day starts.

That night—Friday, the twelfth of March—I was not the only one there. Two boys waited in Ms. Castellon's room with her for the social worker to come over from District. They would be going to a shelter for the night. Not that unusual. At inner-city schools we deal with a lot of extracurriculars. Family problems, mostly. The parents disappear or go to jail or go crazy. Gangs or ethnic groups don't like one another, and kids get caught in the middle. All kinds of stuff.

Mr. Touwsma, the principal, had explained about the boys earlier in the day. At that point all I knew was that they were immigrant kids in a dicey situation. The boys had been brought to the U.S. by their mother, and left with a relative. That's how they ended up in my school.

"The young one said he was afraid to go home."

"Oh boy," I said. The reddest of red flags.

"Not afraid of the guardian," he shrugged. "She's their aunt, I guess. But it's some back home rivalry that's followed them."

"You can't escape the old country."

"Yeah, they actually wanted to go home with Ms. Castellon and bring the aunt with them." Touwsma's dark blue eyes showed he anticipated my next question. "I don't know where the parents are. Doesn't matter. Can't send 'em home with a teacher."

One of the boys is Adam, and he's in eighth grade. The other one, I forget his name, is in Ms. Castellon's sixth grade. They haven't been in school here long, a couple of weeks, maybe a couple of months. When doing my first pass after school, I stopped in to Castellon's room. The social worker was running late. Since the building was going to be locked soon, I told Ms. C to call me when they needed me to let the social worker in. I went back to work, the building emptied out, she still didn't call.

I was finishing up in the library—dumping trash, straightening chairs—when I heard a door open and close, sounded like the one from the parking lot. I didn't think it would be the social worker, since Castellon hadn't called. Probably Kurt had come back to tell me something or pick up something he forgot. He's the Number Two custodian, a good guy. But he's a young guy, music blowin' in his ears all day. Never has those earbuds out. He forgets things. I figured he would come and find me or call my cell if he needed me. Probably just forgot something.

The second-floor library looks out on the courtyard and the back of the office. As I turned to pick up the paper recycling basket, I saw two men walking toward the office. That had been what I heard. Though the doors are locked at four thirty, teachers and others still leave after that, and sometimes they don't make sure the door latches behind them. And sometimes doors stick, or latches don't latch. It's an old school.

I didn't know or much care who they were, but something made me look again. They were obviously Mexican, or Mex-Am, like most of our parents, But two men? Or maybe it was the clothes. One had cowboy boots and a thigh-length gray coat. The other one wore what I'd call a letterman's jacket—short, dark blue, with leather sleeves—and white warm-up pants. These didn't look like concerned relatives, or someone looking to volunteer for the reading program. I thought of the two boys—they were going to the shelter for a reason.

And then I saw, in Letterman's hand, silhouetted against the white pants, a large black automatic pistol. That settled it. I pulled my phone out, and it lit up.

But now Cowboy did something that made me freeze. He stopped at the back door of the office and looked down, doing something with his hands. Then the door opened, I saw a flash of silver metal, and they went in.

He had keys. Not just a key, the whole ring of keys. Kurt had left at six, and these two showed up not ten minutes later with a key ring—that's how they got in the building. I felt a cold, hard stone under my ribs. Those were almost certainly Kurt's keys, and God knew what had happened to Kurt.

I hesitated, scared by what I was about to do. They wouldn't find anyone in the office, but they might find out where Castellon's room was, and I was sure now that that's what they were looking for. To get across to the Fifth/Sixth-Grade wing, I had to move quickly. I knew nothing about this situation, why the boys were in danger, or why these men wanted them. But I had seen that black pistol outlined against the white pants. The only people I knew for sure that were still in the building were Ms. Castellon and those boys. I cursed my luck and took off. If I could get to Castellon's room right away, we could get out through the gym. Once out, we could call the police, the army, and Sheriff Joe. But at the moment, only I could save them.

The Fifth/Sixth Grade wing was at the back of the school. I ran, hopped, staggered through the halls as quickly and as quietly as I could. I had my keys out and opened the door to that wing, then eased it back closed with a soft click. Castellon's door showed light underneath, and I let myself in so quickly that she looked up at me in surprise—was I trying to be funny?

"Geez, Frank! What is it?"

The boys stared at me with wide, fearful eyes. They were handsome, slender kids in thrift-shop clothes. The young one had these round, apple cheeks.

"You have to leave now. There are men here."

Castellon didn't hesitate. "Come on, boys."

She and the young one, whose name was Christian, or Cristiano, I remembered now, were at the door quickly, but Adam, trying to stuff his feet in his shoes without success, lagged behind. He got one shoe on, but he couldn't get his heel into the other one. As we waited, he squirmed his foot clumsily, his eyes wide with terror. I thought I heard the scratching of a key in the door at the end of the hall. Maybe they wouldn't get it with the first key they tried. Adam kicked off his shoe and skipped across the room in his socks.

I opened the door and peeked out. We had to go about fifty feet, past a pair of classrooms and the boys' and girls' bathrooms. A definite scratching could be heard from the locked door at the other end of the corridor. Still looking for that key, I hoped!

"Go!" I whispered, waving them out and down the hall.

We were almost to the exit when I heard the turn of the cylinder in the lock at the other end of the hall, and the thumb latch going down. I don't know how I could hear that, could see it right in the front of my mind, but I somehow instantly and soundlessly scooped all three of them into the boys' bathroom just as the door began to open behind us.

The bathroom door stood open, in airing-out position for the night. We tumbled in, and the motion sensor lights went on. For a second I considered locking the door, but closing it might make a sound that would give us away.

And they had the key.

Castellon whispered to the boys and they went into the last two stalls. I pushed the override button on the light switch and the room plunged into darkness. I slipped into the first stall.

"Up here!" Castellon whispered. In the stray light from the hall I could make out her form. She was standing on the toilet. Her hand guided me as I pulled myself up next to her. She was a smart cookie, or a cop-show fan. If someone standing near the door looked under the partitions, they wouldn't see feet.

That thought took less than an instant, my mind was racing so fast. I listened hard, trying to monitor where the bad guys were and how the kids were doing. I could detect them breathing softly in the adjacent stalls. Propped there with one foot on the toilet seat and one on the paper dispenser, trying to still my body, I had a half-second to remember that in the remodel five years ago, I had tried to get wall-mounted toilets, because they are easier to clean under. They were more expensive, and the district didn't buy them. So as I half-crouched there, maybe a minute from being shot, I wondered: Would a wall-mounted john have held the combined weight of Castellon and me?

I didn't really hear anything, but sensed someone outside the bathroom door for a moment, and then not there. Finally one of the classroom doors opened at the far end of the hall. The thought of them checking up to eight classrooms while I hung there in an agonized crouch made me weak to the point of nausea. On the other hand, every next breath at this point was a reprieve.

They might only be in the classroom for a few seconds, but I could relax a little. Shift my weight.

"Who are they?" I whispered.

"Narcos," Castellon breathed. "Drug gang. They came to kill the rest of the family."

"Jesus."

Out in the hall, a door clicked open, then another one. Probably they just crossed to another room.

I whispered, "This is why they didn't want to go home?"

"I don't know the whole story."

We were embracing to steady each other. I felt the heat of her on my throat and face. Don't know much about Ms. C., even though she's been here a few years. I know if she has a problem with the room, I'll hear about it.

"Mr. Martin, it's too cold in here. We're all wearing coats." Or, "Mr. Martin, I'm still waiting for you to move those boxes out. This is a classroom, not a storage room." Some of the other lady teachers smile when they ask for something, or flatter you. Like the little girl in the nursery rhyme, the one with the curl. Not Castellon. She may spare a smile but lets you know it's your job, not a favor, to do whatever. She's not like that with the kids. I've seen the real feeling she has for them. Not all teachers have that. She does. Her first name is Brenda, I think.

Another door opened and sighed as the auto closer pulled it shut.

Then someone was outside the restroom. The beam of a flashlight shot across the room and bounced crazily over our heads before stopping, pointed now, I was sure, at the light switch, which has no off-on, just the motion detector, which I had disabled. To turn it back on, he would have to hit the override, recessed under the electric eye. You definitely had to know where it was. Because if there was a way to jack with it, kids would jack with it fifty times a day.

I expected the flashlight to come around and shine in the half-open door of the stall, and pointing at us with the light would be a gun. The blood pounded in my chest and ears and fingertips, but I got ready to jump at the light when it appeared. Maybe I'd knock him down before he could pull the trigger. That's a hell of a goal to have for what could be the rest of your life.

But the flashlight shone under the bottom of the stall, back and forth, and then it was gone. We waited, not even breathing now, and finally the doors at the far end of the hallway opened and slowly closed. We crouched there in silence another full minute.

"Oh God," Castellon moaned.

"Are they gone?" One of the boys.

"Yeah."

I helped Castellon down from our perch, both of us a little unsteady. The boys were already at the door of our stall. We crept toward the bathroom doorway and stopped. I looked out into the hall. Empty.

"Okay," I said. They followed me out into the hall.

Cris's face was frozen, but his eyes darted all around. Adam, I noticed for the first time, still held on to his shoes, gripping them like weapons, little clubs. He put them on, easily now, because he was only frightened *half* to death.

"We'll get out through the gym." I had my phone out punching, nine, one—

"No!" Adam grabbed my hand. "Don't call the police. They'll deport us."

I almost laughed. "If you live that long."

"No!"

"He's right," said Castellon. "If they get sent back to Mexico, they might as well be dead."

"What happened down there? Is your family in a gang?"

"No!" Rage burned in Adam's eyes. "My dad killed one of them. Big narco. Very bad man. But it was an accident. Then they killed him and burned down his store. You don't know what they're like." His voice dropped to a pleading whisper. "They were going to kill us and our mother. We had to leave the country before—even before the funeral." Tears burst out of his eyes in a sudden storm. He wiped his face with his sleeve, and as suddenly, the storm passed. "We can't go back."

"And you ended up here in Phoenix with your mother?"

"No," said Cris. "With our aunt. Our mother had to leave. They were going to kill her."

"Come on." As shaken as I was by this story, there wasn't time now to delve into it. Nothing would matter if we didn't get out of here. I led the way, across the breezeway and into the gym. Just get us out and let someone else sort the guilty and the innocent.

Grand Avenue used to be a junior high, so it has a big gym and funky old locker rooms, things they don't put into elementary schools anymore. The lights were still on in the gym, all of them, and it took me a second to remember why: There'd been a basketball game that afternoon. Kurt, and Jonesy, the half-timer, had cleaned up, but Kurt had left the lights on and the folding bleachers rolled out. Kurt forgot stuff.

But I couldn't stop to think about Kurt.

We trotted across the gym to the little foyer by the parking lot door, still half tip-toeing, trying to be quiet. I opened the door and inched outside.

In the orange glow of the parking lot lights I saw Letterman coming around from the office. He didn't seem to see me. I backed up and pulled the door closed.

"We have to go out that way." I pointed. "Through the locker room. You take them," I told Castellon. "I'll turn off the lights. It'll slow them down."

It was only going to take five seconds, I was going to be right behind them. The master switch box for the gym was right there, in a utility closet. I could kill all the lights except in the locker room. I used my key to open the closet door as Castellon and the boys ran out of the little foyer, out around the bleachers. I reached for the gang switch.

"Ahh!" The guttural male voice came from the gym.

All sounds of motion stopped.

"Okay, okay!" said the voice.

Through the crack in the hinge side of the door I saw

Cowboy walking toward them, a nickel-plate revolver at the end of his outstretched arm.

"Here you are," he continued in tense, raspy Spanish, as if biting off each word. "Now we have you little shits. Just park right there." Or words to that effect. Then he said something into a cell phone.

I was hidden from his view by the closet door. I stepped farther into the tiny closet, carefully pulling the door almost shut behind me. They didn't know I was in the building. That was my advantage, if only I could figure out a way to use it.

I heard a sound outside, and suddenly the exterior door next to me opened, I inched the closet door almost closed. Letterman walked by, not noticing anything. After he passed, I opened the door enough so I could see through the crack.

Letterman walked over and shoved Adam in the face. Both men laughed.

Castellon pulled the boy to her and berated the thugs. I couldn't hear what she said, but I heard the tone, I knew that I was obligated—obligated—to have as much backbone as this woman, who barely cleared five feet and was standing inches away from the gaping muzzle of a very big pistol.

I had to do something now or they were going to die. But if I did something, I would die first, unless God wrapped me in His righteousness and made me invisible.

Invisible.

The two men discussed something in harsh, rapid mumbles while gesturing around the gym. Cowboy took a roll of duct tape out of his coat pocket. Letterman pulled both of Castellon's arms behind her and clutched them in one hand. He took the roll of tape from the other man and pushed her out of my sight. They had to be heading to the locker room.

Cowboy gestured with his gun toward the basketball

backboard at the north end of the court and said something to the boys. Something evil.

Now was the time, while Letterman was gone. I pried my feet out of my shoes and looked one more time through the crack, memorizing the position of the boys. I held my hand over my eyes for a few seconds and flipped the master switches.

I opened the door into darkness and silence. As I started to run, a crash came from the locker room.

Cowboy called out, "Yermo?"

The response was more banging and Letterman's distant cursing. By then I had covered half the distance to the boys. In the dim light from the exit signs, I could make out shadows. I reached out and hit Cowboy's hard, heavy arm, knocking it out of the way. I grabbed the boys by their shirts and shoved them. "Go!"

They took off like scared colts. I stumbled after them, trying to keep a grip on their shirts.

I guided them toward the exit sign over the door we had come in. It would take us back through the school.

A gunshot rang out. Loud mother.

We had reached the end of the far-side bleachers, but we weren't going to make it to the door before the next bullet. The shooter could not see us, but he could hear us. He might not miss again.

"Here!" I shoved the boys toward the back of the bleachers. "Go in!"

Another gun blast.

Underneath the roll-out bleachers was a tangle of steel posts, cross members, and angled supports that scissored together when the bleachers closed. But at the very back, beneath the top row of seats, was a narrow passage that could be squeezed through if you stepped over roller tracks and ducked under crossbars.

I pulled Cristian into this passage, and Adam followed. We stumbled and bumped through the metalwork. I could hear Cowboy's boots running toward us.

If we could get through to the other end, there was another door there. We seemed to be getting the hang of it, working our way through by touch rather than sight.

I wondered what had happened to Castellon.

Another shot exploded. A bullet flashed off steel and clanged into something solid. He was down at the end of the bleachers behind us and could hear us, but of course he couldn't see us.

Then there was another shout, and a stab of light ahead of us.

"¡Pa-ya! Pa-ya!" Cowboy yelled. Over there.

Letterman was back, and he had a flashlight. The light shone through the web of steel up ahead. It didn't reach us, but the men were now at both ends.

We were trapped.

Another shot rang out behind us. The bullet ricocheted off somewhere.

Letterman yelled angrily, probably about the shot, which could have hit him. Unable to shoot at us now, they began coming into the maze of steel supports from either end, kicking and stumbling and cursing.

We had stopped in the middle, where, I remembered, there was a little recess in the wall for the electric motor that rolled the bleachers in and out. I pushed the boys in there. It was a move of near hopelessness, but if we could just stay alive a few more minutes, maybe the police would come. Someone outside had to have heard the shots, didn't they? It was probably too late for 911, but I pulled out the cell phone. Deportation was not our problem now. Living was our problem.

Christ, they were getting close. As I flipped the phone open and the screen lit up, I caught a glimpse of the two boys huddled next to me, panting and trembling in the little alcove, eyes blinking in terror.

And I saw the red button on the wall right in front of my nose. A switch. A switch!

With my fingers I followed the metal conduit from the bottom of the switch box to the motor. Was this the backup switch for the bleacher motor? I had never used it or dealt with it at all.

They were almost here. No time for police, no time for anything. I pushed the button.

The powerful motor kicked and whined, and the bleachers lurched and rumbled as they began to close. I held my breath, expecting the gunmen to reach us and start shooting.

They both yelled and cursed in Spanish. Angry at first, and then terrified.

"My God!" said one. "What have we— Save our unworthy asses!"

Or words to that effect.

The pitch of the motor increased as the mechanism met resistance. The rolling bleachers bounced and bumped. The pitch of the curses rose upward together and turned into a brief, gargling scream. Though we couldn't see anything, the scream was very close and cut through the loud hum of the motor. That terrifying scream meant we were safe, but it was still horrible to hear.

Now the metal grid pressed against the recess where we huddled. The motor shut off. The bleachers were closed.

I heard a moan, labored breathing. Strained words that might be a whispered prayer. A soft pop, like a light bulb breaking.

The boys trembled silently in the little space.

"Breathe," I said, as softly as I could. "It's okay now. We're okay. They can't hurt us now."

Adam whispered, "What happened? Are they…?"

I stuck my head into a small space between the folded-up bars and struts and looked right. Letterman's flashlight was caught on something, shining upward. He had made it to within about twelve feet of our hidey hole. He still stood, facing me, but he wasn't moving at all, or making any sound, and there was something odd about his head. It took me a half a minute of staring to understand the problem. A steel elbow had gouged down into his skull, just in front of his ear.

The space was so tight that to see Cowboy, I had to pull back into the alcove, look left, and then push my head out again. Cowboy was stretched out, close to the floor, face down. He was breathing, softly moaning on each exhale. I flipped my phone on, but by the light of the screen I could only see the gray bulk of his coat. He had gotten even closer to us than Letterman, before the steel trapped him.

"What happened?" Adam repeated.

I pulled my head back in. "They're not good. I think one of them's dead, and one hurt."

Cristiano whimpered. "I want to get out of here."

We definitely needed to get out. "I'll start the motor now. The bleachers will open."

I pushed the button, the motor whined again, and the bleachers slowly rumbled outward.

As soon as there was enough room, I used the cell phone light to check on Cowboy. His gun lay on the floor beside him. I stretched my leg out and kicked it a few feet farther away. Just in case.

As the bleachers opened, he dropped to the floor. He wouldn't have any use for a gun. Letterman's body stayed hung up on a brace. It swayed a little but didn't fall.

When the motor stopped, I heard Castellon out in the gym. She called softly, "Frank?"

"Over here. In here. I've got the boys."

"Thank God! Where are you?"

"Come over to the end of the bleachers. Can you see?"

"Not much. Adam, are you alright? Cris?"

"I'm okay." Adam's voice was thick with fear, or maybe relief. Cristiano said, "We're okay. Mr. Martin saved us."

Dumb luck pushed to the limit had saved us. "We're coming out. It'll take a few minutes."

As I stumbled out through the braces, I tried to think what to do. Had anyone heard the gunshots? Were there more killers outside? Since the gym was still dark, I didn't want to turn the lights back on at... 6:55, my cell phone said. It might attract the wrong kind of attention.

Castellon grabbed the boys as soon as they came out. Cristiano bawled, and Adam sank to the floor like his legs wouldn't carry him anymore. I leaned down and gave him a hug and a pat, but we couldn't collapse now.

I went into the gym office and grabbed a couple of big flashlights. Carrying one, I went back under the stands to check on Cowboy. He was unconscious but still breathing. I called Adam and we dragged the guy out. We tried to be somewhat gentle, but he was heavy, and we were stooped over awkwardly, fighting every post and brace.

I wasn't sure why I wanted him out of there. Adam clearly didn't even want to touch the guy, so I put him at the feet end. Anyway we finally got him out, still alive, but unconscious.

Now that the immediate danger had ended, I had to focus. Beating these guys hadn't solved anything. We had survived, but for how long? I could imagine more killers hiding in the dark recesses of the gym, heard again the rough growl of the two men as they laughed at the boys they were about to murder. Someone like that would be coming for us sooner or later.

To Castellon—Brenda—I said, "What do we do?"

Chapter 2
BRENDA

It was early. No one was around. A cool mist had come in off the sea. Everything was gray and damp and quiet, as if the fog, or the dawn, absorbed all color and light and sound.

The vacation in Mazatlán was Shawn's idea. My husband. He said we could take an overnight train from Nogales, and it would be romantic. But it turned out those trains had stopped running by that time—this was 2005. So we flew. Not romantic. The whole trip was, well... he had good intentions. But it meant finding a sitter for our daughter Nicole, who was only six. And the hotel wasn't what we had expected. Not as nice as I expected.

Then the first night, somebody rattled our door, late, trying to get in. We were in bed. Instinctively I called out, "*Qué pasa?*"

More rattling.

Shawn growled, sleepy and irritated. "*Qué pasa?*"

The rattling stopped and the person was gone.

So I was a little on edge. I am Mexican-American, or better

yet, American-Mexican, like my name: Brenda-Castellon. I speak Spanish, but Mexico is pretty foreign to me. Shawn, on the other hand, and not at all surprisingly, had been down here quite a few times, both as a Mexican—he has family in Guadalajara—and as an American, getting drunk on the beach with college friends.

He knew fun places to go and things to do. The second night we had a very nice dinner, then the following morning, we were up early, walking through the fog to the port where we would take a ferry to Baja to spend a night. Shawn said the ferry building was only a couple of blocks from the hotel, and we could have breakfast there. So off we went. I didn't even think about it. He always handled that sort of thing. He had filled a backpack with everything we needed for the trip. I just had my big purse.

I thought it was a school or some kind of office, the two-story building behind an iron fence. Between the fence and the sidewalk, big spreading trees rose up into the fog. I don't know what kind of trees, but their leaves were big and round and dark green.

There was something on the ground there, near one of the trees. A bag of something. But as we walked closer I realized what I was seeing. A small man lay slumped against the fence. He had the haircut of a young man, close-cropped on the sides, sprouting up on top, frosted pumpkin orange.

That was the only part of him that you could identify as being definitely a human being. There was no chance this was someone sleeping, splayed out as he was. His face was swollen in odd places, and thank God it had dropped down and was mostly hidden in shadow, but what I saw was more than enough. The shirtless torso was lacerated and punctured, and the khaki pants were stained dark all around the belt line and the crotch. My stomach contracted and my mouth filled with spit and bile.

"Oh, good God!" Shawn gasped and he turned me away, but it was too late. We walked quickly back the way we came. I looked around fearfully—were they watching us? But there was no one on the street, and that actually terrified me. I glanced back despite my revulsion. Leaning against the body was a square of white board, maybe wood or foam board. On the board was written TE ENCONTRAREMOS PUTO. Basically it means, We Will Find You, Fucker.

We returned to the hotel. I did not know if we should tell the clerk, call the police, or what. I could not think how we would even do that, what we could possibly say. We went straight to our room, both pretty shook up. I lay down in the bed and faced the wall, but I was not tired, I was agitated, my mind racing. Shawn turned on the TV and flipped through channels, as if there would be something there that would explain what we had seen. I asked him to stop, and he snapped the TV off, stood uncertainly for a moment, then went out—maybe to walk on the beach, maybe to call the police. I didn't care.

I had heard of cartel wars and these kind of revenge killings and horrible displays. I had never paid much attention, because that was down here and I was up there, in nice, safe, clean, America. Now I could not stop seeing the odd folds and bulges of the man's torso. From the severity of the gashes I assumed some of what I saw was… I could not think of what it was, but I could not stop seeing the beaten, butchered, and now lifeless flesh. A man who had been alive when I woke up this morning, or at some time when I was slumbering last night in a rented bed. A boy, more like. Someone's heart and soul.

I woke up when Shawn came back into the room. He said he hadn't talked to anybody, but he had hung around the lobby, the cafe, and had not heard any mention of anything like what we had seen. "I even went back there," he said. "And I couldn't find anything. I went to the place where I thought it was, and there were people walking around. The sun is out, it's getting hot. No sign. And I wondered, did we really see it? Then I realized there was no blood. There was blood on the body, but none on the ground. He was... somewhere else, and brought there after he was already dead."

I did not want to hear about how it happened. I did not even want to hear the word blood.

We flew back that night. The trip to Mazatlán had been intended as a sort of second honeymoon. An attempt to revive our marriage, which was slowly failing. It didn't work. When we got home Shawn was still Shawn, and I was less willing than ever to twist reality into knots trying to make it seem like our life together was working. So it wasn't like the dead body we saw was an omen, or a symbol.

But really, I guess it was. And I never forgot the cool, quiet, mist of that morning. And my revulsion. What kind of people did this? And then just cleaned it up and went on with their day? I knew that was a very racist and chauvinistic way to think, but, Jesus! I came from those people, but things are different north of the line. What is it like to live with that? I could not imagine, and just hoped to God I would never have to find out.

Chapter 3
FRANK

I said, "What do we do?"

She stood there for a full minute with her head bowed, hands covering her face. Finally I took her arm and we walked away from where the boys stood studying the injured killer in the flashlight beam. I had suddenly had a bolt of certainty about what we should do, but it would be hard to explain why we should do it.

I stopped and turned toward her. "I think we should take them away and dump them. If he dies, he dies, but we need to get them out of here, and try to hide that they ever came. Because this is obviously part of some kind of gang war or something. And the fact that we killed one of them and saved the boys is going to bring their fury down on our heads. What the boys said about the dead bodies at the schools."

"When we were standing there, they said they would hang the boys from the basketball hoops. Right in front of us, they said this. And they thought it was very funny."

"God. Unbelievable." How far down was the bottom in this quagmire we'd been thrown into? "We're part of this war now. We have to fight. We can't assume anyone or anything will protect us. The police can't save us. I have read about, and heard about from people I know what it is like in Mexico, the fear of these drug cartels or whatever you call them. We have to take action ourselves." Even as I said it, my belief in the idea was fading.

But there was no uncertainty in her answer. "Yes, I think so. I know a lot about the violence. And the corruption." She gripped my arm. "We have to make it seem these two never came here. Someone else may come looking for the boys, but they won't be here. Yes, we have to get them far away." Her eyes were locked on mine. "We've already seen what they can do. And you're right. We have to hide this from everybody. From the school. From the police. Nobody can protect us from these terrorists."

I paused, frightened and unbelieving that my life had suddenly and irrevocably changed. And was now forever bound to this woman and these kids that I barely knew. "You know, your whole future could be at stake if we do this. I don't know exactly all the ways it is illegal, but it surely is. The killing, and the injury to the guy were self-defense, but hiding the bodies, letting a man maybe die that we could maybe save? No. Your whole career, your whole life could be at stake."

She puffed a dismissive growl. "Like you said, let's worry about living that long."

And I thought, this woman is tough. Linda Hamilton tough. I said, "Are you married?"

"What does that matter?"

I had been thinking not romantically but practically. I had read a little bit myself. These people come after families. So the less family the better. I decided that would not be a good thing to say right now. "It doesn't. Can this really work?"

Suddenly she hugged me. Fervently. Her face was buried in my uniform shirt, her body was shaking with fear or anxiety.

I enfolded her, lay my cheek on the soft pillow of her hair. But the swirl of emotions bubbling in me had no particular focus. I looked over her head at the two boys. "Yeah, they've got to go somewhere safe."

She nodded.

A thought spun out of my jumbled brain. "How did you get away from the other one?"

"Oh." She leaned away from me enough to see my face. "When the lights went out he was surprised. I yanked my hand away and ran. He tripped over the bench. I just went out the door and onto the field and snuck around. The side door of the gym was open, so I came back in, very quietly, and the stands were moving. I didn't know what that sound was at first. Then I heard your voice."

"Did you hear the gunshots?"

"I didn't hear anything until I got back inside." She looked straight up into my eyes. "I know what we do may not work. We may already be dead. But if we are, it doesn't matter what we do, and I want to make a fight of it. That means we deal with this ourselves. We lie. We deny. We hide the evidence, and we take those boys where we know they are safe. Until we can give them back to their mother."

"Okay." I agreed. In an impossible situation, you still have to make choices. Dissolving in a puddle on the floor is not a choice.

Once the decision was made I shifted into action mode, with sudden and absolute clarity about what we would do, every step. It came to me all at once, clear as a road map or a slide show. I didn't have to look ahead, because the next step would appear when needed. I had absolute confidence in that. This clarity brought with it calm.

"We'll leave them somewhere, and then call 9-1-1. They've got cell phones. We'll call on one of them, and throw them away afterward. The police won't know about us. If we get the boys away from here, maybe the narcos won't come after us."

Her expression showed understanding. She nodded.

"We'll clean up as best we can. So nothing proves they were here."

Adam, Cristiano, and I pulled out Letterman. A brutal job. He wasn't as heavy as Cowboy, but his legs were like floppy beanbags, catching on everything. We laid him out next to Cowboy. I got spray cleaner and shop towels and sixty-gallon trash bags. While I went back under to clean up the blood and bodily fluids from Letterman, Castellon bagged him up to prevent further spillage.

None of this went very quick. I'd never cleaned by flashlight before, and everything under there had a deep grime from years of neglect. The boys sprawled on the bleachers, exhausted and in shock. After she was finished with Letterman, Castellon stayed with them. Once in a while she would go kneel down next to Cowboy to see if he was coming around.

After the crazy adrenalin wore off, I felt as weary as I ever have been. But I took the time to go get a can of sweepings from one of the trashcans, and I went back under the stands and dusted them over the cleaned area and brushed away the footprints and drag marks in the dust. I knew very well the contempt this amateurish effort at hiding evidence would stir in the "CSI Miami" guy. But, we might be dead anyway, so why not try it?

When I finished under the stands, I went to the switchbox

and rolled the stands up again. Then I checked on Cowboy. His breathing seemed to be getting shallower, and his face was almost translucent in the flashlight beam.

Before we left I had to finish my regular tasks: turn off lights in the rest of the school and check the locks.

"Come on," Castellon said to the boys. "We have to go get your backpacks and coats. You're not coming back here."

They went to her classroom, while I rushed through the school, shutting it down as per normal, half expecting to see a gunman around every corner, behind every door. My knees were aching, but adrenalin or raw fear kept me going. I was back in the gym in ten minutes.

Castellon stood there, her arms tightly folded over her chest like she was cold.

She motioned toward Cowboy. "That one died."

"Okay, good." So we wouldn't need to worry about him. I didn't feel bad about killing them—anything I did was self-defense. Really, just an accident. In fact, part of me wanted to scream it, broadcast it. I killed them. Even then, though, I knew that what I'd done was going to haunt me forever.

I looked around. "Where are the boys?"

"I had them stay in my room. They don't need to see any more of this. The less they know, the better."

"That's smart." I looked down at Cowboy. "Let's get him bagged, and get both of them into my truck." The plan had changed, a little, but after a momentary glitch, a little hiccup in the transmission, I knew what to do. Every step was on that slide show in my brain. We bagged Cowboy, wrapped both plastic mummies in volleyball nets, and I hauled over two heavy volleyball stands. I backed my truck up to the parking lot door and Castellon and I dragged the bodies over and hoisted them in, and loaded the other stuff. Then I dust mopped over the path where we dragged them, even though I couldn't see any kind of trail. I guess it looked okay.

In the dark.

Chapter 4
TEDDIE

I was born in a house with a very large door, or portón, that opened into a room with a high ceiling that was the biggest room in the house. In this room, not too long before I came around, horses and cows could be kept in times of threat or danger. And there were many threats in those days. Gangs of bandits roamed freely in northern Mexico and took what was undefended. The army, or someone who said they were the army, and the police, but who really knew, were also threats who would protect you if it was in their interest to do so.

These are things I was told. I have often daydreamed about those old times, which seem terrible and yet romantic. When the horses and cows were no longer kept, the gate was removed, the opening was walled in, and this room was the first to receive a concrete floor. The rest of the house had pressed dirt floors with rugs. My mama would sprinkle the floors with a water from a soda bottle, just enough to keep the dust down. Eventually all the rooms had cement or wood floors, with tile or linoleum.

All the children slept in one large bedroom divided by a giant dresser or closet, girls on one side, boys on the other. The dresser, I believe, was built in the room, because it was too large to fit through the door. When we moved out, this big structure of heavy, dark wood stayed behind. My parents slept in the small bedroom at the back of the house. When a bathroom was put in between the two bedrooms, their room became even smaller. The family said this happened after I was born, but I could never remember going to the outhouse, which still stood, though boarded up and unused, through most of my childhood. The house had a large kitchen with a high ceiling, and next to the kitchen a small sala held two sofas and a chair, a gas wall heater and the television.

I was happy to have a bathroom, happy to have my brothers and sisters sleeping and dressing and fighting and playing in the big bedroom. When it came time to clean the room, I was happy for so many hands to help.

And I was happy to be the second-youngest son, because as such, it took longer for me to know the things I came to know. The secrets that would soon rule my life. The knowledge from which it seemed like there would be no escape.

I said that my parents slept in the bedroom, but in truth I only remember my mama sleeping in there, almost all the time. When I was three, my father moved to California. For years he was a visitor and a figure of authority, someone who would come into our home and disrupt the order of our lives with his rough voice and intimidating laugh. It would be a relief when he left again. It turned out he had another wife in L.A., and we had some sort of brothers and sisters there. The few times I saw any of them, they did not seem like real brothers and sisters. They had fat faces and big ears. My mother never complained about this fact of the other family, but she had a streak of anger or bitterness in her that I eventually decided came from her resentment of them.

When I was seven, my father stopped visiting, and we were told he had joined the army. Which army, what army, or why he had joined we were not told, and I did not care. I felt proud of this distant but important man and pictured him marching and shooting and charging, wearing medals for his bravery. I later found out he had actually been in prison in California. By the time I found out it didn't matter. I was older and felt almost foolish about my devotion to the image of my father, the brave soldier. In truth, that was the only time when I really admired him, though it goes without saying that I gave him every respect and obedience.

My life also slowly changed. I had started at the local school, like all the children in the neighborhood. I did well there, and had many friends. But around fourth or fifth grade, a group of boys began giving me trouble. Later on, I would understand better what this was about, but at the time, I only knew that a boy named Gustavo and a couple of his friends began to challenge me. At first, I thought that this had something to do with some neighborhood rivalries that involved my older brother Angel, who had now graduated from the primary school. These boys seemed to feel that I was defenseless without Angel around.

They learned that I was not, but it was not easy. The problems with Gustavo went on for weeks, or months, and made my life miserable. I tried to stay away from those boys, but they always seemed to find me. They would call me names, or make fun of my looks or something I did. They would give me a hard knuckle in the arm, or flick my ear. Soon, I did not want to go to school, but the thought of telling this to my mother, and the look that would be on her face, kept me going no matter what. I knew what I had to do. Probably the outcome would be painful and embarrassing. So I steeled myself as much as a ten-year-old can.

One day during lunchtime Gustavo and Miguel and Juan caught me on the playground, out around the corner of the shed, where no one was watching. Gustavo began punching me, and I socked him in the face, and he fell back over a little wall there and my momentum carried me over as well. Gustavo landed on his head with me on top of him and was knocked out. My right arm was under him when he hit the hard ground, and the impact sprained my wrist. But though my arm hurt, I was the one who stood up and walked away while Gustavo lay there twitching. Miguel and Juan just staring at me in wonder.

This was not something I had planned. I just reacted, and landed a lucky punch. As a result of this fight, some of the parents tried to have me removed from school. They twisted the story around to say that I had hit Gustavo without warning, and Gustavo's parents and the other parents were united in saying that I had been picking on poor Gustavo, who outweighed me by at least ten kilos and had a fat, jutting jaw that he loved to stick in everyone's face. The fact that these parents could be so ignorant or so vindictive filled me with anger, and the experience became a valuable lesson for me about the nature of people.

My mother questioned me about what happened, and I told her the truth. She had heard what the other parents had said and did not understand how I could behave like that.

"Why did you fight?" She stared at me with her hard, intelligent eyes.

"I don't know," I said. "They don't like me. But I did not start the fight."

"They do not like you? Who is they?"

"Gustavo and Miguel and Juan."

"Why don't they like you?"

"Because I insulted them once. I called Gustavo a pig."

"A pig? That's not nice at all. Why would you do such a thing?"

"I don't know." I truly did not know, because the incident never happened. I couldn't imagine calling Gustavo a pig and living. But why they started hating me when they had once been friendly, I could not say. But I knew my mama would not accept that answer and would continue to demand a reason for this hatred that had no reason. I only knew that they had made me fearful, and I was ashamed of that. So I told a lie to hide my fear.

"But Gustavo hit you to start this fight, is that right?" My mother stared into my face.

"Yes."

"And then you hit him back."

"That's right."

"And that is all there is to it?"

"Yes. I didn't hit him hard, but he tripped. That's how he got hurt. Not from my hit."

She took a breath and nodded. She clearly had her doubts about my story, but she went to the school and the other parents and told them what had really happened. She was there a long time, and when she came back, it was over. My mother stuck up for me, even though she had her doubts. That is something I have never forgotten.

I stayed in the school, and Gustavo and Miguel and Juan stayed away from me. But my life never went back to what it had been before, at least at school. It was as if I had been painted by a stain that would not wash off. My friends treated me differently and slowly disappeared. That summer, my mother and her sister started a new school, and that is where my sister and I went the next year. There were only about a dozen kids in the school, some older than me, some younger, and two or three my age. Most of the kids there, their parents worked for my father and his partners. So I was used to seeing them around. The two teachers did not seem like real teachers but more like maids, and they did not teach me much. It didn't really matter. I had always got most of my knowledge from reading on my own. Books, magazines, newspapers. My family came to see me as very smart, but I wasn't. I just read a lot.

Years later I would understand what had really happened about the school and how it was perhaps inevitable. It had to do with rivalries and jealousies in the town, which started with the parents, not the children. I would then understand why my mother made sure to tell me, more than once, not to tell my father about any of this. He was in the army and far away, and I wrote to him occasionally, but I was not to worry him with this. That was fine. I preferred to forget about the whole series of events. But later I would understand the reason that my mother swore me to the secret. I would understand that my father was not like other fathers in town, and our family was not like other families. And I realized that the hatred Gustavo had for me came from his parents, and came from the fact that we were different from them. We kept to ourselves, we got away with things they would never dream of doing.

I was eleven when my father came back and began to live with us again, and we moved to a new house. I mean, it was an old house, but not as old as the other one. This one had no gate for horses. It was near the center of town, with big chinaberry trees on the west side to protect it from the hot summer sun. It had wooden floors, a dining room, and three bedrooms. By then Alejandro and Angel had moved away from home, so it was only me and Manny in the boys' bedroom.

When my father came back into our lives he was soon followed by brother Angel. Alejandro was in Mexico City at the university, but Angel was mysterious, like other men who also began to appear at our house. Sometimes they came to talk to my father. At other times, they seemed to be guests or loafers. We children asked for no explanation of these men and their presence, and none was given. Since I had not grown up with many men around, I just assumed that this was the normal routine for men, to hang around houses and then leave for days or weeks. They would take meals, sometimes cook them, watch television, go outside to stand and smoke and argue and explain obscure things to one another. Sometimes they would talk to me, ask me questions about how I was doing, did I have a girlfriend, play sports, do well in school? Angel almost seemed to be one of these men, but of course, he was not.

My mother, when alone, had never had such visitors. Now, when they were around, she would stay either in the kitchen or in her bedroom. So even though the house was bigger, it seemed to have shrunk for her. She had a TV in her room she would watch. And the hardness of her increased gradually, almost invisibly. She was often impatient even with me and my young brother and two sisters, and I would hear unhappy discussions coming from their bedroom.

I hated that he had come and gone from the family when I was young, and the way he had treated my mother. But in public she was friendly with him. They had a give-and-take, and she laughed and smiled. When at home, however, she did not even pretend to have the warmth toward him that she gave to us children. I missed the old house and the old life we had had there with my mother. Without him. I wished he would go away and leave us alone, and take his friends with him.

One day there were more people than usual at the house,

and not just the men I had gotten used to. There were women and kids there, and then everyone but the kids and a few of the women went to church. It was not Sunday. When they came back there was a big meal and the adults got drunk and hung around all afternoon. The men took off their jackets and the women fanned themselves and dabbed at their shiny faces. It was a funeral for Salomón, who I remembered as young and full of jokes. There were several of these funerals over the years, most of them for men who were not old.

When I was fifteen, things changed again, and I came to know what it was that Angel did, and why my life seemed not my own in many ways. The president of Mexico, Calderón, had declared a war against the gangs that supplied drugs to the United States, and this created problems for my father and people he worked with. Even though he himself did not do anything illegal—or so I thought. I was back in the regular secondary school now, the troubles of before long forgotten. One day Angel waited outside for me, and we walked home together. As we walked he talked to me about how many problems the government caused for my father. He told me how corrupt the politicians and the police were, how the wealthy had rigged things against the poor, and that when the poor needed help and could get no satisfaction from the government, the landowners, the lawyers, and the businessmen, my father helped them.

I felt like I already knew much of this, some from history books and movies, and some from things I had seen myself. I knew my father was an important man who had a business in trucking and distributing in Culiacán and Obregón. But he had come from the common people, and the common people respected him and helped him, just as he helped them. But on this day Angel began to instruct me in how I could protect and help my father as he did.

I already knew not to talk to strangers, not to listen to gossip, not to be affected by the jealousy of others who did not understand our family, our way of life.

"But now," he said, "you are going to hear things from the politicians. They will say that our father smuggles drugs, kills people, is evil in every way. You know these things are lies and exaggerations. They take a little bit of truth and twist it and hammer it and build it into a great big lie."

"I know he could not kill anyone," I said.

Angel laughed. "Our father? Can you imagine that? No, but we live in a violent country. People we know, people who have been in our house, some of them have done some terrible things. I don't even know all the things they might have done." He stopped and put a hand on my shoulder. "Other people we know have been victims of violence. But our father has not been part of this. The people who are saying this, the politicians and the newspapers, are angry because they expect bribes, and our father refuses to pay. Do you know what a bribe is?"

"Well," I said, "I think so. They want to be paid money to shut up."

He laughed again. "Exactly."

I found it easy to believe the things Angel told me because of my experience at the school, with Gustavo, where a tiny bit of truth had been taken by people who hated me and twisted around into a lie. Later, I would come to know these things more fully. But nothing Angel said that day was untrue.

Starting when I was sixteen, I began to be given tasks, simple ones at first. Angel or one of the other men—never my father—would ask me to drive them somewhere, and they would leave, go into a building or around a corner. Sometimes they would be gone a few minutes, sometimes all day, but I stayed there and learned to be patient and remain alert, because sometimes when they returned, it would be with something very surprising, some new task I could not have foreseen, but I had to be ready for it.

They sent me to the airport, or the courthouse, or a hotel, and told me to call in when so-and-so came out or went in. They gave me a package to deliver, or told me to drive a car to a certain place and leave it. I rarely received any explanation at all of what these chores were about. And if I asked anything, they gave me a grunt that might mean anything. So I learned not to bother with questions—any questions.

I learned that Angel held some of his associates in high regard, and clearly my father did also. One of these was DeTirro, a man a little older than Angel who became like another older brother to me, but both more fun and more serious than Angel. He took me deer hunting and to the motocross. He owned an upholstery shop, and often in the late afternoon, his friends gathered there to drink a few beers. These times were great fun, and sometimes surprising people showed up at these little gatherings: bureaucrats from the local government offices, lawyers, engineers, and businessmen still wearing their suits. Sometimes even individual members of one of the police or security forces—not in uniform—would join us. These cops were not the brightest or the most convivial of companions. They seemed to share an inability or unwillingness to speak or joke beyond a minimal level. But they were not bad guys, and they accepted Antonio DeTirro and his friends as equals.

Then came the day they put a gun in my hand. I was very familiar with guns and how dangerous they are and how to be safe with them. I knew how to handle a gun out in the desert, shooting at targets or rabbits or birds. One of the most-told stories of our family was the time my father and Angel and I were out hunting javelina when I was eleven or twelve years old.

We were surprised by a boar charging out of the brush, very close. My father and Angel froze, but I had a .22 single-shot rifle, and I pulled it up and nailed the pig right through the shoulder. Normally a .22 might not kill a pig, but this pig staggered another few steps and fell over. We later found out when we dressed it that the bullet went right through his main artery. From then on, any time hunting was brought up, or even if pork was served, I could count on being called *El Gran Cazador*, The Great Hunter, or some variation on that.

I knew about guns, but I did not know how to sit in the anteroom of an apartment suite in Navojoa with a gun, which is what they told me to do. There was a 9 mm Ruger on the table next to the vase with the plastic flowers.

DeTirro said, "There is a man in there," and he pointed at the door which led to the interior of the apartment. "His name is José. He is someone we are protecting. He is fine with that, and we are taking good care of him. He has everything he needs, and he cannot be allowed to leave, and he knows this. He knows there is a man with a pistol out here who will shoot him if he steps through that door. And if he does, shoot him in the heart. Don't talk to him, don't ask any questions or listen to anything he says. As soon as you see him… right in the middle of the chest."

"But what if someone comes through that door?" I pointed to the hall door on the other side of the anteroom.

"If someone comes through that door, that will be me. Don't shoot me."

I sat in the room for ten hours. I heard television in the apartment, some moving around. I had a lot of time to think and concluded that the man inside must be involved in some way in an investigation or trial of some kind. I also realized that DeTirro's humorous remark meant that I was not the only one here, that there was someone outside my door, somewhere in the building, probably downstairs, making sure no one but DeTirro would walk into the apartment.

But then somebody did. At seven o'clock, a man I had never seen before came in from the hall and handed me a note.

The note said, You can go now.

That is all it said, but I recognized DeTirro's handwriting. The man who gave me the note held out his hand and I gave it back to him. He nodded and smiled but did not say anything. I left.

Chapter 5
FRANK

Yesterday I had no plans for this weekend. I've got two bucket seats ready to go into the Duster. Maybe tackle that. But it's my third car, so no rush.

Then the two bad guys with guns showed up. Now my weekend schedule looks like this: One: Avoid being killed by members of a Mexican drug gang.

Two: Avoid being arrested for a double killing which I've already committed, which might have been self-defense—but that's a mighty big might to pin your future on.

Three: Take two boys I barely know, whom the drug gang want dead, to a new home eight hundred miles from here.

Four: Drive back the eight hundred miles by Monday morning and act like nothing happened.

Brenda had followed me to my house the night before—for safety reasons. We did not know who had sent these men, or what was the driving force behind their actions. But I feared that someone might have been outside the school waiting for them, someone who might try to follow us home. And we had to keep the boys with us now. We couldn't just hand them over to an unsuspecting shelter. So Castellon—Brenda—and I now had to make it seem as if the two men never came to the school. Let their superiors or colleagues, if they had any, speculate about what had happened to them. Maybe they'd got drunk or stoned and blew it off. Maybe they had gone into hiding for fear of… well, who knew? But if they never showed up at the school, if we did not stop them or even know they were there, maybe we would be left alone to go about our lives.

Or maybe the hit men came to the school but could not find the boys, because the boys were no longer there. That's what we were working on now.

The cab pulled up in front of the house.

"Okay." I turned to Brenda. "I'll try to make it quick."

She was sitting at my kitchen table, hand on her purse, still wearing her clothes from yesterday at school—where she's Ms. Castellon, a sixth grade teacher, and I'm Mr. Martin, the custodian. That's all we were yesterday.

As soon as I left she would be taking her car to go home and grab a few things for the trip. She said, "I should be back in an hour."

Before leaving the window, I gave the bright green cab a careful scan. The man inside was dark, but most cabdrivers are. The people who were going to be chasing us now would be Mexican, most likely. But you never know.

I turned to go.

"Be careful." Brenda reached across the table to grasp my hand—this woman I'd hardly ever talked to before yesterday. Her face was creased with worry and weariness.

"And you, too." I tightened my fingers on hers.

My son Matt sat across from her. He's just out of the Army, so he's my roommate now. He had stayed with the boys last night and would be staying here with them again while Brenda and I ran our errands. He said, "I'll keep an eye open."

Before we left town there was one very loose end to tie up. The hit men had come into the school late yesterday afternoon using Kurt's key ring. We'd left school late, in a rush, and in all that had happened since, we had not found out what became of Kurt. Had they scared him off, beat him up, tied him up? Or worse? I needed to find that out before we could proceed. I'd called his phone and got no answer. So I had to physically find him.

"Okay. The boys still asleep?"

She nodded. "I'll talk to them."

Matt sipped coffee. I'd told him as little as possible, to protect him and us. But he obviously knew something very bad had happened. "Do they need anything for the trip?"

I had my hand on the doorknob. "Whatever it is, we'll just buy it on the way."

I went out the carport door. The driver was walking around the car toward me. He seemed innocent enough, but I looked him over carefully. He was a portly, baby-faced, swarthy man who could have been anything from Filipino to Egyptian to Peruvian. He examined me just as warily, this swarthy man approaching him. I'm dark, but also hard to pin down—not obviously Mexican or Indian or black—but then again, maybe.

Seeing that I had only a small backpack, the driver turned and climbed back in the car.

"G'mornin'," I said as I got in. "I just need you to drive me around on some errands. First, let's go to Twenty-Third Avenue and Thomas." Kurt lived on the west side. The school was on the way, and I wanted to see if maybe his car was still in the parking lot. I hadn't looked for it last night.

The cabbie nodded and we took off. The Ford Crown Vic smelled a little of air freshener, and a little of... lunch meat? The aroma of many people a day in a place where the windows were hardly ever open.

The first thing I had to do required some casual stealth. I slid my fingers under my butt and into the crack between the seat and its back to make sure there was enough space. Then I pulled two cell phones from my jacket pocket. These were the dead guys' phones. I powered them on. They were already set on silent mode, no vibrate. Then, as nonchalantly as I could, I pushed them into the crack until I felt them drop into the space below. Hopefully the cab company did not clean that space too often—or ever—and the phones would ride around being tracked for at least a few days all over town, helping to reinforce the idea that the hit men had never arrived at the school.

The best knowledge I could acquire on short notice was that cell phones cannot be tracked if they are off. This seemed like pretty good Wikipedia info. I had turned them off last night, as soon as I got them from the pockets of the dead men. If my information was correct, they would not be trackable until turned on again, as they were now, so there would be no way to say they had gone to my house. And if they were tracked now, they would be all over Phoenix in what I hoped was a confusing manner.

The cab approached Twenty-Third Avenue I said, "Left, up here." The driver made the turn. I had a feeling he might be East Indian. I didn't know if that was better or worse than any other group in terms of hit man tendencies.

We approached the school, which is tucked into a half-industrial neighborhood northwest of downtown. Coming from Thomas Road, you see the ball fields, and then the classroom wings built in the '50s, and behind them, the original high-ceilinged 1920s building and the gym. These buildings that I have taken so much pride in now filled me with dread.

The place was deserted on Saturday morning. We rounded the corner, and there was Kurt's car in the parking lot. I leaned back into the seat to stifle a shudder.

After a moment, I was able to croak, "There it is. Safe and sound. My son borrowed it, and…" I had no idea how to finish that sentence.

"Ah." The driver nodded. He turned into the parking lot.

It had thrown me, but I had to keep going. First, get rid of the cabbie. I reached forward with fifteen bucks in my hand. I wanted him to forget he ever saw me. I wanted to be as average as possible. Fifteen bucks included about a twenty per cent tip on the fare. As average as can be. "So I guess I won't need you anymore."

"Thank you sir." He glanced at me with bulging soft eyes.

When the cab left I walked around the car, surveying the surroundings. The school faced the back side of an apartment complex, mostly blocked from view by some scraggly pine trees. There were a few houses on the left, a motel parking lot on the right. I took out my phone and called Kurt's number. I heard the ringtone through my phone and felt a twinge of relief, sure he would answer in a moment, then he would come down and get me and his car and then—I heard a muffled chirp from the car. From the trunk. Alone in a deserted parking lot in the middle of a giant city, I was almost knocked down by a wave of emotion.

Now what? I tried the door. It was open. I found the trunk latch. I pushed it, and the trunk popped up. I went around to rear of the car and pulled up the trunk lid.

He lay inside, curled up, facing away from me. Even though I was half expecting it, the sight punched me in the gut. He did not move or make a sound. I leaned into the trunk. His half-open eyes did not flicker. He did not breathe. He was dead.

I pulled the trunk lid down and held it. It was a beautiful Arizona spring morning, the kind that people come from all the cold places just to breathe in and feel on their skin. Lacy clouds against an intense blue sky. "Jesus, Kurt." I said in a strangled whisper. Or maybe I just thought it. "What did they do to you, boy?"

There was nothing else to say. Much as I might wish otherwise, I had to keep going. I opened the trunk again. Kurt's wallet bulged in his hip pocket. A wallet containing a life that was over. Fighting a shudder, I slipped my fingers into his right front pocket and pulled out a lanyard with his school ID clipped to it. I reached back in and, yes, the car keys were in there. I wouldn't have to turn him over, thank God. As I pulled the keys out between two scissored fingers, he moved. I jerked and the keys slid back in the pocket.

"Kurt?" I leaned over and stared at the side of his face. A breeze lifted a feather of his light brown hair. I could see the corner of his half-open eye, and there was a glimmer there, a reflection of sunlight. But no life. He hadn't moved. That had been me spooking myself.

He was a good young man who probably didn't get enough credit from me—casual and laid-back about almost everything, a good worker, but not someone who was going to be a school janitor for long. He always seemed to see himself in some bright, interesting, pleasurable future.

"Sorry, son. I killed the sonsabitches that did this. And I'll take care of you." I gripped his shoulder. I had to rid myself of him, and I felt bad about it. "But right now there's things we got to do."

Reaching in again, I snared the keys: a GM key with a plastic grip, and a house key. There was also a medallion that had the word Nebraska embossed on it, and a picture of a covered wagon. Was Kurt from Nebraska? I never knew that.

I closed the lid, walked around, and got into the driver's seat, trying not to think about what was in the trunk. The car was not new, or particularly clean, but it started right away. I wheeled around, looking in every direction, and I did not see a soul. The killers had probably come up to Kurt last night as he was getting into the car, probably played dumb or helpless, and Kurt, friendly to the last, would have offered to help. I had no trouble believing they would cold-bloodedly murder a stranger just to shut him up. How they killed him I could not tell, could not even think about. I didn't see any blood on the ground or in the car. The incredible waste of it, the stupidity and heartlessness, pressed against my chest like a block of iron. Poor Kurt. Poor guy.

I had to get him away from the school. For our cover-up to succeed, it would be much better if his death—his murder—happened someplace else, at the hands of an unknown person.

That might mean that, officially, his murderers would never be caught, and his case never solved. But of course, that had already been taken care of, by me. Somewhere on the Great Ledger it had already been entered.

It was not yet ten thirty in the morning—still cool, but looked to be a pretty warm day coming on. I didn't want Kurt to cook. And I couldn't leave him in a place, such as a public parking garage, where there might be surveillance cameras. I knew an old shopping center, not very busy, where the high wall of the end store would probably shade the car for at least an hour.

I called Brenda. "Are you back already?"

"Yes."

"Meet me at the corner of Thirty-Sixth Street and Indian School."

"When?"

I triangulated our locations. "If you leave now it'll be about right. There's a Circle K on the northwest corner there. Just wait. I won't be long."

"The north-west corner?"

"That's right. Northwest corner, Thirty-Sixth and Indian. But hurry. But don't hurry, y'know? Just take it easy and everything will be fine."

I drove to the old shopping center, pulled into the parking lot, shut off the car, wiped off everything I had touched with a handkerchief, and walked away, pocketing the keys. Brenda's Camry was already parked at the Circle K on the opposite corner.

I took over the driving. We went a couple miles south, until I saw a pay phone in front of Lee's Liquors. There aren't too many of these public phones left, but convenience stores usually have one. I wrapped my hand in the bandanna before touching the phone. Probably not necessary, but my fingerprints, like those of all school employees, are on file with the state. And the army probably still has a set.

I called the Crime Stoppers number, not 9-1-1. "There's a

silver Chevy Malibu in the parking lot next to the antique store at Thirty-Sixth Street and Indian School. There's a body in the trunk." I wanted to say his name, to say something more, but that would complicate matters. It felt like I was disrespecting Kurt, denying his life in a most cruel way. That I had to do it did not make it easy.

As we drove back to the house, I told Brenda what I'd found in the trunk.

She stared at me. "Kurt."

I nodded.

"And he's—"

"Yes, he is—" Suddenly I couldn't breathe. I had to pull over on a side street, stop the car, and cover my face with my hands to keep the sorrow from overwhelming me. What is the meaning? I thought of all the random death and destruction and joy and hope that seems to be part of human life. What is the meaning? What is the point?

We sat there in silence for a few minutes.

She laid her hand firmly on my shoulder. "These animals are not going to beat us."

I took a big raspy breath and tried to compose myself. "We saved the boys, but we didn't save Kurt."

"He was really just a boy himself." Her eyes glimmered.

"Yes, we'll beat them," I said. "If they come back, we'll kill them all. I don't know how. But we'll beat them."

She found a tissue somewhere, and dabbed at my eyes, then her own. Her tender gesture touched me. If this were a movie, we would be falling in love. But we weren't in a movie, just a strained, frightening experience that had forced us into a series of actions we could scarcely believe. We struggled every moment to understand what was happening and what we should do. I hadn't had time to think about her personality or her attractiveness. She had dark eyes and a pretty and plain face. She was a small, intense, smart, and warm woman, ten or more years younger than me. That was the sum total.

But I now knew plenty about her character. In the long night just past, I had learned things about this near stranger, and had feelings about her, that I'd never had about anyone else. That was because of the circumstances, of course, but whatever the reason, we would be linked in a unique way until the ends of our lives, no matter what else happened to us or where she or I went.

I took a deep breath, and turned the car around to get back to the main road. While doing that, I noticed a storm drain on the north side of the street, close to the corner. I looked around. Some kids were playing a few houses down, but they paid us no attention. I stopped and pulled Kurt's car keys out of my pocket, and handed them to Brenda. "If you open your door just a little, there's a storm drain right there. Drop these in."

She opened the door, looked down, and dropped the keys. "Okay?"

"Did they go down in?"

She nodded.

"Okay."

Chapter 6
TEDDIE

The trouble started when my father set up a plastic-recycling business. It is ironic to me that so many terrible things began with this attempt to do something very good for the society and for our family.

In Mexico, recycling is nothing new, but we used to call it scavenging. There are people who make, and have made for years, a fair living doing this. They even specialize. *Cartoneros* pick up cardboard and paper, and have regular depots where they take the stuff. They don't get paid a lot per unit, but there are tons of cardboard and paper being disposed of every day, so a couple of energetic guys with a truck or a cart can move a lot. There are other people who pick up glass bottles, tin, and aluminum cans. But over time, more and more stuff came in plastic bottles, which there was no easy way to recycle. This is a shame because more and more, it is in plastic that sodas come, and Mexicans drink a great, great deal of soda. You might say it's our national drug.

So a group of businessmen my father knew in and around Obregón and Navojoa put together a consortium to begin collecting plastic to bring to a warehouse where we would have the equipment and people to sort it and bale it. The bales could be sold in the U.S., and even shipped to China. My father explained these plans to me in detail, and gave me reports to read. It was a new thing for him to be so open about his dealings and interests, and I was happy to be treated like a man, if not like an equal. He was still my father.

It was a good business, and he wanted me to have a future, and he wanted someone to follow in his path in business. Alejandro was studying the law, Angel was involved in other parts of the organization, and my two sisters and younger brother had other things going on. I still had a difficult time liking my father, a kind of gnawing resentment for the way he had abandoned us before. But my mother had just died of cancer, and I could see that he was sort of self-consciously stepping up to try to fill that loss for all of us kids in whatever way he could, which in my case, since I was now old enough for it, was with responsibility, and work, and money.

I never felt like I was getting a hand-me-down business or a rich man's gift. My father always worked hard, and as little as I knew of him, I already understood that sitting at a desk and thinking hard, reading something and really concentrating, talking on the phone, or going to meetings, that was all work. As much as driving a truck or building a house.

Anyway, I was working on this project, but then the government announced that they were starting the exact same business in our area, a joint plastics-recycling project of the municipal and national governments.

"This is so typical of Mexico," said my father, "and the federal government in particular. A good opportunity arises, or individuals develop something, and the *chilangos* take it over, the PRI assholes, and screw it up, and—"

"And once again," I said, "the people are left with dust in their mouths."

"So the local big shots and the suits from far away try to fuck us. Just as we're about to open up."

My father was very clear about one thing: "The issue is not whether the investment we have already made is to be lost. The initial investment is not that great. The key cost factors are labor to collect the plastic, and transport. Obviously we haven't spent a peso in either area yet."

"Why should the government compete unfairly against private business?"

"Well," he smiled. "To compete… when you decide to truly compete, there is no fair or unfair. It's a fight, a real fight, with no rules. There is no fair. We are going to compete, and win."

Our recycling plant opened for business as planned. We recruited collectors, hired people to sort and to work the baling equipment, finalized contracts with two buyers in California. We got to market first. Then the municipal recycling plant opened. They offered the collectors a higher price. But we knew there was only so high they could go. They had overhead and restrictions that we did not have. So we bumped up our ten kilogram price and managed to keep our supply chain going. We were shipping bales, they weren't.

But one man was a problem. His name was Vicente Padilla and he owned a trucking business and an appliance store and other things, and he was one of the old oligarch class who resented the things that poor, hardworking people like my father were now able to accomplish. That small traditional group wanted to keep the mass of people poor, servile, working for nothing while they, in their wisdom, guided the society in ways that would enhance their own lives. I hated this group of upright, uptight, hypocritical pricks. Padilla treated the municipal government and police force as personal property, using them to gain business advantages and to punish those who went against him. We might have been able to find a mutually beneficial accommodation with the government group if not for Padilla. We made an offer to, in essence, combine the city's program with our business, managing the collection of the plastic and processing at their plant for a percentage of the revenue. We would continue to run our own business independently, and there would be enough work and profit for everybody.

I attended a meeting in which the city leaders responded to this plan. Vicente Padilla—for reasons I do not understand, and to his eternal regret—opposed our plan very adamantly. Because we could not come to an arrangement, a conflict arose. They did not want to see their program fail, and we did not want to be driven out of business.

After that, city health and safety inspectors came to our warehouse and found a number of supposed violations, so we were forced to pay for things like wider doors, fire alarms, and street improvements. The insurance on the truck we contracted for hauling was cancelled, so we could not make our deliveries for several weeks. We were forced to sell our baled pallets to the city at the same rate they paid the scavengers, even though we had already done all the processing and should have been entitled to a higher price. Under typical customs of government and business, which DeTirro called "a nod and a wink," the city consortium should have acknowledged that unfair advantage was being taken, and some other type of compensation or allowance should have been given.

So we nodded, and waited. The wink never came.

My father did not want to do business under this traditional system anyway. He might have made money through crime, but he had earned it honestly. He did not think he should be forced to bribe his way through everything; recycling was a legitimate business, and he thought it should be conducted in a businesslike way. He decided to pursue a legal solution. He had lawyers, too.

But we did something else, as well. We knew that one of Padilla's trucks was headed to Guaymas on a certain day with a load of baled plastics. Our plastic, some of the stuff we had sold to the city at a loss. The city consortium was sending it to port for shipment. DeTirro and I and several other men intercepted this truck, disconnected the trailer, and sent it north behind our own tractor. This would satisfy our contract with our U.S.

plastics customer. We held on to the driver until we knew the load had crossed the border. Then we sent him and his truck on their way. It did not matter that he knew who had done it. In fact, he sat with us the whole time at DeTirro's upholstery shop.

Our approach was that this was almost a prank. But Vicente Padilla did not see it as such. While we continued to try to reach a compromise with the city, Padilla and a few of his allies took a hard line against us.

My father made it clear that we had made our point and there would be no more pranks. But DeTirro heard about a truck full of electronics that was coming in. It was like he had gotten a taste for hijacking and liked it—just like they say that if you have a dog and chickens, if the dog kills one of the chickens, he will develop a taste for it and keep killing them until you have to get rid of one or the other. DeTirro decided to hit this truck himself. He chose two of his most trusted friends but did not tell me about it, even though I consider myself one of his most trusted friends. The day it was happening, I found out what was going on. I knew it was a mistake and tried to divert him, but I did not want him to know that I had found out, because then the person who told me would be in trouble.

"So, let's go down to the civic center tonight," I said to him. "See the car show." Cool cars and sports cars are a shared interest of ours.

"Yeah, okay," he said. But he called me about six and begged off, as I knew he had to. He was going to be busy that evening. I let it go. Loyalty and good business should have led me to talk him out of this project, or to rat him out to my father, who had the power to actually forbid it. But I didn't do anything. I didn't see any real harm. I knew that custom demanded that he would soon be spreading around some of the wealth while apologizing for having broken the rules. It's easier to get forgiveness than permission.

In a way, I could see that he was following protocol by not getting me involved, or even letting me know what was going on. To do so would have put me in a compromised position with my father. Besides, if something should go wrong...

Then DeTirro disappeared. The next day he had been planning to go to Las Vegas for a week off. Or so he said. He was going somewhere, and I was going to stay at his apartment while he was out of town, as I would sometimes do. I was young, single, short on money, and living with roommates in a dumpy place, so it was a nice break for me. And he liked having someone staying at his place to keep an eye on things.

I was also going to take him to the airport. But he did not show up in the morning and did not answer his phone. I went to the shop, and they had not seen or heard from him. There was no news of a hijacking—actually, there almost never is. I talked to a couple of people who might know, and they did not have a clue. It was like DeTirro and the two guys with him had just disappeared.

I got more and more worried as the day went on. Part of my worry was that unless they showed up, I would have to tell my father about it. Finally, around six, I resigned myself to the worst and went to catch him at his office before he went home. I told him what I knew, and what I suspected.

My father rarely looks surprised, but this did get a reaction from him. Quickly stifled. "I think I have given Antonio a little more leeway than I should."

I knew he was also talking about me.

My father does not yell. He will take you down one peg at a time: how you screwed up, like those other times, this one and that one. With me, he professed great sadness, since my lack of character or intelligence must be his fault, etc. This is much worse than being yelled at. Finally he switched the topic slightly.

"You need to understand that this works against everything we are trying to do," he explained with a show of great patience. "The key to organized crime is that it is organized. We are as much a part of the society as anyone else. We are shrinkage to businesses—a small and acceptable and inevitable loss. We are that little fish that cleans the parasites off the whale. We protect the society from wild banditry, from thug violence."

This was the first time my father had talked to me so openly about his underworld life.

"I understand," I pleaded. "But I trusted him—I trust him—to know what he's doing. You trust him, too. He would never betray you."

"But he might cheat me a little and that might be alright a little?"

"No, no. Definitely not. But I only heard a rumor. Antonio kept me locked out of it. He knew I would try to talk him out of it."

"I sure hope so." He wagged his finger. "You haven't been around very long. And maybe you aren't quite as smart as you think. For instance, did you know that this truck was going to Vicente Padilla?"

"You already know about the truck?"

He scoffed at me and looked at his watch. "You come to me at six o'clock. I haven't just been sittin' on my ass all day. Antonio knew it was Padilla's truck. Three days after I told him specifically to lay off Padilla."

What an idiot I had been. I could see now what I should have done. Because I am the son, my loyalty and energy should go unswervingly to my father. And I had utterly failed to realize that. "I don't know what to say, really. I'm sorry. I was just wrong."

He relented slightly. "You'll learn." He smiled. "Maybe."

The next day we found out that the hijack had been an ambush. Police had surrounded the truck and taken the three of them to jail. We found Jesse and Nando there, but could not get any word about DeTirro. Days went by, and the police would not admit that they had him. Of course, we knew what had happened to him. He had been disappeared: Taken to a secret prison or, more likely, shot and dumped into a pit or the ocean.

What we did learn was that the ambush had been engineered by Vicente Padilla. Exactly what his role was, we did not know. Was he involved with the details, or with the carrying out of the ambush? Was he responsible for DeTirro's disappearance? We did not know, exactly. But my father made the decision that something had to be done, even though he knew there would be repercussions.

One night I was at my father's house for dinner. Afterwards he asked me to move some wood out of the storage room. He was an amateur carpenter, a good one, and he had decided to put some hardwood flooring in one of the bedrooms. He already had the teakwood in the storage room, left over from a previous project.

As we stood in the storage room, he put his hand on my shoulder. By this gesture, and by his somber expression, I could tell he was not really thinking about flooring.

"It has come a time," he said, "for you to stand up and be counted. You bear blame in this incident because you felt it was more important to be independent, to be agreeable, than to inform me of an important matter—"

"Pop, it's not that. DeTirro is older than me, he's worked for you for…"

"You were wrong not to tell me. And because of it, Antonio is probably dead."

I couldn't argue with that. I also couldn't escape it. It was haunting me.

He leaned against the workbench. "Angel will be here tomorrow. You will go with us to a meeting with Padilla. We are going to get the truth from Padilla, no matter what it takes."

"Okay."

"No matter what it takes. Got it?" He gave me a piercing, commanding stare. "I want you to be ready for whatever happens."

"Got it." I understood that this was to be my blood initiation. That was why Angel was involved.

But something had changed by the next day. My father decided not to go to the meeting. Angel had talked him into letting him handle it himself. And I was still to go along.

We met Padilla that evening at his appliance store. The store was closed and dark. We parked in the back and went into his office and sat down. From the start, he had a stiff attitude. It was clear he felt affronted by us, though I don't really know why. Our father had set up the meeting, and I assumed there had been words of conciliation on both sides. There was no one there with him, so he obviously was not afraid of us.

He sat behind the desk in what wasn't really an office, but just a cleared spot in the warehouse area at the back of the store. We sat in plastic chairs opposite him.

Angel began. "Your missing trailer can be picked up in Nogales."

"Then it's still missing," he scoffed. "When it's back down here, then it's back."

Angel considered for a moment, stroking the edge of his jaw with his thumb. "Will that satisfy you?"

"As to the trailer, certainly."

"We also need satisfaction," said Angel. "The police have a friend of mine, from the hijacking incident last week. Of course, I don't—nobody condones what he did, but the police have been holding him incommunicado. They won't give out any information about him, even to his family."

"I thought the hijackers were in jail."

"Two of them are. The third one, they do not have a record of. Obviously he is being held secretly."

"Well, that may be." Padilla shrugged. "I don't know. That's the way things go now."

"But you have considerable influence with the police," said Angel.

"Oh, no. Not at all. I support the government, but—"

Angel had gradually been straightening up and leaning forward in his chair. "But you have friends. We don't ask for anything but justice. This man tried to pull off a stupid little robbery. So let him be tried and punished. Nobody I know even wants to defend him. But we want to be assured that he is still alive. Because, as you say, that's the way things go now. His name is Antonio DeTirro."

He shook his head. "Don't know him."

"Of course not. Why would you? But we know they have him, and we need to be assured of his safety. We want to move forward on the issues we have to resolve. But we can't do it without we solve this thing."

"I'm not going to bargain with you." Padilla spoke with a vengeful resolution. "You stole my truck and my goods, you tried to do it again and got caught. I don't know this guy, and I don't give a fuck about him. The issues that need to be resolved, as you put it, are already resolved, as far as I know."

Angel sat staring at him for a long minute. When he raised his hand there was a pistol in it. He pointed it at Padilla's chest.

Padilla was arrogant. "You can't threaten me."

"That is not my intent. We need to find a reason—"

Angel's gun went off, but it didn't seem to hit Padilla, who just sat there smiling. It was Angel who slumped forward. A man came out of the hallway behind Angel and I realized I had heard two shots, not one. The man pointed his pistol at me, but somehow I managed to fire from the waist and shoot first, and he collapsed on the floor. He never pulled the trigger on me.

Angel had been shot in the back of the head. He was leaning over the desk. Now I realized Padilla had been shot in the chest. He was sprawled back in his chair, fluttering his hands weakly. I gave him a shot in the face using Angel's gun, and he stopped moving. Next I dragged Angel over to the door. I put Angel's gun in the stranger's hand, and my gun on the floor below Padilla. I went out and pulled my car up to the door, hoisted Angel into the car, and left.

Chapter 7
FRANK

I backed the Camry into my carport to load the trunk. If a neighbor happened to be paying attention he'd see that I was going somewhere. But I wouldn't do anything to catch his eye. I walked into the house. If someone was watching they would have seen some new people come into the house last night. But they wouldn't have seen anything else unusual. They might notice Brenda getting out of the car, but a woman visiting me was not entirely unheard of. Just a rarity.

Brenda and the boys had slept in Matt's room last night, and he was on the couch. Except she and I barely slept. We had to find a safe place for the boys, and the best we could come up with was with Brenda's brother, who is a police officer in California. (Her other brother is a state highway patrolman.) That actually seemed like a pretty good solution, if he would do it. And he didn't hesitate. "Bring 'em on up, Sis."

So that's what we were getting ready to do this morning. When I walked in, Cristiano, the younger one, sat on the couch watching television. Matt sat at the other end of the couch. He held up a plastic bag. "I got a change of clothes for each of 'em.

A little too big, but they'll do. It's my old stuff."

"Thanks." I turned back to the kitchen and poured a cup of cold coffee.

Matt followed me in.

"Seen anything funny?" I asked. "Anyone drive by?"

"Nah. Just the usual dog walkers." He lifted the lid on a small ice chest. "There's water and soda and cheese in here. Those string cheese thingies. And some bread and stuff in the bag there."

"Thanks, son." I really appreciated not only Matt's help, but his not asking me for more than I told him, which wasn't much more than that I was leaving town with these three people he'd never heard of. "We found a safe place for the boys. I'll be back tomorrow, late."

"You've got a—" He pointed at his chin.

"What?" I said, and walked into the bathroom. In the mirror I saw a seeping scrape from the left side of my neck to just past the corner of my jaw. I had not felt any discomfort from it at all, but there it obviously was. I remembered that I got it late last night, stumbling around in the dark. The overdose of adrenalin I was running on—or something—had completely masked any awareness of the small but ugly injury. And now I could feel it.

Brenda had gone to the back of the house. She emerged from the hallway with a very somber Adam. He was a tall and skinny eighth grader. High strung, I sensed, though he'd managed to keep himself together during the terror of the previous night.

"Adam has something to say."

He frowned at me like he knew I wasn't going to like it. "We have to take my Tía Aida. My aunt."

I didn't like it. "We do? Who says?"

He was ready for an argument. "If we don't bring her, they'll kill her. She took care of us when our mom had to go. Now we have to take care of her."

I almost said, *we can't save your whole family*. But that would be cruel. I still didn't know the complete story of what these boys had gone through.

"We can't judge her," said Brenda. "Aida asked me to take the boys for their protection. She knew there was danger. She has no one."

I calculated what this did to our plan. It could blow it all to hell. "But she's probably the one who told them the boys were at the school."

Adam leaned toward me, defiance hardening his features. "She wouldn't do that."

Brenda was on his side. "They could have found out some other way."

"*Somebody* told them." To buy time, I turned and walked out to the carport. I grabbed the small toolbox out of my truck and put it in the trunk of the Camry. I always try to have tools on a long trip. This gave me a moment to think. Were we inviting the very germ that had almost killed us?

Brenda followed me out. "He might be right. If they found the boys through her, they might do something bad to her.

"It's nuts. What will your brother say?"

"Well, we also have to think about what the *tía* will say if we take off with the kids. There are rules."

Adam came out too. We stood around the open trunk of the car. I had lost on this one. "Where does she live?"

"2906 West Flower. It's an apartment."

"Alright. I'll go get her. They might already be watching her."

"Be careful," said Brenda.

"I'll go with you." Adam smiled, like he was making it better.

"Yes," I said. "You will."

The building was a one-story fourplex of green cinderblock, set in a scraggly Bermuda grass lawn under a couple of mountainous pine trees. Adam led the way to apartment D. For Damned.

I knocked. We waited. A tall, rather beefy young woman finally opened the door.

"*Adan!*" She gave it the Spanish pronunciation. Ah-*don*.

"Hi." I wanted to get inside with no muss. "We need to talk to you. Can I—?" I guided Adam through the door ahead of me as the *tía* stepped out of the way.

She gave him a smothering hug. "Thank God you're okay, *mijito!*"

"Yeah, they're okay," I said.

She ignored me, cooing over the boy.

Adam broke down in her arms. "These men came to the school, they wanted to—"

I patted his shoulder. "I think it's best we don't talk about that now." I did not trust this woman. She could come if she wanted, but I wasn't telling more than I had to. "I'm from the school. I helped the teacher, Ms.... You're Aida?"

"Yeah."

I patted Adam again. He had quickly regained composure. "They're safe. Is there anyone else here?"

"No." She gave Adam a final squeeze, then closed the door and sat down at the kitchen table. The apartment was small. The living room and the kitchen were the same room.

"Did anyone talk to you or follow you?" I asked her. "In the last few days?"

She glanced at me, then at the TV, which was not on. "What happened?"

I sat down at the table, facing the door. "The boys were threatened. They're safe now. Did you see a tall guy who looked like a cowboy?"

"Not a cowboy." Aida frowned at a bad memory. "But someone was watching me. They had a blue truck. But they're gone now."

"I sure hope so."

Adam stood by the refrigerator, his eyes flicking over the stove and kitchen counter in a way that made me wonder if he'd eaten breakfast. I hadn't had a thing.

I leaned closer to her. "We have to get them out of here, and we want you to go with us."

Now I had her full attention. "Go? Where?"

"I can't tell you right now. It's a safe place."

"Why can't you tell me? Why should I?"

"They're going to come back. They're on their way now, maybe, and who knows what they'll do. So you need to get dressed and come with us."

"I am dressed," she sniffed. She was wearing gray sweatpants that were too small for her, a tank top, and a ragged blue long-sleeve leotard. "I can't just—I work and…"

Adam turned to her and hugged her awkwardly. "You've got to!" He gripped her arms. "They'll kill you. Mr. Martin knows what he's doing. He's going to protect us, I know it!"

Aida looked from Adam to me, her annoyance melting into realization.

"You're in danger," I said.

She stood up and walked around the room, looking at the furniture and pictures as if she was going to start packing things.

"You don't have to bring anything," I said. "In fact, you can't. We have to go now."

"How long? What about my rent? What about my job?"

"I don't know. We'll have to figure out a lot of stuff later."

"But I have to know where."

"It's California. That's all I can tell you now."

She walked over to the sofa, picked up a gold satin pillow, and began beating the arm of the sofa with it, whining. "Why does this shit happen to *me?*" She stalked around the room, twisting the pillow, then came up to me. "I have no money, so…" She looked up. "Forget it, Johnny."

I followed her eyes. In the bedroom doorway stood a small man, not much bigger than Adam—a pale, bony man in his underwear, holding a small pistol. That it was small didn't make me quiver any less.

Chapter 8
BRENDA

This morning, before we left for California, Frank and I took the boys into the bedroom and closed the door. We went in there specifically to lie to the boys and try to get them to lie. It's an awful thing to do, but we were in desperate circumstances and facing unknown dangers. They sat on the beds, and Frank closed the door. They wanted to know what happened to the two men.

"I took them to the hospital," said Frank. "They were both, you know, already—"

The boys nodded.

He went on. "I haven't told your *tía* what happened last night. I will eventually, but for now I just think it's best to not talk about it."

"Where are we going?" asked Adam.

"To California. To stay with Ms. Castellon's family. Phoenix may not be that safe right now."

Cris, very somber, said, "Will our mom be able to find us?"

I said, "Yes. We'll make sure of that. This move is just temporary, until she gets here and can decide what to do."

The boys were quiet, and complacent. Still in shock I think. Their lives have been chaotic for a while now, and they woke up this morning in a house they've never seen before, with people around they barely knew. But they seemed to understand that, at least for now, the less truth we told, the better. They seemed to feel the same way I felt, that the four of us were now bound together in the memory of something awful that had happened to us. Like them, like Frank, I had been thrown into this. There had been moments last night when I wondered if I would ever see my daughter again, wondered if I was about to see two children murdered in front of me. Those moments had changed my instantly and forever. And from then on my job, the job of all four of us, was to move on, to take in the horror but not let it overwhelm us.

By 1 P.M. all was ready. Tracy, where my brother lives, is almost to Sacramento. We wouldn't arrive until well past midnight, Sunday morning.

My car would have been comfortable with four, but now we had five. Tía Aida was a large woman and seemed to take up even more space with her self-centered attitude and grating voice. Her presence bothered me because of my suspicion that she had given up the boys' location to the gangsters. I knew we could not leave her behind, but I didn't trust her.

I had spoken to her when Cris enrolled and came to my class. Since it was well into the second semester, I wanted to get a feel for the home situation. Sometimes this kind of contact with parents, stepparents or guardians can be useless or even disturbing. What I found with Aida, who said she was Cris's aunt, was a person already fairly overwhelmed by life and now willingly taking on two boys. But I did not sense fear, or anger, or conflicted emotions that sometimes come from people living on the edges of the law or society or their emotional capacity. I felt the matter-of-factness of families. This is what needs to be done and I am doing it.

Cristian sat in the middle of the back seat because he was the smallest. He leaned affectionately against his aunt, arm across her tummy. On his other side, Adam, the eighth-grader, hunched up within himself in a defensive pose. I had to wonder how this all would turn out for these boys. You do what you have to do to survive, and then you deal with that survival for the rest of your life. These boys, just since I'd known them—less than a day, in the case of Adam—had been threatened and shot at, had seen a man killed practically right in front of them. Then they had helped move the bodies. What would their minds be like at sixteen? At sixty?

Frank drove west on the interstate. There was very little talk like people might normally engage in at the beginning of a long trip to someplace new. Miles and hours crawled by with agonizing slowness under a bright, colorless sky. I slept and woke up and I did not know why I was in a car, who these people were, or where we were going. I remembered what happened the previous night but, for a few seconds, nothing about this morning. Then I started to reconstruct it, which is not the same as remembering. It was very strange. I felt, in a way, like I was still asleep.

We crossed over the river into California and continued north on a smaller highway. Frank and I had each withdrawn as much cash as we could before leaving Phoenix—credit and debit cards would be for emergency use only. And cell phones had been left behind. We could buy some at a drug store. We wanted there to be no trace that we had left Phoenix, or where we had gone.

Cristian dozed off, and Aida pulled herself up toward the front seats and let him lie sideways on the seat behind her. She had a ring with a flashy rhinestone butterfly on it. As she leaned toward us, her hand was on the back of my seat, and the jeweled insect on her finger flicked around the edge of my vision.

She looked at Frank. "So when are we going to figure

everything out?"

"Now is fine," said Frank.

Her face hovered near my shoulder.

She said, "I want to know, where are we going?"

Again I had that odd, disoriented sensation. I had called my brother but could not remember doing it. Yet here we were, on the way, so it obviously happened.

"Tracy," I said, feeling a little panicky. "Up north. We're staying with my brother Willy. He's got a big house, and all the kids have moved out. He's an officer on the town police force. You'll be safe there."

"What about you?"

"We have to go back tomorrow." Frank glanced at her.

"What?" Aida sort of reared back. "You're just going to leave us there?"

"We are trying to keep your location a secret. So we have to keep to our routine. As long as nobody connects you and the boys to us, you're safer."

"So you go back?" she cried. "But what about us? I don't know these people. How will we live? Your brother, does he know we're coming?"

"Of course," I said. "He insisted on it."

Adam mumbled something.

Frank looked at him in the rearview mirror. "What?"

"I don't want to be in Phoenix," he said, not taking his eyes off the scenery, his voice a monotone.

Aida slapped the back of my seat. "This is bullshit!"

"What's bullshit?" Frank's voice rose. He hadn't wanted to bring her anyway. "I don't know what happened to you people before, but you're my problem now. Mine and hers. This is the solution we've got. You got a better idea, let's hear it."

His resentment and suspicion were natural. But he needed to make the best of this. I gave his shoulder a pat and he sent me an apologetic little smile, or smirk. I twisted around so I could see both Adam and Aida. "We don't know what else to do. I'm sorry. At least you'll be safer."

"But I don't know what I'm going to do!" she whined. "I've got responsibilities, a job that I need. Can't I even tell Johnny?"

"Johnny?" I said.

Frank glanced at me. "There was a man there with her."

"He's a friend," said Aida, pouting. "He was worried about me."

"Look," I said. "We know it's tough. But you don't know what these kids have been through. At least you'll be safe here. Can you call in sick? Tell them there was a death in the family?"

Adam growled. "There was a death in the family. And maybe my mother, too."

I turned more to see him better. "I'm sorry."

"They shot my father." His voice barely rose above the road noise. "Someone betrayed him." Adam's voice grew firmer. "Someone in the town."

"Was it the police?" Frank asked.

"No, he was helping the police, and the judges. They were fighting the narcos. The narcos and the police hate each other, and my dad was on the side of the police. He rode with them sometimes. But they couldn't protect him."

We continued down a long, straight stretch in respectful silence for his father.

"What was his name?" I asked.

"Vicente. My father, a brave and strong man."

I felt a rekindling of resolve. The fact that a police force could not protect the boys' family seemed to confirm that Frank and I were doing the right thing.

We caught I-40 to Barstow, then cut across to Bakersfield. I spelled Frank driving and he put a cap over his face and tried to sleep. But the setting sun was coming right through the windshield. Neither of us had slept much the previous night, maybe not at all, depending on how you define sleep. Finally the sun went behind a hill, and we were driving through the shadow of dusk, down a nearly deserted road through green fields, where sprinklers shot long arcs of water into the air.

This is where I grew up, around these endless fields, with the water flowing through ditches and spraying out of pipes; the warm, dry summers when you can almost hear the crops growing; the tule fog in winter; the long lines of farmworkers moving so slowly down the rows.

But I lived in the town. No one in my family ever worked on one of those farms. We never herded goats or smuggled drugs or saw a drive-by shooting. Yes, I come from one of those families. Everyone in my family did well in school and got out in the world through sports, clubs, activities, groups. And we all went to work for the government in one way or another. My father worked for the parks department. I became a teacher, my two brothers policemen, my sister an accountant for the irrigation district. My sister and I were overprotected, of course, while my brothers swaggered all over town like little macho pricks. But Willy went into the army, and from there to the police academy. The younger one, Jerry, got into the highway patrol through community college. We called him Eric or Chip, because of the TV show about the Mexican-American highway patrolman on the motorcycle.

Being Mexican-American, we were all affected by the big migration that started in the '90s, just about the time I was getting out of high school. As law enforcement officers my brothers were very aware of police prejudice against Hispanic Americans, but they were Americans first. American taxpayers paid their salaries and gave them their ideals.

"We're doing a lot of stops on these braceros," Willy would say. "They just have a look about them. They're not like us. They don't even try to fit in. Like our parents did, like we did. We were better, and stronger, because of that. These people just don't get it."

"But they are people," I said. "Like us. Who could be us."

"Well," he said, "they're not us."

"But is it their fault? The father gets deported. And the mother and kids stay. She works, they take care of themselves. But the parents, or the parent, don't speak English, so they are at a disadvantage. Most of the economy is closed to them."

"Well, anyway," he said, "it'll stop soon. The immigration will slow down. They'll get it under control and that'll be the end."

But nobody did anything about it and it never stopped.

We headed up I-5, pushing on through the night past towns, or turnoffs, anyway, to places like Wasco, Kettleman City, Mendota. The freeway was a tunnel of light through the flat, farmy darkness. We ate dinner at a Subway at a truck stop. The back seat fell asleep, and Frank and I switched places every couple of hours and drove on, staring through the windshield at the few things there were to see, definitely victims of highway hypnosis by this point. I felt like I had reawakened from my disorientation, though my memories of the day were still in a jumble.

Then, to pass the time, we started to tell our stories. Me: single mom, college-age daughter, love my family but had to leave Modesto, where I grew up, to live my own life. He: divorced a few years ago, one son.

I said, "Someone told me you're Panamanian."

He glanced at me. "Yeah, my grandfather came to Arizona from Panama in 'thirty-eight to work in a copper mine. But Panamanian really, it's code for African. Somewhere back there I had a great-grandfather who came from Jamaica or Cuba to work on the canal. The Big Ditch. And of course, most, or at least many, Caribbean islanders are black."

"Really! That's fascinating."

"Yeah, Panama is a real crossroads. Indians, blacks, Europeans, and a lot of U.S. citizens. And my grandfather married a Mexican girl. And then my mom married an Irishman."

"Jeez, you got all the bases covered."

"No kidding."

Ten more miles droned by.

"It seems safer out here where it's dark all around. Like no one can find us now." I said. "What a way to come home."

I thought I should clarify one thing. I glanced over my

shoulder at Aida. She seemed to be asleep. I leaned closer to Frank. "I didn't tell my brother that we... took care of the visitors."

"Don't you think he should know?"

"The fewer people who know, the safer we all are."

He gave me a doubtful look. "But for their own protection they need to know what they're up against."

"They're not up against anything," I said. "No one will know the kids are up here."

"Well, okay. I don't know. One day at a time, I guess. One hour."

It was after midnight now, and we were in the last few miles. The lights took on a different pattern. We were there. I directed Frank off the interstate and tried to remember the landmarks and street names that would lead us to Willy's. He has lived in the same house for at least fifteen years, but I'm always afraid I won't be able to find it.

Willy came out on the driveway as soon as we turned in. He's my big brother and has the burly build that runs in the men in my family, and the thick, dark-gray hair. The garage door was already opening, and he waved us in, where his wife Gemma stood waiting, wrapped in a blue robe. The door closed behind us and we got out. We shared quiet hugs and murmured greetings. In this enclosed, echoey, room, after hours on the road, the stillness was almost oppressive. Again I had a feeling of unreality, and it was beginning to feel natural. Our lives, after all, had been uprooted in a sudden and shocking way.

Willy greeted sleepy-eyed Adam and Cristian like a long-lost uncle and seemed unfazed by Aida. He and Frank grabbed the few bags and we all funneled into the house. Gemma showed the kids to their room. Willy, Frank, Aida, and I remained in the big, open kitchen.

Willy opened the refrigerator. "How about a beer, Frank? Sis?"

"Sure," I said. After a night and a day with really no sleep, what I wanted was to find a pillow and some sheets. But my head was still buzzing from the highway. I sat on a barstool and sipped the cold beer. Frank also had a beer. Aida had a soda.

I was dead. We were all too tired to talk. Frank and Willy chatted a little about the drive up, but nobody said anything about why we were here. And I thanked Willy for responding to our need so quickly and completely.

"We'll do what we can to help," said Willy. "I talked to Gemma. We'll take care of them until things get straightened out." He addressed Aida. "And that goes for you, too, young lady. We won't turn you away."

"I'm very grateful." Aida flashed a previously unseen shyness. "I was afraid, there. I was so afraid I asked a friend with a gun to come and sleep on my couch."

Willy chuckled. "This is probably a better solution."

After half a beer I was hearing that old line from the song, *and weariness amazes me*. I couldn't remember the rest of the song or who sang it. The Beatles? No. An American. Mariah Carey? I loved Mariah when I was young... or she was young... someone was young....

Chapter 9
TEDDIE

The most important thing to remember, and please remember it always, is that I am not responsible for the death of Vicente Padilla, or of Ruben Saenz, the corrupt police officer who ambushed us. Shooting Saenz was purely an automatic reaction, and purely self-defense. I can still clearly see the exact angle of his arm as it swung toward me, even though I actually have no idea how I pulled my pistol out of my jacket and fired before his gun was aimed at me. It was like he was in slow motion. He may have thought I was unarmed. My first shot hit him in the chest or arm, and he staggered. The second shot was aimed square at his chest, and he absorbed it without flinching, so I was afraid I had missed. But then he dropped straight to the floor. I never checked to see if he was technically dead at that point.

With Padilla I was only finishing what Saenz had started. When Angel pulled a gun on Padilla, he had no intention of using it. As far as I know, and I have asked people, Angel never killed or hurt anyone in the course of his work or his personal life. I am sure his shooting of Padilla was a reflex reaction to having a bullet slam into his brain while he was holding the gun with his finger on the trigger. Or perhaps it was an emotional reaction to being shot. Perhaps he knew what had happened—he heard the blast of the gun behind him, felt the impact, maybe saw an expression on Padilla's face, and decided to take his revenge instantly. I will never know because he never spoke again, or even looked at me.

He was still breathing when I carried him to the car, but he was dead weight. His head wasn't bleeding that much. I leaned the passenger seat back and laid him on it. I started to pull the seat belt over him, but then stopped, thinking what a ridiculous thing that was to do. But then I thought, He's still my brother. He's Angel. I put on the belt.

That's when it really hit me. I choked up, buckled him in, pressed a rag against his head, and drove away. I drove as fast as I could, but it still seemed to take forever. I spoke to him as we drove, encouraging him. And I really believed he was going to be alright. He was obviously hurt, but just seemed to be asleep. The bleeding had almost stopped. He was breathing normally.

I called my father. Because we knew the phones were tapped, we rarely used them and never said anything important. All conversations were matters of code words, inflections, and inference from what was not spoken. On this night all I said was, "Angel had an accident."

"I see. What are you going to do?" He could not even ask me what had happened. That is what our lives are like.

I said, "I'm taking him to the hospital."

There was a moment of silence, and in that silence, I thought I heard understanding—maybe he read the tone of my voice.

He said, "I will call Ayuda."

Ayuda meant Dr. Flores, the physician who handled things for us.

The doctor arrived at the hospital soon after they took Angel in. He went straight into the trauma center where Angel was. My father arrived a few minutes later and we waited in the hall. Time had stopped. I told my father what had happened, how we had been ambushed.

"Where was this man?" At that point we did not know he was actually a state police officer.

"He must have been hiding in the rows of shelves behind us. The desk where the fucker was sitting was actually in the warehouse, in the back of the store."

"Didn't that tip you off?" His face was slack and pale. His eyes were red.

"Well—"

"Didn't you search the room? You just assumed everything was alright, that the son of a bitch would meet you, all alone?"

I've never felt so miserable, so guilty, so worthless. "Well, it was just a meeting. We have meetings all the time, you have meetings. You don't expect to be shot."

"But Angel pulled out a gun."

"He wasn't going to do anything. He just wanted to, you know, impress on the guy that we were serious."

"That's not how you do it. I thought he had more sense."

I had to defend Angel. "The guy was being an asshole. He wasn't talking. He was giving ultimatums."

My father pressed his hands over his cheeks and mouth, looking up at the ceiling. Tears wet his eyes. "I thought he had more sense." He hugged me and we both cried. He said, "I don't blame you, *mijo*. I could have lost both of you."

We sat there and sat there. Finally Flores came out with the surgeon. We stood up.

"We did a brain scan," said Flores.

We stood there.

"The bullet has done terrible damage."

"Will you do surgery?"

"Your son is barely hanging on. We're trying to keep his blood pressure up and keep him breathing."

"And then—"

"I think it is extremely unlikely he will regain consciousness."

My father broke down. "Can't I...," he whispered, "...can't I even tell him goodbye?"

Flores hugged his shoulders, also very emotional. "You should go in the room. Be with him. Pray. That's all we've got."

My father took my hand and we went into the room. The bed was propped up at the head a little, so he was kind of facing us. His neck and jaw were held in a brace, and hoses and tubes had been taped over his mouth and nose and ran to various machines that clustered around him. My father looked away, for a moment—we both did. Then he gripped my hand hard and we approached the bed.

"Thank a merciful God that she is not here."

He meant my mother. She died of cancer two years ago in January. She and my father had not lived together for several years, though they never divorced. She had to put up with a lot of turmoil and uncertainty when he lived with her, and she had been glad to be rid of that. If she ever felt a bitterness that her life was being taken too early, she never expressed it. That was an almost unbelievable stoic and self-sacrificing aspect of her that I never really appreciated until she was gone. But thank God she did not have to see this.

My father sent a man to pick up my older sister Rosalie. Her expression, when she arrived, was mostly questioning. My father met her in the hall, and when she came in a few minutes later the tears were fresh in her eyes.

We stayed in the room all night. We talked to him. My father was calm at first, but after a while he broke down and wept uncontrollably. My thoughts were filled with scenes from the past, of Angel as a boy and a young man. Angel and I were not close as children. He was more oriented toward our older brother Alejandro, relegating me to play with the girls and the babies of the family. But he was still my brother, a huge part of my life—sometimes an annoyance or a roadblock, but also an inspiration and a protector. And in the past few years, as I slowly came into the business, we grew closer.

Soon Angel began having seizures, arching as if from an electric current and feebly moving his arms and legs. Rosalie reacted strongly to this, weeping and hugging me. My father leaned close to Angel, almost in the bed with him, whispering. As dawn approached the seizures became weaker, and further apart. I knew this meant Angel was dying, but watching him writhing in pain, I hoped it would come quickly. At seven o'clock in the morning he died. He never regained consciousness.

We called the mortician, my sister was taken home. I sat with my father in the room with Angel. I did not know what would happen next, and I feared the worst. I could hardly believe that no police had shown up the whole night. After all, there had been a shootout, three people killed.

After they took Angel away, I walked with my father out into the morning light.

"What should I do?" I asked him. "Are they going to come and arrest me?"

"No. Sit tight."

"How can I sit tight? I don't want to go to prison."

He put a hand on my shoulder. "I am going to see to it. Believe me, I will go to prison before you. And I will never go. So."

Three nights later, Antonio showed up. I was at my father's and drank too much and fell asleep on the couch. The sound of voices woke me. Familiar voices. I walked into the kitchen to find my father sitting there with Antonio. For some reason it seemed very natural that Antonio would be sitting there at the small square table in the green-tile kitchen, looking healthy, happy, unbothered, untouched. My father sat across from him, a strained expression on his face. They both sat there sipping coffee as if Antonio hadn't disappeared suddenly two weeks ago. As if we had not assumed he had been killed by the cops or the prison guards. As if that disappearance had not been the cause of the meeting that ended so terribly.

Antonio stood and embraced me. I did not respond.

"Sit down," said my father. "Let's talk about the future."

"The future?" I was angry. "Where has he been?"

My father ignored that. "Antonio has been talking to the authorities about you."

I sat down, hoping that explanations and understanding would be coming to me soon.

Antonio stood leaning against the counter. "The police know that Angel shot Padilla. And that Padilla shot the cop accidentally. They know you were there, and that you took him to the hospital. That's all you did.."

This statement raised more questions than it answered. "How do they know—?"

My father said, "This is what the evidence shows."

Did this mean that my ruse of switching guns had actually worked?

Antonio sat down next to me. "I went over it with them point by point. You are not going to be prosecuted."

"So it's all going to be swept under the rug?"

"No," said my father. "It's going to go through the system. After all, a prominent man was killed. A police officer was killed. My son was killed. But you are being kept out of it."

"Then I am free?" I could not believe this.

"Yes. But there is a price to pay." My father leaned toward me, his eyes red and tired. "No one else can ever know, you cannot ever admit, that you did anything there but take Angel out of there, to the hospital. And there are to be no recriminations against the police, or the Padilla family. Their businesses will continue to operate." He looked pointedly at Antonio. "With no interference from us."

I was still trying to catch up. "The prosecutor said that? The Padilla family agreed to it?"

"Yes. The brother agreed to it, I'm told." Then my father continued. "The police and the prosecutors are going to regard this as a private dispute between Angel and Padilla that got out of hand."

"I can't believe they are doing that."

My father sat with his elbows on the table, tapping the tips of his fingers together. "We are entering a new era of cooperation with the authorities. Our business is going to change. We're going legit. We're getting out of shipping. It's something we've been moving toward. It's better this way."

By shipping he meant drug smuggling. That was a code word. I could hardly believe this. Shipping was our most lucrative business. "How can we get out of shipping? Will we have income?"

"Yes. Our revenue is going to be smaller, but adequate. It's going to be a real business now. Margins are smaller. We're going to be downsizing. We're getting rid of most of the shipping department. Some will join us, others will—"

"They aren't going to want to be downsized," I said.

My father and Antonio both smiled at me. It was that calm, self-assured smile that lawyers and professors and bankers give you. It said, *we know you don't understand now, but you'll see.* You'll see. I understood that there had been other things going on that I was not aware of and suddenly felt very much like the apprentice I had thought I no longer was. And I felt sick of the whole thing. Why was this my life? Why did I have to deal with these terrors? It made me sick at that moment—physically sick, almost to the point of puking.

But this was the world of mirrors and shadows I lived in. That Padilla and my father both were connected to some of the same business and political people while also rivals was not unusual. The bounds of every person's role in such a situation are well defined. And knowing what to say to whom without crossing or retreating from those bounds is the essence of both business and politics. Even a bloody shootout could be managed.

Two days later, nine people stood in the cemetery as Angel's coffin was blessed and lowered into the ground. This was how my father wanted it. Only the immediate family was there. Angel lay in the plot next to his mother. My mother.

The town was wild with rumors. Padilla's widow, Miranda, had disappeared, along with her two children. She had disappeared immediately or possibly even before her husband was shot. On the afternoon of the day Angel died, one of our people went by her house and reported that no one was home. Neighbors had seen the family leaving in a stranger's car or a rented car late the previous night, and they did not come back.

It was widely believed among my father's pals that Miranda had set up the fatal meeting. Padilla was causing us major problems, but his alignment with the regional police, along with the changing climate brought about by Calderon's war on narcos, made dealing with him very difficult. It was said that Miranda Padilla somehow communicated with my father that her husband was willing to meet with him to settle their differences, but with no specifics of what might be discussed. My father never said anything about these particular rumors, but if he had gone to the meeting as planned, he would surely be dead now. Angel had talked my father into letting him and me go instead.

And I found out where Antonio had been. A judge who knew him had ordered him released from the local jail after the botched hijack attempt and turned over to the federal police for his protection. We had feared he had been killed or disappeared, and he probably would have been if he had remained in the hands of the local police. In return for this very big favor, Antonio had been questioned about his activities, and he had realized that the feds, or maybe the DEA, had thoroughly infiltrated our organization. This was when he was given the ultimatum that he delivered to my father: Get out of the drug business and cooperate. Somebody was going to go down. Antonio conveyed this to my father, and the decision was made to sacrifice the man who was in charge of the drug operation. None of us knew this when we set up the meeting with Padilla. Whether my father found out that day I do not know. Maybe that was why he sent Angel and me, because he knew that Antonio was safe, so there was nothing really to negotiate. Maybe Angel knew this as well.

The morning Angel died, Antonio was released. As part of the deal, I was given immunity for the Padilla killing. I felt humbled and grateful. "My father did that?"

"Actually," said Antonio, "I insisted. I couldn't let you go into the hole."

Chapter 10
FRANK

A dog barked somewhere, not very close. I woke with a start. It was dawn. I didn't remember going to bed, but waking in the near dark I knew where I was right away: At Castellon's brother's house in California. Willy. And Jemima or something. I briefly felt an urgent need to get up and make sure everyone was safe. But I could not move, and as I slid back to unconsciousness, being safe didn't seem so important. They might kill me, or all of us, but I wasn't getting up right now.

I slept again, sort of, replaying all the things I had done to cover our tracks, and also how I would explain myself if caught. In the whole trail of evidence and motives, there was one glaring error: What had become of the school key ring that belonged to Kurt, which the killers had used to get around the school? I was almost positive I had not left this in my truck, which was the vehicle I had at school Friday, or in the house. I had stripped the bodies of identification, had taken their phones, but could not recall checking Cowboy's coat pockets. Unless one of them had dropped the keys at the school, or maybe under the bleachers. I would look when I got back, but in the meantime, there was nothing to do but gnaw on the worry.

After an hour that seemed like five minutes, I got up and dressed and found my way through strange, pleasant rooms to the kitchen. Willy seemed to be the only other person stirring. He provided me with some coffee, and motioned me to come into the den, a small room with a desk and chairs near the kitchen. To my surprise Brenda and Aida were sitting there, stone-faced, like they had just heard some bad news.

"Well, it's interesting." Willy closed the door behind me. "We had company this morning. A guy watching the house. He's not out there now, but we'll see if he comes back."

"What?" It took a moment for me to realize what it meant. We had just driven a thousand miles and accomplished exactly nothing.

"Is it them?" Brenda asked in a soft voice edging to hopelessness.

"Of course," I said.

"Oh god!" Aida moaned.

It was her fault. I said, "You called him, didn't you? That boyfriend or whatever he is."

"He's a friend! I didn't call him. Do you want to see my phone?"

"Yes."

"Well I left it at home."

Willy said, "We'll find out who he is and what's going on. I'll let you know."

Brenda sighed. "Let's keep it under our hat for now. The boys."

Willy nodded and winked. It almost seemed like he was treating it as a game.

Gemma made pancakes and sausage. Everyone was hungry and eager to put the weariness of the last two days behind us. I contemplated Aida's every word and action. Had she called the boyfriend or someone else? She gave no signal I could read. And if not her, who? How?

After breakfast, Willy suggested I come with him to the

store—the fridge was already depleted. We walked out to where his Tahoe was parked in the drive.

"How do you like it?" He beamed at me.

"Nice."

He motioned me to the rear of the truck. "Tailgate." He pointed at it. "Most of 'em have barn doors. I like the tailgate. You can carry big stuff if you have to. And the rear view is less obstructed."

"I guess you're right," I said. "I have a camper shell. Pretty much the same deal."

He opened it. "See?"

He really liked his tailgate.

We climbed in. As he started the truck, Willy said, "Nacio Figueroa, from San Bernardino."

"Nassy... what?

"Our visitor."

"How did you—?"

"I had a friend drive by and get the license plate number while he was parked here on the street."

I felt a little put out, as if I had become merely an observer of my own life. But it was actually a not-unpleasant feeling. Someone else was in charge now. Someone else was taking care of things. I could relax a little. It was mid-morning, I'd had some sleep and some food, and it was alright. I assumed we were going to the grocery store, but we seemed to be touring random residential streets.

We talked about how the drug gang could have found us so quickly—assuming Aida, as she claimed, hadn't told anyone.

"It's hard to fathom," Willy said. "Is there any other way they could have found out your destination?"

"It's possible someone followed us without being seen—but I was looking, believe me."

"Do you believe her?"

"I guess I have to. The boys insisted she was in danger. She might be the only family they have left."

"That's a nasty-looking scrape on your jaw there. Did they

hit you?"

"Naw," I said. "They never found us. I got this moving my boat last night. I've got three cars and a boat, and a two-car carport."

"Your boat?"

I realized how lame that story sounded. "Yeah, to get Brenda's car into the carport. You know, to be less noticeable."

"Yeah, sure."

Willy's smooth flow of conversation was not as casual as it sounded. The small talk mixed with questions about what had happened, what we'd done at various points. His eyes were casually alert at every moment. He had a police radio in the truck, but it only sputtered out routine business as far as I could tell. His cell phone rang. He held it to his ear and listened, grunted a couple of times. "Okay. Right." He lowered the phone. "Señor Figueroa is a U.S. citizen with a minor criminal record."

We had passed from the tract houses out into what looked like fields of corn, about a foot high. A recent rain had soaked the fields and the sides of the road. Knowing the name of one of the gangsters made me a little sick to my stomach. "Is there only one?"

"If we pick him up we might flush out someone else."

"Do they know who you are? That you're police?"

"Don't know. We'll have the sheriff pick him up. Shouldn't take long to find a warrant for a Fig-er-owa."

I understood that he was making a pretty redneck joke about Mexicans. I also got that he could do it because he was Mex-Am. Maybe he thought I was too. My hair, when I let it grow, is wooly gray, my skin is brown. I grew up in a mining town in Arizona where being around working class people of all races was pretty routine, and I had friends of all stripes. There was no ghetto culture. The men and women were there to work hard, get paid, and raise their kids to do the same. The goal was for them and their kids to get out of there at some point, and most did.

"So you work at my sister's school?"

Or maybe he was testing me in some other way. "Yeah. I didn't really know her until this happened. They think a lot of her there."

"We should get down there more. But this job, it's like a Chinese grocery. You can't get away."

He was free with the ethnic clichés.

The police band crackled something unintelligible.

"I don't know anything about her personal life," I said. "But I know she's got character. Fearless. The way she dealt with this."

I wanted to tell him about the confrontation in the gym that had led directly to the two hoods being killed. But I had agreed, I guess, not to tell that. I wavered for a moment. Instead I related how we'd successfully hidden from them in the bathroom, just minutes before that, how she had had us stand on the toilets so our feet couldn't be seen.

"That's my sister," he chuckled. "Go, Brenda!"

I wavered but did not say more.

We came to a stop sign and turned onto another farm road, but which direction we were going I could not say. The roads stretched out long and straight, and clouds hid the sun. It was just farms and more farms.

Willy gazed in his rearview mirror at something behind us. I turned and looked. A police car with flashing lights was pulling up on another car.

"Got 'im!" Willy slowed down and turned right, onto a dirt side road.

From there, looking across the corner of a field, I could see the orange flashers of the police car, now stopped on the road behind the other car. A row of scraggly bushes blocked seeing much more. Another police car pulled up. We were too far away to hear anything. "The guy outside your house?"

"He was outside when we came out. Down the block. He followed us. Then someone was following him." Willy flicked his phone, looked at it, and chuckled. He turned it toward me.

For a minute I thought he was showing me a video of that TV show *Cops*. The camera approached a gray car. I realized this was happening at the moment, right over there.

"That's the car," He glanced at the screen and showed it to me again. "And that's the guy." A bland-looking kid with a fade haircut stood beside the car. "Ever seen him?"

I shook my head. "He was outside your house? And followed us? And you knew it?"

"Yeah." Willy tapped the phone and held it to his ear. When someone answered, he said. "That's the guy."

"That's why you showed me the tailgate. To make sure—"

He turned the truck around, and we headed away from the stopped cars on the paved road. I thought we were coming to another town, but we went under a freeway and were back in Tracy. Maybe this guy was as good as Brenda claimed. He'd been awfully smooth. I had no clue we were participating in a bust, really. I thought we were just riding around and talking.

"We need to figure out what to do," he said.

"Brenda and I have to go back to Phoenix."

"I think that's okay. We'll keep the kids under wraps for a while."

"But what about these gangsters, or whatever the hell they are? They were here right away. They'll be back."

"Maybe." Willy slowed for a red light. "How much are they willing to invest in this, what, revenge thing? I think they'll lose interest fairly quickly. Unless it's something else?"

I felt a flush of panicked indecision. What if they—whoever they were—came after Willy and his wife?

Willy patted my arm. "But they're on our turf now."

His attempt to reassure me made me realize that he couldn't understand because he had not been through what I had been through. But maybe he was right—or at least seeing more clearly than I. After all, he was an experienced policeman.

"We don't get much of this international cartel stuff up here. Not directly. But the local gangs know when someone new comes to town. Sometimes we do a little strategic data sharing."

Had I heard that right? "A local gang cooperates with you?"

"I wouldn't say cooperate." He thought about his words. "Sometimes we have to deal with them. But we'd still pop them tomorrow if we could connect them to the things we know they do."

"Aren't you afraid of, I don't know, retribution? I mean, gangs and such, they don't seem to follow any of the rules of society, or even life."

He considered a moment. "They know we have weapons. They know we will use them if they go too far. And I'm not just talking about courts, law and order. Sometimes law and disorder is the way to go."

"So you have an understanding."

"Absolutely. They're human, though sometimes what they do is inhuman. You have to have a Jesus flashlight sometimes to see that and just do your job, not become a monster yourself."

I could visualize his reaction if I told him everything. He would be calm. He would help us. I walked up to the line, then stepped back. "We're driving back, but we've got to leave soon to be back in school tomorrow."

"I don't know," he said. "If they are following you, I'd hate to see you driving across the desert in the middle of the night. You'd be better off flying."

We had arrived back at his house. Now that the morning's work was over, he gave me a little tour. We went to the back, where the lawn adjoined a sloping pasture that ran down to a creek. It was quaint and pretty in a way that California can sometimes be and Phoenix almost never is. Willy pointed to an old, peeling, wood shed in the corner of the property. "That was part of the old farm here."

Brenda came out on the patio. "We need to have a discussion."

I wondered if it would be about lunch. We went back in to find everyone gathered in the living room as if they were waiting for us to tell them what to do.

I seized the reins. "Well, everything is cleared up, and after talking to Willy, I'm real confident about the plan."

"We'll have fun." Willy smiled at the boys. "Take a little vacation from school. We'll do some things."

They all just stared at us. Adam on the yellow chair in the corner, Tía Aida and Will's wife Gemma on the couch, Cristian on the other chair, and Brenda behind him.

"The boys want to go with us," said Brenda. The other adults both shrugged. The boys were stone-faced.

"Really," I said.

Willy bent over Cris, hands on knees, a smile on his broad face. "A friend of mine has a cabin up at Lake Berryessa. How'd you like to go up there—?"

Cristian didn't even let him finish. "No. We're staying with Miss Castellon. We know they followed us here."

I resisted the urge to find out who had told them. It scarcely mattered.

Brenda was clearly exasperated "We've been trying to talk them out of it for an hour."

I turned to Adam, appealing, I hoped, to his greater age and maturity. "But it's more dangerous with us. We have to go back to Phoenix. Where will you stay?"

"With her." He glanced at Brenda.

The obvious response to that was, *she doesn't want you*. The one response we could not use.

"You should stay with her too." Cristian pointed at me. "That'll be the safest thing."

"Don't worry, you'll be safe here." Willy turned from Cristian to Adam. "I know I'm not as pretty as my sister…."

"I even told them I'd stay here with them, if they stay," said Aida. "I'm going to stay, anyway. Gemma told me it's alright."

"And we have to drive all the way back." I was frankly pleading now.

Adam shook his head. "No. We're going with you."

I looked over at Brenda, and her gaze met me and held for a long moment. Whatever else it meant, this turn meant that the story, or incident, or chapter, or whatever it was, was not over.

The sudden and drastic turn our two separate lives had taken was going to go on now. For how long?

I saw in her eyes a tinge of regret, but also a strength and willingness to endure.

Chapter 11
TEDDIE

Because the accused killer—Angel—was dead, the media—which is to say, the man who owned the local newspaper and a television station, and who was a crony of Padilla's—let the story drop. Padilla's brother, who had been the junior partner, reopened the store. Now my father's business would focus on legitimate trucking and transport, and now there would be no opposition to our move into the recycling business. All was quiet. It seemed too good to be true.

It was.

For one thing, the divestiture of our shipping business was going to be tricky and cause a lot of bitter feelings. The man in charge of shipping was Berto Abella, a ruthless killer and brilliant organizer. He had developed most of the smuggling network, both the supply end and the distribution end. As such, he believed he was the most valuable player on the team and should be the heir to my father, and that his reign should begin soon. I had personally observed his chafing in his tone of voice and facial expressions, which never took place in front of my father, but in other situations, among other associates. In fact he rarely saw my father, since we were pretty sure he was under constant observation by the DEA.

Now, with Angel dead, what would he do? "He is going to try to push your father aside," said Antonio. "He controls the flow of product. He has the people. He thinks your father is too old, takes too much of the profits. He thinks the legitimate businesses are a drain, are just a distraction."

"So now he will get his wish," I said. "We get out of shipping, he can have it."

"No," said Antonio, "Part of the deal, is that we have to give Abella to the government. They don't want to see the operation transferred to a new leader. They want to destroy it. And we are going to help them."

I was confused, to say the least. "But we will be setting up people who have helped us, have been loyal to us. There will be vendettas. We'll all be in danger."

"That is why we have to be very smart and very careful. It cannot look like we set him up. The blame has to be shifted to someone else."

"To whom?"

He gave me a conspiratorial grin. "That is the question."

But nothing went smoothly. Despite the supposed agreement with prosecutors, within days we began to feel the pressure. Our associates who are involved in moneylending, escorts, hijacking, and emigration began to be rousted. Abella's men also were being arrested for minor or trumped-up crimes, which complicated the plan to divest the shipping business. This harassment, though it did not result in big drug bursts, meant that our associates could not make deliveries, so product was now sitting, and cash was not coming in, and everyone still needed income. Our expenses were tremendous, and a large part of those were payoffs and favors to corrupt officials.

But the pressure was not coming from the local police, it was coming from the army drug-busting units and federal prosecutors.

"It's the DEA," said Antonio. The U.S drug agency. "They've

got the leads, the wiretaps, informants. They have lists of suppliers, transporters, distributors. They know names, addresses, brothers, wives, girlfriends. The killing of Padilla made us a target."

I knew about the DEA. They were everything the Mexican police were not: smart, determined and well-funded. Their network of undercover agents and spies extended throughout Latin America, probably throughout the world, and it existed to destroy the drug traders, not to make the DEA agents rich. That gave them a big advantage over the governments and the criminals that they faced. They had already crippled the big Colombian cartels, which is what created the opportunity for the Mexican organizations to step into the breach. Now they were backing the Mexican government in its effort to squash us.

"They are hitting Abella's guys hard," said Antonio, "and he's pissed. He blames you and your father."

"Me? I'm nobody. I don't know anything."

"So we're thinking maybe now would be a good time for you to take a vacation."

This surprised me. By vacation, I assumed he meant go somewhere safe, like Michael Corleone to Sicily. But why now? I was tempted to dismiss the idea, but sometimes hearing things from Antonio was like hearing them from my father. "I don't know. I think I should stay here and ride it out."

"It's not just law enforcement. It's Abella now. We think it's coming to a full-blown war with him. We were going to set him up, but we may never get the chance. It's possible he's already out of reach. We don't know if it's going to come down to shooting. It might."

I did not want to go anywhere. I already felt lonely and isolated. There were images I could not remove from my consciousness: Saenz raising his gun toward me and dropping like a sack of cement after I shot him; Angel's blank, glazed eyes as he lay in my car. And my mother, shriveling up from cancer and years of suppressed heartache.

And strange and fearsome things were happening to me. I

got a phone call—and my number is not widely known.

"Is this Teodoro Soto?"

"Yeah, who is this?"

"Do you live down near the lagoon?"

"No. Who is this again?"

"Oh, my mistake."

Click.

I got several more calls like that. Did I drive a green car; did I own a German shepherd dog? Nonsense questions followed by a hang up. This was very disconcerting to me. I began to question everything I was doing. I began to feel trapped in a life I had not chosen—or had I chosen it? When did I choose?

I did not tell anyone about these calls, or about my feelings. Who would I tell? I had no friends, just associates. I had no woman, just women. My sisters had shut themselves off from me. Angel was dead. My mother long gone. Antonio seemed to have become my father.

Miranda Padilla remained out of sight. Rumor said she had gone to the U.S. Her absence sure made many of us wonder if she had tried to set up my father, and why she might have done that. She was from the same town as my father, and there were hints of something between them, ranging anywhere from a love affair to a blood feud. None of us would dare—or anyway I wouldn't dare—ask my father about these stories. But her disappearance led to a rumor that the Mangos had killed her and her kids. There was no way to refute this kind of talk—in fact, even acknowledging it would be a mistake. Given our arrangement with the local authorities, it was obviously a very dangerous thing to have floating around.

A few weeks later I was pulled over by traffic cops for no reason and made to wait a half hour standing outside my car on a busy street while officers stood nearby and whispered about what to do about me. Then they told me to leave. This was clearly just intimidation. As Rudy Soto's son, I was subjected to a certain amount of harassment, but I also had a certain degree of immunity. This incident made me angry, but when it was over I just felt sad and helpless. Who would I tell?

At that point I decided to just leave town. There were just too many unknown factors. My father and most of those close to him had dealt with these sorts of tensions before. I had not. I arranged to visit a friend of mine in San Diego. That meant I would be out of the loop for a while, but I was beginning to question how much I had ever been in it.

To justify my trip and give me something to do, my father wanted me to work in two areas: recycling and rail transport. The rail line was sort of a grand illusion, but it was one that my father and I shared. He had told me more than once his memories of riding all night on the old diesel train from Mazatlán up to Mexicali. He wanted to reestablish long-distance passenger trains, and had already explored this idea with businessmen and government officials on both sides of the border. Of course, there is no going back—a new train service would require new lines, new equipment, new technology. This was the part that interested me—the mechanics of railroads, the huge and powerful equipment, the massive scale of everything. We didn't have enough money or expertise or connections to make this happen, but we wanted to meet other people who shared this dream of passenger rail. Maybe if enough people cared and worked together, Mexico could do something truly remarkable.

Recycling I knew more about. However I was left largely on my own to make whatever contacts were needed. California had a booming business and trade in recycled materials, and I was able to set up some meetings. But I did not have much to do. I stayed with my friend Michael for a while, did some small deals for extra income. Michael is going to San Diego State, and has lots of friends. I enjoyed being a fake college student and began to wonder if I should become a real one. I looked into applying, to see what would be involved. I would definitely consider engineering—electrical or computer.

Michael's friends went to classes, and stayed up late studying, but their lives seemed so free and happy. I met some nice girls, had some interesting conversations, became aware of aspects of the world I had barely glimpsed before. That was exciting, for a little while. But I also recognized that I was now basically rootless, pointless, without direction. How far would I get into a college program before I lost interest? Each morning, looking at the coming day, I felt like a dead man walking, as the expression goes. Some of this was a kind of grieving for Angel. But I also had a very deep and real frustration about my life. Why was I here? What was the point? I was twenty-one years old now, and I wanted to make a mark. The beach was the perfect place to walk and think, but soon I got tired of trying to figure it out. So I drank and sniffed coke and partied. The ladies liked me. Everybody liked me.

Then Antonio showed up and told me the news, and my life suddenly had a point.

Chapter 12
DEA REPORT

Phoenix Office: Undercover operations
Report of Contact:

Informant phoned into control at approx 1930 hours. Stated that he was a driver on what he believed was a drug sale, or possibly a drug buy. Informant has shown by actions and by quality and amount of intelligence supplied, that he was at best a low-level grunt in the mangos organization. States that he dropped off two men at vicinity of 23rd Avenue and Thomas, assuming they might be headed to the Velda Rose motel on Grand Ave., which is a known retail site.

Why a Mango operative, even a low-level one, would be engaging in activity at a small time drug house is unknown. The hiring of what informant describes as local contractors (of unknown background and unknown intent) and their transporting in a Mangos vehicle leads to no obvious explanation.

Background:

The Mango organization is associated with Culiacán cartel.

The Mangos main activity is smuggling of cocaine and heroin into California and Arizona. They have a chain of wholesalers they deal with and are known as a "clean" organization in that they avoid territorial conflicts, focus on providing supply and services to established orgs, and generally avoid confrontation and violence. They have evidenced little interest in infiltrating or influencing government or business in any great degree. They run prostitution, hijacking, protection, car theft and other local rackets in and around Navojoa and Cuidad Obregón, Sonora. DEA AZ and CA have ongoing intelligence operations re the Mangos, and continue these operations. Informants say the recent killing of Angel Soto, son of org boss, has created a power struggle within Mangos, which may offer an opportunity for strategic disruption and takedown of the drug operation.

Summary:

Contact from Informant _____ acknowledged. No action taken. Will continue to monitor informant.

Chapter 13
FRANK

I saw them as soon as we walked into the terminal. More important, they saw us.

We had decided that we couldn't drive and still get to school tomorrow. So I used Willy's desktop to buy us four airline tickets, and we slipped out of Tracy hunched down in the back of the Tahoe. So Brenda's car would be left here until... who knows? As we got out at the departure door at the Oakland airport, Willy said, "I've got a guy inside. He'll keep an eye out."

But the eyes we'd caught were a couple of not-very-subtle Latin gangbanger types, one in a green nylon Eagles football jersey and one in a black shirt with the sleeves rolled up. They began to move toward us as we walked through an arcade of restaurants and gift shops, heading to the security gate. My heart sank and anger flamed in me, so hard and high I almost could not contain it. I was bloody sick of being chased and threatened by Mexican thugs.

Cristian pointed at a bright red-and-yellow sign. "In-N-Out Burger. They're good."

Brenda glanced at me. "The boys are hungry. Is there food

on the plane?"

"On Southwest?" I said, irritable.

Brenda slowed down. "We've got plenty of time."

She obviously had not seen the two men. I wished I had gotten details from Willy as to who was waiting for us. Bringing the boys had been foolish. I should have stood my ground. Now we were stuck.

"What's wrong?" she said.

"Nothing." I tried to regain my composure. "They have the same kind of shops on the other side of security," I said. "Let's get that over with."

She gave me a look.

"Just, I'll feel better when we're in a secure area."

We walked around a sort of mezzanine where some escalators were partitioned off by a short wall. I took advantage of the little ripple in traffic to hitch up the strap on my bag, half turning and glancing back. They were there, easily within sight, but I did not catch them looking at us.

We came to the line for the security check. It wasn't a very long line or a very crowded area. Ahead of us, uniformed people directed passengers through the familiar routine: shoes off, objects into tray. Armed officers stood on either side of the corral, attentive and calm. I felt better already. Standing in line, I turned and glanced back again. Our new admirers had disappeared. I scanned left and right for them, trying to stay casual. Nothing. If they were still watching us they were well hidden. No one else looked suspicious either.

I began to relax a little, conceding that I was just a *bit* on edge and could have misconstrued the glances of a couple of Mexican-looking dudes. In fact, what kind of reaction might my red-eyed glare have produced in them? If they were illegal aliens, or even if they weren't, a visual going over by an old man with an attitude might have made them at least a little uncomfortable.

Someone was giving directions. A slim, exotic-looking woman in a blue Southwest Airlines shirt spoke to the couple ahead of us, pointing to her left. "Gates thirty-six, thirty-seven, thirty-eight, and forty, forty-one, forty-two, you have to take the elevator. Yes sir, it's construction. Yes, the elevator will take you down one floor, then you just follow the passage. Los Angeles, yes."

We were headed to gate forty-one. As my eyes followed her pointing finger, I saw a large group of people crowded around a single elevator. That couldn't be right, yet it clearly was. I looked at the woman. "We haven't gone through the security gate yet."

"That's right," she said. "They have security down there. Just follow the passage."

"Oh, great." I muttered.

"We've still got two hours," she said.

"Of standing in line."

But there was nothing we could do. And there was plenty of annoyance around. As the crowd swelled behind us, more people noticed that there was only one elevator, no stairs, and the elevator held maybe a dozen people at a time. No one was happy.

Something poked me in the back, the corner of a suitcase or something. I flinched badly. That could have been a knife. A man and a woman just ahead of us jabbered softly in a foreign language, not Spanish. A tall hipster dude next to them stared at me with eerily bright blue eyes. What was he staring at? I looked around for the two men who had followed us, for a green jersey, a black shirt. I didn't see anything. But in truth, anyone around us could be an assassin.

I leaned to Brenda's ear. "I don't like this."

She gripped my arm and gave it a pat.

We shuffled slowly forward, hemmed in by people and their luggage. Suddenly the jam broke free for a moment, and the boys were moving ahead without us. Brenda let go of me and snared Adam's jacket. But Cristiano kept moving ahead, oblivious. She said, "Cris—"

He didn't hear her, but the movement stopped, and he turned and look at us. As the crowd shifted he wormed his way back.

"Don't get separated," Brenda whispered.

We were stalled again. It was hot. The tall guy was not looking at me, but I could sense his awareness. He had edged closer, and now stood an arm's length from Cris, hand inside his leather jacket, like Napoleon. What the hell was he doing? He fumbled with something in there. I gently pulled Cristian around me and eased toward the man.

Beneath his jacket, the man's thumb pushed something repeatedly. His hand withdrew from the jacket. Empty. As the coat settled around him, I glimpsed a phone, and saw the thin wires that ran up past his collar to the buds in his ears.

Jesus, did I need a break.

Once down the elevator—one floor—we entered a crowded makeshift security checkpoint. Unlike the tense logjam upstairs, this was chaos, with security people directing groups from one line to another, and doing baggage checks on the floor by the wall. A female officer looked at our tickets and double-checked our driver's licenses, which didn't match each other in any way other than showing the same hometown.

"These your kids?" The woman watched us for a reaction.

"No," said Brenda. "My sister's. We're taking them while she and her husband go on a cruise."

The kids stood there placidly, obviously with us. The woman handed back our IDs, already dismissing us from her attention.

We walked away, free of the crowd at last.

"Your sister? On a cruise?"

"Whatever. She just wanted to hear something normal. Not 'we're running from a drug gang.'"

"You are a cool customer."

Her eyes flashed merrily. "Just trying to keep up with you."

We followed a windowless hallway to a junction where a makeshift sign showed arrows pointed right for gates thirty-six and thirty-seven, and left for the others. Most of the people turned right, we turned left, came to a stairwell, and went up to a broad concourse that smelled of new carpet and paint. It was almost deserted, and you could see spaces where shops and restaurants were going in. None of them were open.

"There's nothing here," said Brenda.

I had promised them something to eat. "Are you really hungry?"

"No, no. It would be a hassle to go back now. As long as there's a bathroom."

There were people movers—horizontal escalators—running down the side of the concourse. Cristian and Adam lit up at this minor thrill and pulled Brenda and I onto the belt. The boys cackled as they strode ahead.

"Don't run!" I said.

They passed unaided walkers in the concourse as if winning a race. Then they went into reverse until Brenda and I caught up, then took off again, matching giant steps. Fortunately there were no other passengers on the belt, so the hijinks didn't bother anyone.

The concourse stretched out past one gate, then another, and into the distance. A burst of passengers came out of gate thirty-eight, heading inbound. As their excited chatter diminished behind us, I could see the passageway ahead was almost deserted. Having no one around relaxed me a little.

We arrived at our gate. The area was so empty I double-checked the tickets. Yes, five thirty flight to L.A. and Phoenix. Yes, the same flight number. But it was only three forty-five.

After the two days I'd just had, I should have relished the chance to sit, relax, maybe even catch a few winks. But I couldn't quite get there. What if those two Mexicans showed up again? What if I'd been distracted by them, or the crowd, and missed our real pursuers?

We took seats among the rows of connected chairs. The sun slanted through the glass wall behind us. The boys walked up to the glass, drawn by the jets and baggage carts moving around on the concrete apron and the taxiways beyond.

I walked back to look down the concourse. Still largely deserted. I wished for food, but there was not even a vending machine. I took another longing glance up the concourse as I turned to go back to my seat.

Someone was coming. Someone in a black shirt, coming at a trot. I walked over to Brenda, in a fit of indecision. Should I tell her of my fears? But I didn't know who was coming. And what were the odds he came here to kill us? Pretty low, but should I be measuring the odds?

As I walked up to Brenda, a door next to the boarding gate opened, and a young black man in the blue button-down Southwest Airlines shirt came into the room. He wore a friendly-looking goatee—some goatees can be fierce looking or squirrelly. He glanced at us, then looked again. Perhaps sensing my anxiety, he walked toward us. If there was an out, I wanted to take it. Maybe my fears were groundless, but maybe not. This guy had to help us.

He stopped in front of me. He smiled. "You doing alright, folks?"

"No, actually. We may be in danger."

Brenda gave me a sharp, surprised look.

The ticket-taker, or whatever he was, appraised us for a moment. "Alright. You can come with me."

"Boys!" Brenda called softly, and gestured.

Adam and Cristian came over, still energized by the novelty of the airport.

To the man I said, "Where are we—?"

"Security." He nodded confidently. "Just right this way. It's right down here, by the restrooms."

I couldn't believe our luck. A security station, right at hand. I felt a little bit of my anxiety draining away. And it didn't hurt that it was a brother helping us. We walked up the concourse not more than a hundred feet. The man in the black shirt was closer now, but not running, and he did not look at us. I couldn't tell if it was the guy I'd seen before or not.

The airline man opened the door. "Right down the stairs." We trooped down the metal stairs. "Just at the bottom there," he said.

Three men stood on the landing in front of a door which

seemed to go out onto the runway. I turned to ask the man behind me what to do.

And got clubbed in the face by something very hard.

I sagged against the banister, head spinning. The men grabbed Brenda and the two boys.

The ticket taker was holding a gun now and jabbed me with the barrel. "Just come along," he muttered. "Or I'll pepper them right here."

We all shoved into the tiny space in front of the door. "Okay," one of the men said, and the door opened. We walked out onto the apron. A panel truck was waiting there, just a few feet away. A bakery truck. The two rear doors opened and we were guided up and inside. A stout man with a camo pistol stepped in behind us and the doors closed. He remained standing at the back as the four of us bunched up near the front of the tin box, crammed between metal shelves. Dim light filtered through translucent panels in the ceiling.

The truck began to move. I turned toward the boys, who were backed against the wall, and Brenda kneeling down next to them. Nobody said anything. What was there to say? Confused thoughts about the meaning of life flitted between my ears and out into space. Who the hell knew what it all meant? At least I'd had a life. But the boys were different. To take them now would be too great a crime.

I measured the distance between myself and the thug. Reading my thoughts, he raised the pistol and pointed it right between my eyes.

So there was no action possible. Then what we had to do was bargain for every minute and hope for a miracle. I leaned against the bread rack. The man smiled and lowered the pistol, holding it in a relaxed grip, pointed at my gut. The box creaked and the sheet metal sides boomed when we hit a bump, and we hit a few. The side of my face, where I'd been hit, burned like fire.

We rode back there for maybe a half-hour. Every time the truck would stop or turn, our anxiety would spike, expecting that the terrible thing that was going to happen to us would start now.

Finally, the truck stopped again, the doors opened, and the guard slipped out, the doors closing behind him. After a few minutes, the doors opened again, and a different man, a tall man wearing aviator glasses, stood at the back of the truck, a grip on both doors. I intuited that he was going to throw the doors wide open, and they would shoot us right here where we stood.

"You get out now. You come with me." He had a Spanish accent, and spoke in sharp, clipped sounds. "Comport yourselves nicely. Okay."

We stumbled out into the parking lot of some kind of marina. Rows of yachts and fishing boats gleamed in the lowering sun. Seagulls tottered around on the asphalt. The man motioned us through a gate and onto a dock. A large houseboat blocked the rest of the marina from view. The thug with the camo pistol directed us onto a cabin cruiser.

I thought, *why don't they just do it? Why all this buildup?* The answer to that was too obvious. They planned to do terrible things to us. Things that could not be done just anywhere. I had never been afraid of the water, but as I stepped onto the boat and looked out across the darkening bay, I felt a physical repulsion at the sight of the broad expanse of water, still and gray as iron, that covered the deep, crushing silence beneath.

Chapter 14
MALLORY

He said, "You think we're going to roof you? Please, *chica*. We're class. We love women the old school way. Charm and sweetness." He was the one who called himself Ralphlauren. Like one word: Ralphlauren. I would later find out his name was Teddie. But coming to find out his real name is part of the story. He had this ability to draw you in by pushing you away. So Ralphlauren for now. And I'm Mallory, by the way.

"Very classy," I said. "Isn't that classy, Carissa? They refuse to drug us on principle."

Carissa pulled that serious face of hers that is so funny. "Old school, Mal. Old school."

She and I were at the beach. Pacific Beach. It was Friday afternoon, and we were done with classes—I'm finance, she's nursing—and I had an extra day off from work. It was still the chilly time of year, so the beach was not crowded. Only people with wet suits were going in the water. We walked toward the pier, just talking, but also keeping an eye out for whatever. These two young talents became very interested in us. And they weren't too awful. Quite young, obviously Mexican, but not cholo. Since it was at the beach, they weren't wearing much, but one of them had on this pretty sharp-looking hoodie—almost like cashmere?—and they both had markers. Expensive haircuts, tasteful bling, and tattoos. One, Michael, was very good-looking. In a romance novel he would be on the cover with his shirt off. The other one, Ralphlauren, had self-confidence, if not actual charm. He had dark eyes and okay features, but his eyes were too small and his forehead too big to be really good-looking.

So we let them bother us for a while. If things got too rowdy we would just leave. They said they were staying at the Pacific Terrace, which is a very nice place. You could see the tower of rooms from where we stood on the sand. They said, come let us buy you a drink, buy you dinner. Since it was three o'clock in the afternoon, they might have figured there probably wouldn't be dinner until they had us sloshed.

There was no chance of that by me, or by Carissa. We put on our cover-ups—mine is sort of an Arabian tunic. Maybe little blonde girls or Beyoncés can trundle through Pacific Beach with their hiney hanging out. Not I, said the bubblebutt from Grant Hill.

We walked into the bar of the hotel, also not crowded, and sat down. The waitress came over. RL placed the order, and we all showed IDs. I was a little surprised that the boys were of age, they seemed like such pups.

Of course the boys wanted us to ask them about the hotel and how come they were so rich they could stay there. They wanted us to ask so they could pass it off as nothing. And I had some curiosity. So we kind of teasingly asked them about themselves. They both said they were going to school and that they came from good families that owned various businesses in Mexico or somewhere. They were interested in making an impression, but not so much in details. They didn't say what school, but I assumed not San Diego State, because why would they stay at a hotel? I figured they were spring breakers, or just plain liars.

Carissa and I both ordered Coronas and kept a death grip on

them. We only drank those beers, or water we had seen the waitress bring. Not because of these guys so much, just standard procedure when having drinks with strange boys in new places. They noticed what we were doing, which led to the previously mentioned conversation.

Carissa said, "Yeah, Mallory, try to act cool."

"Oh, I'm cool," I said.

"Mallory," said the tall one. "That's a funny name."

"You think my name is funny? What was yours again?"

"Michael."

"Okay, Michael, plain old Michael. You know anything about cars?"

He shrugged.

"My dad was a car nut. He named me Mallory and my sister Holley. He would say Holley's the fuel and Mallory's the spark. You got to have both to get anywhere." This family joke went completely over the head of the two amigos, but as I was saying it, I heard the words in my dad's voice and saw him out in his garage in Long Beach with his old Dodge muscle car. It was a good memory.

"But," I took RL's hand, "you ain't no college student. At least not at SDSU." I turned his arm and touched the Movado watch. "That's a thousand dollar clock on your wrist."

"Naw," he said. Again, *No Big Deal, Sweetheart, but do feel free to be impressed.*

"D'ja steal it?"

He laughed.

I inspected it. Gold, heavy, black face and, like all the best watches, no unsightly numbers or indicators for irrelevant things like hours and minutes. "I used to sell these," I said. "You know, you really have it backwards. To impress the girls at the beach, you have a cheap but fancy watch, and you tell them how fine it is."

He slipped the watch off and handed it to me.

I looked it over for a second. "Yep. It's new, too."

"Yeah." His smile was like, a little embarrassed to catch

himself being so shallow.

"So you're buying! I am ready for a *drink*. I think a Manhattan. Carissa?"

"Just a beer."

"Well, well," said Ralphlauren, nudging his tall but quiet buddy. "Now it's a party. We party like da hooood!"

The way he said that was so Mexican, I had to laugh.

"The hooood!" said Carissa. "Dat wha you think we from? No. We party all over town. We been to this place lots of times. But we never stay late. We always have a lot going on. I can't be gettin' up in the morning with a head full of cotton."

I could see the pool through the big window. I asked no one in particular. "Is that pool heated?"

"Yeah," said RL. "You want to go in?"

"Well, we are dressed for it."

He glanced out at the pool. "You wanna go *sweemeen*, Miguel?"

The tall one shrugged.

Carissa said. "Yeah, let's do."

Michael/Miguel said. "You have to put your drink in a plastic cup. No glass at the pool."

RL held up his hands. "Give me a minute."

I assumed he was going to the bathroom, but he was back in a minute with a waiter. "Okay."

The waiter led us to the other side of the pool, where a row of cabana tents stood, entirely unoccupied. The waiter turned to RL with a questioning expression.

"Yeah, OK," said RL.

"Can I get you anything?" said the waiter.

"We'll let you know," said RL.

"There's also a minibar there with beer, wine, and soda," he said, then he left.

RL looked at me. "Will this do?"

I was not impressed with the tent, but Ralph did seem to have kind of sweet, naive quality. Like he was still learning how to be a rich asshole, and wasn't sure he could pull it off.

"Looks like they have enough towels." Carissa pointed to a pile of fluffy tangerine-colored towels that had been rolled up and stacked in a pyramid on the sideboard about four feet high. I laughed. The boys didn't seem to get it.

If I say I was up for something on one hand, and say I'm not that kind of girl on the other, it may be confusing. Let me explain: My life is alright, I guess. But I get frustrated and depressed about where it's going, why I can't, shouldn't, and whatever whoever fuck that shit.

Here's my life: I had to work last Saturday when I should have been off. Sunday I went to a picnic with my ex-boyfriend's family, his brother and wife, and their kids. That's how lame my life is. Go ahead and read that sentence again, particularly picnic… ex-boyfriend's family. He doesn't know he's my ex-boyfriend, though. So on the surface, not quite so lame.

He doesn't know he's my ex-boyfriend because he never accepted that I wasn't his girlfriend. There was never two in that tango. Let's just keep his name out of it. Doesn't matter. I'll call him ex-boyfriend for simplicity.

We had a pretty good time at the picnic, for what it was. But on the way home late in the afternoon, a darkness enveloped me. Sadness and emptiness, and I just had to be alone. It wasn't about anything that happened at the picnic, or with Tray (whoops!). Again, it was more about what didn't happen. He got miffed about it, needlessly. It wasn't about him.

It goes back to when I was a kid, when I was not allowed to see friends on Sunday or do anything fun. Go to church, go to Sunday school, then something with the family, usually just sitting around at someone's house, wandering around the back yard. At the end of the day I would feel sad and lonely. Even now, too many Sunday evenings, I look at the setting sun just feeling bleak. Monday's coming, it's starting all over, but where is it going?

My life is boring. And here it's another Sunday afternoon, empty and pointless—not because of my generation, or my race, or my gender, or the times, but pointless because the people I spent it with. People I don't really know or much want to know. Who are boring and witless and repressed, involved in unhappy marriages, bad jobs, bad real estate deals. They don't know how to fix their cars, or their finances, or their lives, or do much of anything beyond paint the bedroom again.

In other words, they are just like me. Rats on a treadmill, each and every one of us, headed into another week of work and worry to get to another pointless weekend. There's no narrative there, no development. Why is my life an unending stream of uninteresting people, please-just-shoot-me conversations, dull nonevents, depressing days, and lonely nights?

Chapter 15
FRANK

Through a horizontal slit window I saw the lights of San Francisco coming on in the dusk. The boat we were in made a slow wide arc around the wharves and the waterfront, as if it was headed to the Golden Gate and the open sea beyond. The four of us prisoners were crammed into a tiny cabin in the bow, and we sat together on the bunk, staring at the glittering lights of the offices, apartments, and hotels rising high into the graying sky. I had a sudden, very strong urge to be in a tavern somewhere among those lights, anywhere among those lights, having a cold beer, with nothing to do but totter home for dinner.

It kept tearing at me. "How the hell did they find us at the airport?"

Brenda stared straight ahead. "I don't know. But they did."

"We should just give up!" hissed Adam, full of anger and hopelessness. "Give them what they want. Me and Cris."

"No, we can't." Cris chopped his hand at the air, just as angry.

"Shut up!" Adam punched him in the chest, which jostled all of us.

"Knock it off." I held Adam's skinny forearm. He didn't try

to break free.

The boat churned its way forward. I pushed cautiously on the cabin door. It was not locked, but there were armed killers on the other side of it. The slit window was not big enough for even the kids to squeeze out of, and there was no other exit and no hiding place in the little cabin. We had rescued the two boys from a swift and simple death to... what now? A slow and terrifying drowning in icy waters?

I touched the door again. A suicide rush? What good would it do? Besides, they'd probably know I was going to do it before I even started, just like they'd known, seemingly in advance, every move we'd made so far in our "escape." How the hell had they known we were driving eight hundred miles to California? Maybe Aida had somehow made a phone call to her slimeball boyfriend, and from that somehow they knew we were in the area. But how would they know the exact address where we were headed, which we'd never told Aida? They got there almost as soon as we did.

Then when we'd tried to go back to Phoenix, they'd beat us to the airport, known our gate number, and been waiting there with a bread truck. That would only have required someone hijacking a vehicle with an airport permit, disposing of the bakers, and finessing their way into one of the most tightly controlled areas in any city—the working area of an airport—with almost no advance planning. Or maybe they had people working in that particular bakery ready to spring into action. The odds of all this defied logic. The difficulty of the puzzle added to my anger over being threatened and abducted.

But anger would get me nothing now. I would have to bide my time, know the moment to strike, and then move. It would surely be a suicide rush anyway, but if Brenda and the boys could somehow get away, survive, I would pay the price. Just, how?

The engine growled, the hull shuddered from the smack of big waves, or pattered through smooth water. Out the window I could see the lights of cars moving slowly on the ramp leading to the south end of the Golden Gate Bridge. We would be under it soon. The tension was unbearable. My stomach churned with a nausea that had nothing to do with the motion of the boat. It grew darker outside, and in the unlit cabin. Streaks of fog blocked the city lights. The choppiness of the water increased. Soon we passed under the ghostly light of the bridge, a sight so awesome and final I realized my life was leaving me at that moment.

I circled the three of them with my arms. "I will do something to disrupt them or bother them. I don't know what. But when I do, you try to get away somehow. However you can."

Cris nodded. Adam stared without comprehension.

Brenda said, "I don't think they should try to swim. It's too far."

"Maybe there's a float or a life jacket you can grab. I don't know. We have to try something. Try to get to their guns." Wait. "No, don't. I don't know what, but we're not going down without a fight. Okay?"

Adam nodded. He seemed to shake himself. That was what I wanted to see. We—or they, if I were gone—would need his wiry strength somehow. We were in almost complete darkness now, and the boat's movement changed. It was rising and falling on the swells of the ocean, a slow, regular motion that changed the sound of the engine.

The cabin lights went on, the door opened outward, and Camo Pistol stood there. This was my chance, but the gun was pointing right at Cris. The man stepped in, grabbed Cris, and yanked him out the door.

Brenda cried, "No!"

The man quickly reached back in, pointed the gun at Adam, and motioned him forward. This was my last chance, but it was Adam in the line of fire. For a second I thought he might resist or struggle, creating an opportunity, but in that second he was gone, and the cabin door slapped shut.

I sat there, stunned. Brenda turned away. I could feel the heat of anger and fear coming off her. My moment for action had come and gone because I was not in the proper position to do anything. If I had been sitting closer to the door I could have hit or kicked the gun arm when he came in. Maybe. Maybe it would not have gone off, or would have missed. Maybe the boys would have been alright. It was a risk but also a chance, and now it was gone, and the boys were doomed. My stomach heaved but only produced a bubble of foul acid. I spit it into the corner of the bunk behind me and wiped my mouth with my hand.

Ever since this adventure began, despite the odds, I had felt a kind of strange, even mystifying confidence that I could do what needed to be done, that somehow we would win. But now it seemed all I had done was to plunge us deeper into a horror from which there was no appeal and no escape. For this I deserved to die. The others didn't.

The engine slowed, coughed, and stopped. The boat pitched forward as the wake caught up with it. I was sure the next thing I would hear would be a gunshot. I pulled Brenda to me, and she folded into my arms. We heard a high-pitched grinding sound—the starter of the engine. It whined once. Twice. The engine coughed but wouldn't start. Indistinguishable rapid words came from several voices. There was a loud creaking sound and a thump, and the boat rocked unevenly for a moment. Then came another try of the starter.

The door opened, and the man with the aviator glasses—he seemed to be the boss—stood there. He waved at me to come out. I gave Brenda's hand a quick squeeze and staggered out the door and up the two steps onto the open back part of the boat. In the center of a sort of well, the engine cover had been tipped up like the top of a piano. Above my left shoulder, one man sat behind the steering wheel and controls. Bright lights shone down from a sort of rack that arched above his head. Gusts of wind were blowing a light, chill mist. A man in a gold cap stood at the rear of the boat, his hand clamped on the back of Cris's neck. At his feet, Adam lay on the deck, face down. Camo pistol guy stared at the exposed engine. Above us, maybe a quarter mile back, the Golden Gate Bridge glowed through the fog.

"You a mechanic. Fix it," said the boss.

I looked him up and down. He didn't appear to have a gun. "I'm no mechanic, and anyway, why should I?"

The punk in the gold cap said, in Spanish. "We have to kill them all now."

The boss didn't seem to have heard him. "You know how. Fix it or he goes over."

The punk holding Cris shook a chain. He draped it over Cris's shoulder, looking at me with a dead-eyed grin. The chain ran through the handles of a couple of five gallon buckets that sat on the transom. Obviously full of something heavy.

I wanted to scream, "So what?" But this was a chance. A few more minutes. I was in a position to do something. Working on the engine gave me time to think. "You got a flashlight?"

The guy sitting at the wheel flicked on a light and handed it to me. He was a chubby guy in yellow nylon shorts, who didn't seem to even notice the chill, damp breeze that was numbing my hands. Camo Pistol handed me a small plastic toolbox that held a pair of channellock pliers, a crescent wrench, and a couple of screwdrivers.

I forced myself to concentrate. The way the engine was set in the deck you had to bend down very awkwardly to get at anything. Practically lie on the floor. The engine was a six cylinder, basically an automobile engine. I didn't know too much, but I knew spark and gas. That's where you start. I pulled off a plug wire and held it with the plastic-grip pliers. I looked up at the boss. "I need him to crank the engine."

"*Prendelo*," he said to Yellow Shorts.

The engine cranked for a few seconds, and sparks snapped across a half-inch of space from the end of the wire to the engine block.

"Okay!" I waved my hand. The engine stopped. We had spark. I reattached the plug wire and sat up, running the flashlight over the engine while glancing around, trying to account for every gun. Camo Pistol squatted down on the other side of the engine. He seemed to be the designated mechanic. I wanted to know how much of this he was getting. My guess was, not much. He held an automatic 9 mm loosely in his left hand, pointed at me. Yellow Shorts could have had a pistol laying on the console before him, but I couldn't see up there. The boss did not seem to be armed, but he had on an oversized windbreaker, and anything could be underneath it or in those pockets. And the punk with the chains had a pistol laying on the seat cushion next to him.

To no one in particular I said, "I think it's either the fuel pump or the fuel filter."

"Can you fix?" said the boss.

"I don't know yet. May take a little while." I looked up at him. Above and behind him I could see the towers of the bridge swinging slowly past as the boat slowly circled. So we were still more or less in the middle of the channel. Distant lights glowed on the bluffs of the San Francisco side, but no boats were nearby. In the fog, though, a ship or boat might come up at any moment.

"Do it fast," he said.

I shrugged. Again the question—why? Who gives a shit where you kill us? As I turned back toward the engine, I realized that it didn't matter to them where they killed us, but how they got away from wherever it was. Therefore, if the boat couldn't move, they couldn't kill us. They couldn't exactly call the Coast Guard for a tow.

I looked at the boss again. "I just have to ask."

He stared back at me, his face a blank.

"How did you find us at the airport?"

He didn't chuckle or smile. He was a serious guy. "We hacked your reserva—we got into the airline computer."

"You broke into the airline's computer system? And you saw the reservations."

"That's enough." He turned and sat down on the bench seat that ran along the side, near Adam's feet. "Jes' work."

I shelved the information about the airline reservations for later. I had another question: How did he know I was a mechanic? Just a guess? Or do they actually know who I am?

These people had a lot of resources.

Then I almost laughed. For later? What later? What later did I still have?

But I had a plan. Just delaying wasn't enough. This was our only chance.

I bent over the engine again, but this time I kept my legs curled under me. That meant I had to stretch my back more, but it wouldn't be for long. With the flashlight I found the clear bubble of a fuel filter in the gas line running to the carburetor and flicked my finger at it. It was full of gas. I pulled the throttle arm a couple of times and flipped the choke flap on top of the carb. "Okay, okay," I mumbled.

I unscrewed the clamp and pulled off the fuel line from the carburetor. I looked at Camo. "Okay, I need—" waving to him to bend down. I flipped the choke flap again, and held it open with my finger. "Like this. Finger here. *Dedo aqui*."

He leaned down, bracing himself on his gun-hand elbow, the gun still pointed in my direction. There was no mechanical reason to hold the flap, but he did not know that. It got his face right down there next to me.

I held my finger over the end of the fuel line. I looked up toward Yellow Shorts and called, "Again! *Prendelo*!"

The starter whirred. I took my finger off the end of the hose and pointed it at Camo's face. Gasoline shot out of the tube in rapid, strong bursts, right into his eyes. He squawked and tried to rear up, but I hooked him behind the neck and held him long enough for him to get a good face full. I let go of the hose and shoved a fist at him, making contact with his throat. He rolled backward. I thought he dropped his pistol into the engine compartment, but I didn't have time to think about that. I pushed myself up and fired my body into the punk holding Cris. I smashed into his chest, and we both went over the rail. As we fell, I realized that Cris, and the chain around him, had come with us. I could somehow hear the chain clinking.

We were in the water. Punk grabbed my shirt. In the light from the boat I saw the dripping burr of his hair. He pulled me close and punched me over and over. Small but strong. Lifting my arms to protect my face, I felt the chain. I grabbed it with both hands and held it up as a block, but he punched it back at me with his forearm. Cris was not near us. I didn't know where he was.

We went under, then came up again. In the dark, and the bone-chilling cold, and the foam he and I were making, there was no up or down or thought. When I felt air on my face I breathed. That was all I knew.

He was punching, but he was tiring, too, and the force of his blows weakened. Neither of us had anything to push against except each other and the tight side of the chain that was caught on the boat. He missed a punch and sort of spun toward me. I looped the chain over his head and used it to pull the side of his neck into my chest and hold it there. We were both under now, and he pushed his fists and forearms against my chest and gut. I pulled tighter.

But I was running out of air. I scissored him with my legs and looped the chain around his middle. My lungs were bursting and my head was spinning toward blackout. I was aware of the chain being yanked painfully from my fingers, breaking them, it felt like. Now nothing held me and I clawed my way to the surface. I glimpsed the night sky and sucked in air. Once, twice, and I knew I would live.

The man I was fighting was gone. Just gone. I spun around, looking for someone, and kicked my legs. Nothing to be seen or felt. The chain was gone, too. There was about twenty feet between me and the corner of the boat. The water was gently swelling. I could not see Cris. A man—the boss—stood at the back of the boat, maybe holding a gun in his shadowed hand. He seemed to be looking down, maybe at Cris. I heard gunfire, but saw no flash from his muzzle. Another shot, again no flash. The boss tumbled off the end of the boat, landed in the water, and sank.

Who'd shot him? Cris? Adam? One of his own guys for some reason?

"Cris!"

"Here!" I heard him and saw him at the same time, off the stern, just out of the light, treading water. I tried to swim over to him, but my pants were inside out and hanging off my shoes. I couldn't kick the shoes off, so the pants trailed after me, slowing me down. I pulled for the boat with my arms. Someone—Brenda!—looked over the back of the boat and said something. I reached the little platform that hung off the stern. Cris was there.

Brenda looked down at us. "You can come up," she shouted against the wind. "It's okay. I've got one of the guns."

"You shot him!"

"Just hurry up!" She disappeared from view. "Adam's been shot."

I hoisted myself up and reached back to lift Cris. We both tumbled over the transom onto the bench seat. My clothes were more off me than on. My shirt hung down to my knees, and my pants were still dragging from my shoes. I wedged my shoes off and pulled my feet out of the sopping pants.

Adam lay on the other side of the engine hole. Yellow Shorts was propped in the corner, quietly gasping for air. He'd been shot, too. Brenda stood braced against the rail, pointing a gun toward the front of the boat. "The other one is up there. He crawled around the steering chair."

I guessed that would be Camo Pistol. I gripped Cris's shoulders and positioned him behind the upturned engine cover. "Kneel down here and don't move. I scuttled over to Adam and knelt over him, dripping. "How are you?"

"It hurts," he moaned. That was good. Complaining about the pain is a sign a wounded person is going to live. He waved his hand over an ugly dark area on the side of his T-shirt, and emitted a whimper.

I reached down to the hem of his shirt and tried as gently as I could to tear it. But my fingers were weak and painful—it wouldn't give. No time to look for a knife. I grabbed the hem again in two fists and rolled them against each other, and the fabric gave way. I tore it up to his armpit.

A hole in the side of his chest was bleeding pretty badly. "We've got to get a towel on that," I said. I wondered if there was a hole on the other side too and rolled him over a little. His scream ran out of breath quickly. There was no second hole—it was all one long hole, a shredded mess. But it was seeping blood, not pumping it. That made a difference for a while. "We've got to stop the bleeding."

"Are you okay, *mijo*?" Brenda knelt down and stroked Adam's forehead, still pointing the gun to the forward part of the boat. "He was so brave. He attacked that son of a like a… wolf or something."

I crawled over to the cabinet by the passageway, where I found a hand towel.

Brenda handed me the pistol and took the towel. She pressed it against Adam's side. He howled and kicked weakly. But the bleeding had to be stopped.

"Where did you get this?" I hefted the pistol.

She pointed at Yellow Shorts.

"What happened to him?"

"The one with the glasses shot him, aiming at Adam. Them fighting made the boat rock."

As if part of her story, the boat began to rock. We were catching the wake of a ship that was now nearly to the bridge, inbound.

"Does it work?" I waggled the pistol.

"Sorry, *mijo*!" She stroked Adam's forehead but kept her other hand firmly on the towel. "I shot the guy with it, so I guess so."

"Where was that one?" I pointed to the front of the boat.

"He was leaning there, coughing. Then you came back. I turned to look at you, and he was off like a rat, crawling over the cabin."

"Does he have a gun?"

"I don't know."

I looked around the deck, but there were no guns to be seen. The engine compartment still gaped open in the middle of everything. "Cris, do you see a gun back there?"

"No, nothing." He sounded exhausted. Done for.

"Did the guy drop his gun when he fell in the water?"

"He still held it."

In a second I assessed our situation. Adam and the other guy wounded, a bad and very angry guy in the front of the boat, maybe with a gun. And we had a gun. But the engine was not running. Should I fix it? No way we had that much time, with Adam's condition. I began to shuffle around looking for a cell phone, a radio. There was a black box in the cabinet beside the steering wheel, with a microphone at the end of a coiled cord. I turned a knob and it came on. The bar of overhead lights flickered. Now I noticed we were losing them. Jesus, what about that? Get the engine running to keep the lights and radio on? Maybe we had a few minutes of juice left in that battery.

I pushed a button on the radio mike. "Hello, hello, anyone hear?"

If this was like a CB radio, you were supposed to… what? I hadn't seen one of these in thirty years. There was no response. I twisted the knobs. "If anyone can hear, this is SOS. We are stranded on a dead boat in the channel outside the Golden Gate. We have wounded people, and we're in danger. There's a man with a gun on the boat. Mayday, mayday."

By fiddling with the two knobs, I managed to get a staticky sound.

The boat jarred sideways with a crunch. Then it bumped again. In the fading light of the overhead bar I saw rocks. We had run up against a couple of boulders, behind which rose more rocks and a steep slope. We had drifted to the north shore of the strait.

"We could get off," I said to Brenda.

"We can't move Adam."

There was a shot. I ducked down. It seemed to come from the rocks above us. There was another shot, and wood crunched somewhere nearby. I rolled over against the side of the boat. "Cris! Stay down."

"What is it?" His voice was remarkably calm now.

"That guy must have got off. He's up on these rocks. We have to get these lights off and get away." I wormed my way to the captain's chair, looking for the light switch. I pulled a knob, twisted it, found a toggle switch and flipped it. No effect.

There was a smashing sound above me, and I ducked. The lights went off and glass sprinkled down. Cris was drawn up to his full four-feet-nothing of height, with a long boat hook in his hands. He gave it another full swing against the overhead bar. There was another shot, from farther away.

I reached for Cris. "You okay?"

"I'm okay."

"That was very smart and very brave. Here." I took the boat hook from him, reached over the side, and pushed the boat away from the rocks, expecting a shot. We were off the rocks, but it wasn't enough. I knelt down by the engine compartment, found the disconnected fuel hose, and after a couple of minutes working by feel, I was able to reconnect it to the carburetor. I clambered up to the captain's seat, found the throttle, and pushed the starter button. The engine spun but wouldn't catch. The battery wouldn't last much longer. I threw the thing into reverse and hit the starter again. With the prop engaged, this pulled us slowly back, away from the cliff. We got about a hundred feet before the battery died.

Lights appeared behind us, and through the wind, I heard an engine. It took a moment to realize that another boat was approaching.

"Brenda! Boys?"

How did they know her name? Brenda yelled and waved her arms. It was her brother. I couldn't think of his name. I was exhausted now.

"I'm here," Brenda called.

"Look out!" shouted Cris. "There's a guy up there with a gun. On the rocks."

Someone on the police boat said okay. A spotlight pointed toward the shore.

I sat on the padded bench at the stern. Looking down, I saw that my wet T-shirt had been stretched and sagged down almost to my knees. Which was a good thing, because I had nothing on underneath it.

Chapter 16
MALLORY

We all went in the water, and that was fun and changed the pace. But in the splashing around, it became obvious that RL had latched on to me. It was not a mutual thing. I preferred tall, handsome, and shy, just as Carissa did. But it was just a fling, anyway. I was already thinking about driving home. Since we were wet now, we would have to sit on towels. Maybe we could borrow some from the hotel that had so many.

I got out of the water and went to the cabana, which was really a sultan's tent, white and tangerine. It went well with my cover-up. I sat down to dry my legs.

He followed me.

"What's your name, really," I asked.

"Ted. Teddie."

"Teddie Bear. Guess you've heard that before."

"Oh, yes."

"Shall I call you Teddie?"

"Sure, that's alright. Why fight it?"

He had a small gym bag he'd been carrying around the whole time. He reached into it and pulled something out. He flashed a small amber bottle. "Wanna do a line?"

"Oh boy." I already regretted leaving the others. Carissa and Michael were still down at the other end of the pool. And there was literally no one else around. "I will pass. You're some kind of crazy party animal, aren't you?"

He smiled, but it wasn't one of those lizard smiles that real players give you. "Me? Not at all."

I arched an eyebrow at him.

He laughed. "Well, a little crazy. You do it to me. You're very attractive, and a little crazy yourself, though you try to hide it."

"Thank you. I think."

"You wouldn't scream if I touched you."

"No, but I might destroy you in the crotch with the broken end of a whiskey bottle. But no glass around the pool. But don't try me."

"I have a fantasy."

I was still laughing him off. "Here we go."

"It's really very innocent. Can I see your..." He made a cupping motion with his hands.

"What's it worth to you?"

He held up his arm, with the Movado.

I looked around. We were half hidden by the tent. I didn't care if he saw my tits. I pulled the bikini top down, it became a sort of pushup bra. Which I don't need, since I'm pretty big. "No touch."

Teddie took a swig of beer. "Nice." He held up the little vial. "May I?"

"Knock yourself out."

What he did next so stunned me that I could not move. He leaned toward me and carefully tapped out a thin line of cocaine on my left breast. Then he leaned closer, and with a small tube he sucked it into his nose.

"No touch." He laughed softly.

I've heard of boys getting kinky, but never this. I wasn't afraid, but my body was electrified with surprise and wariness.

He looked at me with sparkling eyes, exactly like a little boy who just swiped a cookie.

"No," I said. "You are a crazy party pokie loco."

"Other side?"

I laughed. "I am never letting you near me again. You're too weird. So go ahead."

Same thing, right breast.

I pulled my top up, and adjusted. "Okay. That was different. Now you get back in your lane, playboy. And stay there."

I wondered for a moment if I had been violated, harassed, or abused just now. Did he take advantage of me? Yes, but not any more than guys I've been with who lied to me, or moved too fast, or just smelled bad or felt scaly or whatever.

He took off the watch and handed it to me. "I'll be good. I respect you and all women. I *am* old school."

"All right. Keep the watch."

"All for fun. The purest sex is sex in the mind. Edging up to a fantasy, and then turning away. Just put it on your wrist. It's not real, it's a fake, so don't feel weird about it.

I took it. "I won't feel weird about the *watch.*"

He laughed. He had these big dark eyes, very expressive. I decided they were a large part of his charm or charisma or whatever it was that let him get away with stuff. He put the vial back in the gym bag.

"What else you got in your bag of tricks?" I asked. I don't know why I asked. I didn't really care.

He pulled out a smaller zipper bag, like a purse, and opened it. It was packed tight with cash.

That's when I got scared. "You're not a rich kid. Or a student. That's drug money."

"No it's not. I don't do that. I just carry cash because I can't use a credit card. Because I can't let people find me here in the, you know."

"In the U.S."

"Yeah."

"And why is that?"

"Because people I know are being hunted by corrupt officials. Let's leave it at that."

Fine with me.

We lay on the chaises side by side, not saying anything. I was very conscious of the big watch on my arm. I had no feelings about what had happened. At least, none that I was willing to admit to myself. I felt like I wanted to have a beer bottle in my hand now, but not to drink. Just to have to have something in my hand to stop the tremble that kept trying to crawl down my arms and legs.

I stood up and waved to Carissa to come over.

So: Wrap this up; get her dried off; leave.

A fully dressed man walked up to us. He did not belong here, and I went on alert. But then he tapped Teddie's chaise with his shoe. "*Chavalo*."

Teddie looked up. "*Hola*, Grandpa."

"How's the vacation?"

"Over, I think, now that you're here."

The man was older that Teddie, and had long sideburns. He looked around at the setting but did not seem to notice me.

Teddie said, "Sit down! They've got your Bud Light in the cooler over there."

"You guys," he said. "I bet you that beer cost you fifty bucks."

"Don't worry about it, my wise old uncle."

"That's better than Grandpa."

Teddie opened his hand to me. "This is Malmarie."

"Hi." I said.

The grandpa reached out and took my hand.

I looked at Teddie. "Is this one of your professors?" I asked.

They both laughed. "Oh, that's brilliant," said Teddie. "Would you say so, Professor?"

"I think it is, yes, probably true." Grandpa or uncle or professor walked over to the icebox and bent down. He was even more Mexican than the kids, with his stiff jeans and long-sleeve shirt. He held a beer up.

"Okay," said Teddie.

"Okay," I said.

Teddie moved to the couch. The uncle stood next to the minibar. "Malmarie. Is that your real name?"

I laughed and shook my head, suddenly giddy with what had happened. This had been a hell of a ride, the last hour. "No. He doesn't know how to pronounce it."

He shrugged. "I'm not surprised."

"What's yours?"

He shrugged again. "I don't know how to pronounce it."

Teddie guffawed at this. "Don't give her a hard time, *Tío*. His name is Antonio."

Carissa and Michael were walking up to us now.

"We met these nice young ladies on the beach," Teddie explained to the professor. "And they were kind enough to agree to have dinner with us."

"No, no," I said. "Thanks and everything, but I have to get home."

"Nonoooo!" said Teddie. "We are leaving tomorrow. This is our last night."

Carissa's expression showed that she not only accepted this, she expected it. But she had not been through what I'd just been through. I found myself in the weird position of wanting to get away from there, but thinking the easiest way to do that was to go along. While I was contemplating this, Carissa made up her mind.

"Whaddja have in mind?"

"There's that famous place, down the boardwalk," said Michael.

"That's not a bad idea, Mikey," said Teddie.

"I have to be home by ten," I said. Lame, but I felt a little cornered. And I felt safe with Carissa there. And the old man, for some reason, gave me a feeling of things being okay. I would not, of course, be getting close to, or being left alone with Teddie.

But I did walk with him to the restaurant. "So you don't really go to college."

"Well, I do, but I work, too. I work as a consultant. Transportation."

"Oh?" I didn't know what to think of this guy. He seemed to change from minute to minute.

"Yeah, we are working on starting a new railroad that will go from the west coast of Mexico to L.A., Phoenix, everywhere."

"Don't they have one?"

"I mean passenger." He flipped his hands out. "The passenger trains in Mexico went out of business years ago. But we think it can be revived."

"No shit? Like the Surfliner?"

"Kind of. The Surfliner is more for commuters. This would not compete with that, but would extend it to Tijuana, maybe Ensenada, and down the mainland west coast to Mazatlán. So it's more of long distance. Maybe high speed. It's already been done in Europe and China. That's what we do. Move shit around. We also ship recycled plastics to China."

"Really!" I have to admit, I was a little impressed. I had seen him as basically a chadwick, a playboy, and a drug dealer, with all that cash. But I was not afraid of him anymore. Being in a crowd made me feel safe, or even a little cocky. I know drug dealers. They are usually no more remarkable than sales clerks. If you want the product, this is what it costs. If you don't, then good day. It is more often the drug customers that are crazy or threatening. Of course I have heard stories about turf wars and such, but I've never known anyone who was involved in those things. Close, but not involved.

During the dinner, a couple of things happened. First, it became obvious that Carissa and Michael were now an item. I could tell this because they both seemed more interested in talking to me, but about themselves. Carissa told me something about her work that I'd already heard, and Michael talked about flying a glider. My reply to any of this didn't matter, because they were really only listening to each other.

Because of this, I was mostly ignoring Teddie or at least appeared to. He and the professor were having a straggling guttural conversation that seemed casual, but wasn't. They spoke almost all in Spanish because they thought Carissa and I would not be able to understand that.

But they were wrong. My Spanish is excellent. And what they said was so interesting, it distracted me from being Carissa's wing-girl. Here is a summary, without all the quotes marks and spaces in between, and without all the questions I at first had that later were answered or figured out by me—though some of what they said I still don't understand.

Teddie's father, whose name was never said, had a business in Mexico that involved customers and couriers in the U.S. His name was never said, but let's call him Raul, for the sake of clarity. I later asked Teddie what was his father's name, and he said something that was not Raul, but he may have lied.

I assumed that the business was drugs, but no drug was ever mentioned. The words drugs and dope and coke or whatever were never used. Of course, I had known all along that Teddie, back when I knew him as Ralphlauren, was a druggie, and a dealer. I had not realized what a true criminal he was.

The father had a rival or enemy who was causing problems, I'm not sure about what. But there was true and deep hatred between these two. He must have been another drug man because they each tried to steal the other's product and create trouble with the law for each other's workers or friends. From watching shows and movies about drug dealers, everybody, including me, knows that words like product and stuff mean drugs, and I pictured a scene: Bundles of powder wrapped in plastic, and they open one of the packages with a switchblade knife and put a dab of powder on their tongue, and then they nod like snakes and smile.

Anyway this gang war had degenerated to the rivals stealing each other's stuff and getting each other's guys arrested. And there had been some sort of shootout in which Teddie's brother had been killed, and so had the rival. This part of the story disturbed me so much I had to eat a French fry to calm down and totally missed what Michael was saying to me at the same time, so I just nodded.

There had also come a rift in the organization. One side felt that the murder of Teddie's brother was a challenge, and that they were fighting for their lives. Others seemed to feel that the score had been settled. Teddie's brother had been killed, but the rival had also been killed. There was a balance to it, and now it was time to get back to business. Teddie seemed pretty neutral, but the fact that he did not readily agree with the older man about the need for revenge told me that he favored the making money point of view. It also told me that despite his youth, Teddie was higher in the organization than the older man, maybe because he was a son of Raul.

What I heard made me realize that my first intuition had been right. That these men were dangerous. But sitting there, face to face, it struck me that Teddie resembled, or sort of acted like, some of the managers I have worked for—I've been in retail one way or another most of the time since I was seventeen. Like in a planning meeting or a staff meeting, a department head or team leader trying to make decisions without all the facts, knowing they could face stubbornness or opposition from others, that they could be blamed for a wrong decision, that they could not win either way. Teddy had this unenthusiastic quality, like someone forced to eat or smell or look at something unpleasant.

Yet somehow, the setting, the evening, had become quite relaxed. Everyone seemed comfortable. Just having dinner. Teddie and the older man were not engaged in an intense, hushed conversation, as you might expect from the business they were talking about. It was seemingly casual, interspersed with relatives, ex-wives, girlfriends, funny things they thought or their friends said, *chingado* this and *jodido* that.

We went to the bar of the restaurant for a drink and then walked back to the hotel. It was obvious that Carissa was going to hook up with Michael. As we walked she lagged behind, pretending that there was something wrong with her shoe, leaning on me for support.

"He wants me to stay with him."

"Okay," I said.
"I can't do it."
"Well, that's up to—"
"I mean, I would."
"Well."
"Can you stay?"
I laughed. "No. How could I? Where could I?"
"It's a four-bedroom suite. Even if that guy stays, there's still another room, all to yourself."

This seemed ridiculous to me. It's one thing to spend the night with a guy and walk out in the morning wearing the same clothes. It would be another to go into a room and sleep in my clothes and then be uncomfortable in the morning because I'm not really with anybody—and when are we leaving, etc. And I would sleep in my clothes, for sure. The bedrooms probably wouldn't even have locks.

"If you don't stay," she said, "I can't. I would be too afraid."
"You, too?"
"Seriously. It depends on you. I really want to."
I was swaying. "I haven't been invited."
"Michael invited you."
"No—"
"He invites me, and he invites you." She beamed at me. "Believe me, it was his idea."
"So is this your plan or his?"

She just laughed, and we caught up with the boys. They must have been talking, too, because Teddie gave me a key card. "I'm going out with Antonio. You are welcome to stay in the suite tonight. Take the room by the kitchen. It's yours. No one will bother you. Order anything you want. I guarantee no one will bother you."

So I did it, and slept in the big, flat, firm bed all night. There was a fluffy orange robe folded up in the closet, and I slept in that. Very comfortable. No one bothered me. It was safe, like he said.

Chapter 17
Airport kidnapping ends in struggle on a boat in Golden Gate channel
Four victims safe, two kidnappers dead; one may have escaped

SAN FRANCISCO—Four people were kidnapped Sunday from Oakland International Airport but they managed to kill two of the kidnappers and escape. A man and a woman and two boys, all from Phoenix, were targets of a revenge killing ordered by a Mexican drug lord. They were taken from the airport to Ballena Isle Marina, where they were forced onto a boat that then headed out to sea. The boat developed engine trouble in Golden Gate Channel, and the intended victims overpowered their attackers and killed two of them.

The names of the kidnap victims were being withheld. They were a man, age 48, and a woman, age 41, both employees of a Phoenix elementary school where the two boys are students. On Sunday afternoon they arrived at the airport several hours early for a Southwest Airlines flight to Los Angeles and were forced into a delivery van that had a food-service permit for the restricted area of the airport. The van was trailed by Drug Enforcement Agency officers who had been alerted to a possible kidnapping at the airport. DEA alerted Oakland PD and other agencies, and harbor patrol attempted to intercept the kidnappers' boat. A Coast Guard vessel was also closing in when the incident ended.

The motive for the kidnappings has not been revealed by authorities, but the boat showed "no signs of preparation for a long journey," said FBI spokesman David McQueen. It has not yet been determined how the boat, which is registered to a Castro Valley man, was obtained by the kidnappers. It may have been rented or stolen.

According to McQueen, all of the kidnappers have links to a Mexican drug cartel. The DEA agents on the scene were monitoring the airport for drug smuggling activity when they got an anonymous call informing them of the kidnapping, and identifying a French Market Bakery truck that had just left the terminal...

Chapter 18
BRENDA

It was like we had to make up lives from scratch. The most basic decisions stood before us. Were we a family, or just a group of refugees? The terror at the school—only four days ago! That happened only to us, in the dark of night. But the airport kidnapping, the drama under the bridge—that was all out in the open, with police reports, media coverage, many questions from many people.

We had hoped that if we got the boys away from Phoenix, and just carried on, the whole night at the school would just fade away. But then we were involved in a very public altercation with known members of a drug cartel, and now we were going back to where we'd started. So what was the new plan?

We spent a whole day answering questions, from an FBI guy, a DEA guy, a woman from the airport security. How had they known where we were? The police searched my car for some kind of locating device but found nothing. And what had happened in Mexico to drive those people to such crazy risks? Frank and I answered the questions, but I felt very strongly that we could not give complete control of our fate to others just because they had an official title and an important job. Deep inside, I felt like it was still the teacher and the janitor and the two kids against... well, the world? Maybe not the whole world, but an unknown and dangerous part of it. Frank and I had become protectors of these two boys. And part of what we needed to protect was the story of what happened to us, how, and why.

And actually the questions were pretty easy because we were victims, not perpetrators. And because all the questioners were more concerned with what happened here, not in Phoenix. We reviewed for the FBI guy the confrontation with the two bad guys at Grand Avenue School, and how we escaped by hiding in the bathroom, which was almost true, and had some indelible details that we all remembered, like standing on the toilets in the dark. He said someone would contact us when we got to Phoenix. The only time they talked to Adam or Cristiano was quite brief, and in the presence of Frank and I.

The most important thing was that Adam was not seriously injured. It would be painful, and the wound required some home care, and a doctor would look at it when we got to Phoenix. But he was very lucky. Of course, we all were. So it was time to go home. And the only way to get there was to drive back the way we came. Nobody wanted to do it, but nobody had a better idea. We certainly were not going to fly! Frank and I had briefly explained our absences to the school—though certainly longer conversations would be necessary once we returned.

But we needed to get back. The boys insisted that they had to remain with us. That overrode their fear of returning to Phoenix. That and the fresh terror of our experience in Northern California. If there is no safety anywhere, where should you go? Aida had ceased to function. She could not make a decision beyond that she was not going back to Phoenix. So Frank and I had become the boys' de facto guardians.

That was one of the main issues now—where was their mother, Miranda?

"She drove us to Nogales," Adam told us. "We crossed the border and went to the bus station. When we got off the bus in Phoenix, our *tía* was there. Our mother said she would come in a few weeks. She will come." He looked at Frank and me with impatient conviction, as if daring us to argue the point. Aida provided that Miranda had said something about going to Puerto Rico. What had she said? Did she have a connection of some kind there? Aida shrugged and went silent.

We left Tuesday afternoon. We were not going to try to make it to Phoenix in one day. That I was firm about. While we drove we tried to figure out what we were heading toward. The first question was: Where were we going to stay when we get home? My house has three bedrooms. "It's not big," I told them. "The rooms are small, and it only has one bathroom."

"I have two bathrooms," Frank said. "But only two bedrooms."

I had seen it and could not see how it would work. And his son was already living there. "My house has a living room and a den, or family room, or whatever you want to call it. It has a hide-a-bed in there. In the den, I mean."

I think Frank actually liked that I was volunteering. "And you're located on…?"

"Forty-Eighth Street and McDowell," I said.

"Nice neighborhood?"

"Yeah, I like it."

"If we stayed at my place, Matt would move out. He wants to move anyway."

"I like Matt," said Cris.

"That's because he let you eat Trix for breakfast," I said. "I don't have Trix at my house."

"You could get some," said Cris. "I know where to get them."

"Oh, really?"

"Right next to the Lucky Charms." He smiled innocently.

"I see."

Frank said, "So you have three bedrooms?"

"One is my daughter's. One is full of junk."

"Maybe I shouldn't be there."

"No," said Adam. "You should be there. Me and Cris can sleep on the floor. If you're not there, it's weird. There should always be a man living at a house."

"I think we can make room," I said to Frank. "I think I will feel safer with another adult there. With you there."

That was a very subtle statement. Another thing we were making from scratch: What were he and I? We had become a couple, but a couple of what? Volunteers? Traveling companions? Cellmates? Not lovers. Not even really friends.

But certainly co-conspirators.

And the miles passed.

Because there were still investigations going on, and we were still under a continuing threat, the FBI agent had helped us craft a story and then told it to the Bay Area media. The story was that the two boys, unnamed, were victims of the drug wars in Mexico. No further details. The DEA guy knew about the killing of the kids' father, and knew a lot about the gangsters that had come after us. None of it got to the media, and very little was shared with us.

That night, halfway home, Frank and I had this conversation on the second-floor walkway outside our motel room in Bakersfield. Or Barstow. Anyway it started with a B. The kids were watching TV in the room, and we both felt the need to catch up on what had happened, and coordinate our response. And neither of us was all that sure that what we were doing was the right thing, or the smart thing.

"You know..." I leaned against the painted blue railing, "...there are going to be questions when we get to Phoenix."

He nodded, "I know. And we'll have to answer."

"The closer we get, the more scared I get."

"That's the drive. And the stress. I know you're looking for someone following us. We all are."

"Will we ever be able to relax?"

"Yes," he said, folding me into his arms. "Yes. It will happen. I can see the future."

I let myself curl into him. "Oh, let it be so. From your mouth to God's ear."

"We're in this together, and we did what had to be done. I don't expect the law, or the world, or anyone else to understand. But if we stay strong, keep it simple, we'll get through this."

My relief at his words could not conquer all my doubts. "You're sure you want to—"

"Yes. At first I was dubious, but the more I think about it, the more perfect it seems. They came to the school, looked around, and left. What happened to them after that has nothing to do with us. We did nothing to them, so any retribution is, you know, not relevant."

I looked up at him. "But we did do something to them."

"Yeah," he growled. "Well, we have our secrets."

"Unless someone else was, you know, watching." I patted his shoulder and leaned back a little to see his face. "If someone was outside watching or waiting, then the truth will come out, and it will be much worse for us."

He yawned. "Worse for me."

"For us. There will probably come a time when telling the whole truth will be possible. Let's hope that happens." I gave his back a short, encouraging rub. A gust of breeze blew some papers and cups across the parking lot below. "Where are we, anyway?

He laughed. "Actually, I don't know. We went through San Berdoo, and they have motels here. That's about all I know."

We went back into the room. The boys were lying on one of the beds watching a cartoon, but they looked pretty bored. Frank turned the TV off and sat on the other bed. "When we get to Phoenix, the police are going to ask us more questions about what happened at the school."

Adam stared up at the ceiling, Cris was trying to scrunch himself around a pillow. Adam said. "Uh huh."

"They are going to ask you what happened."

Cris spoke into the pillow. "We got away."

"That's right," Frank said. "Do you remember that we went outside, and you got in Ms. Castellon's car and left? And I got in my truck and we went to my house just like nothing had happened, right? Only something did happen, didn't it?"

Silence. No eye contact.

"The two men were badly hurt, weren't they?"

No response. Adam was showing signs of great impatience, as if tired of our nagging.

I sat down next to Frank and reached over and took Adam's hand. Then I reached toward Cris until he stretched out and grasped my arm, his face still buried in the pillow.

"So, Cris," I said. "You were hiding in the bathroom in the dark. Were you scared?"

He looked up from his pillow, made a goofy face, wagged his head up and down wildly, then hid behind the pillow again. This flip attitude, in a moment that demanded seriousness, disturbed me a little, but I decided not to react.

"So then we left the bathroom. Then what happened?"

Into the pillow he said, "We ran outside and drove home in her car."

Frank said, "What happened to the men who were chasing us?"

"I don't know."

"I see." It occurred to me that I don't know from a boy Cris's age was a pretty solid answer. I turned to Adam. "Is that what happened?"

He nodded.

Frank said, "Did they point guns at you and threaten to shoot you?"

Adam looked at us with scorn. "Don't worry about us. We know what to say, and no one will trick us. We know what to say."

I pondered the boys' responses. I have known enough kids to know that they have, almost all of them, profoundly deep cores of character and strength that they can call upon in time of need. In other words, they surprise you, over and over again, mostly in a good way.

Frank said, "The most important thing now is to protect you boys. Ms. Castellon and I are determined to do that."

Adam stared toward the blank screen of the TV, but he was seeing something far away. "I am going to live long enough to make them pay with blood for my father. I will do anything you want."

"Me too," said Cris.

These were brave words from two boys. Could they be relied on? A whole lot depended on it. But I wanted to hug them and scream with joy or relief. And I did hug them. But I did not scream.

Chapter 19
FRANK

We got to the motel after dark. The room was on the second floor, and the elevator was right outside the office, so we all got in there. The doors slid closed. Everyone was tired and uncomfortable. The elevator said, "Going up," in this weirdly warm female voice, and I suddenly felt an overwhelming panic, like an explosion. The door was going to open and the men with guns would start firing at us. It was the voice that told me. The woman's voice. The elevator stopped, the voice said, "Second floor," the doors began to open and I almost screamed. Brenda and the boys trundled out and I followed, my heart hammering like it was about to throw a rod. We found the room. I forced myself to settle down. Everyone went right to bed. I took a hot shower. Being closed off in the shower, unable to see or hear anything going on outside the bathroom, made me nervous again. What if killers broke into the room and strangled or stabbed everyone? But I fought to stay calm, to take my time, because there was something else I was nervous about: getting into bed with Brenda.

I turned off the shower. All was calm, all was bright. While toweling off, I glanced in the mirror and was startled, again, by the dark red scab under my jaw. One reason it kept surprising me was that it did not hurt. I dried off and put on my pajamas, which consist of a T-shirt and an old pair of very comfortable seersucker Bermuda shorts. These are also my pajamas at home. I hadn't expected I would be displaying them on the trip, but I always wear pajamas if possible. Sleeping in the socks and underwear you wore all day is, to me, beyond the pale. Even after facing death.

I opened the bathroom door and stepped out. The only light in the room was from the bathroom behind me, and exterior lights leaking in around the front-window curtains. The boys were two lumps under the covers in one bed, Brenda a not much larger lump in the other.

The window a/c had been on high since we walked in, and the room was now quite chilly. I turned it off, then went back and closed the bathroom door so only a sliver of light showed, in case someone had to get up during the night. I walked to my side of the bed and slid in, back to her. We had held each other in fear, and relief. We had cried together, plotted together. We were united in purpose, travelers on the same road, But getting into bed together is different..

I lay for a while, almost too weary to sleep, facing the soft orange glow of the window. My hip acts up sometimes when I am tired like this, and keeps me awake until I get up and get a drink, or an aspirin, or both. I had some aspirin in my kit, but I really didn't want to get up.

I didn't hear her move, but her arm slid across the soft space between my hip and my ribs, and her hand found mine and gripped it so gently. I did not move, but my heart suddenly surged with pure emotion, too strong to describe. Not love, or anger, or fear, or relief, but all those, and a simultaneous cherishing of all I have known and seen and done, not just today, but every day, forever. And of her.

Tears wet my eyes and a wonderful peace came over me, and I slept.

The next morning we were up fairly early, with seven hours of driving ahead to get to Phoenix, where we needed to set up a new household. Or at least begin. We had breakfast at a coffee shop where the checkout was in a foyer stuffed with curios, T-shirts, toys, and candy. As Brenda and I finished eating, the boys went exploring among the shelves. When I went to the check stand to pay the bill, Cris came up to me, holding an action figure of a gorilla. It was pretty cool looking, but it cost seventeen dollars. Brenda said he should put it back on the shelf, but I hemmed and hawed and finally said I would get it for him. During which I avoided looking at Brenda.

She said to Cris, "You should tell Mr. Martin thank you."

"Thank you."

I looked at Adam. "You can get something, too."

"No thanks."

I studied him for a moment. We had all been traumatized by the kidnapping, and the violence on the boat. But Adam had been a hero. A thirteen-year-old hero. And he had been injured. Today he seemed fine—though a little crotchety.

I handed the restaurant bill and toy to the lady on the other side of the counter, and reached for my wallet. Cris plucked a package of grape gum out of the display and held it up.

"No," I said.

"Oh, please!"

"No."

"Please, please, please." He made that aggressively comic face that was starting to become annoying.

"No. Put it back."

"No. I want it."

"But I'm not buying it."

"I'll buy it."

Brenda cut in. "He already bought you something."

The cashier put the toy in a yellow plastic bag and handed it to me. I held the bag in front of Cris, just out of his reach. "Put the gum back and let's go."

"No!" He batted the bag and it flew across the floor. Of course, by now, the cashier and the other people in the restaurant were all giving us the eye. I reached out, grabbed him by the wrist, and pulled the package of gum from his fingers. He screamed and began to thrash about. I picked him up and carried him, screaming, out the door and across the parking lot. As we approached the car he went silent and limp. When I set him down, he collapsed to the pavement. At this point the thing had become a ballet, a gymnastics routine without right or wrong or reason. I opened the car door, placed his sagging body inside, and strapped his seatbelt.

By the time Brenda and Adam took their places, Cris was staring out the window. I turned and looked back at him. "What was that all about?"

He didn't respond. Brenda twisted around in her seat. "Cris, I'm a little disappointed in—"

"Can I have the toy?"

"No!" she snapped. "That kind of behavior is… you are eleven years old, not a little baby." She lapsed into silence.

"Let me put it this way," I said. "We are going to be together for a while. You boys said you wanted that." I did not want to even hint that we would consider abandoning them. Even then I understood that this was a kind of acting out that had nothing to do with gum, or money, or my authority. I did not have any authority. I did not even really have good intentions, just an awareness of the situation and the proper response. I had somehow become a sort of vessel of souls, set adrift with a tattered sail and only stars to guide us. If I could, I would deliver this little crew to safety. "Now, for this to work, we have to be able to count on you. It is going to be hard. You are going to have to fight off your anger, your fear—"

"Can I have it?" Cris said.

"Can I count on you?"

"Yes."

Brenda said. "I need to hear an apology. And a promise."

Cris stared at his knees. "I'm sorry. And I promise."

I wondered if rewarding him with the toy was the right thing to do. Especially since it involved going back into the store and picking up the damn thing, or maybe the cashier would have picked it up—Did I really want to make that effort for this ungrateful, manipulative little…?

Brenda pulled the yellow bag from her purse, gave me a level glance, and handed it to Cris.

We started home. For the next hour, Cris played with that toy in total silence, deeply absorbed. Moving its arms and legs, mumbling to it, walking it along the armrest and the window ledge.

I dumped my bag on the floor. Everything in it was dirty.

Matt walked into the bedroom. "You're back!"

He walked over and we shared a brief hug. There was an asymmetry of emotion to it, because he knew nothing about what had happened to me in California.

But he felt it or saw it. "You okay? Everything alright?"

"Let me buy you a Coke."

We went in the kitchen and sat at the table. There was no Coke, so we had glasses of cold water. I told him about the trip to California, how the spy had shown up almost immediately, the kidnapping, the boat, the investigation. He listened with due respect for a while. But the California incidents had not made the news in Arizona, so he began skipping through screens on his phone and found a story easily.

He looked at this while I talked. "So there will probably be police calling me, local police, because someone, the FBI, I guess, has told them about the incident at the school. Which is not in any of the news coverage."

"Jesus!" He said softly, and he gave me a concerned look. "Are you sure you're alright?"

"Well, I'm here. Still breathing. I'm a little sore from getting knocked around. But not too bad."

"And her? And the boys?"

"Brenda's fine. And the boys? Well, we'll see. I am going to be spending most of my time over at Brenda's house. We don't know what kind of danger or legal shit we may be facing, the boys have no home—I said everybody's fine, but that's not true. They're scared shitless. And I'm pretty worried, too."

As I was speaking, a strategy appeared before me. A way to let sleeping dogs lie—or, rather, tell the truth. "Do you remember, Saturday morning, when I took the cab? I was going to try to find Kurt, and I took the cab because I didn't know if any of the bad guys were still around. So I didn't take one of my vehicles."

"But you never found him."

"No."

We tell our children tales about Santa Claus, about how we never did drugs, how we loved their mother. When they grow up, the lies may become smaller, more subtle, downright ambiguous, but there are still times when you have to tell them.

"Now, I am going to be essentially living at Brenda's. Almost in fortress mode. I will be taking the 9 mm. But I do not want this violence to come to this house, to threaten you. And, depending on how things go, we may need this place as a refuge. So I am trying to keep the police or anyone else from connecting this place to what happened."

"The fact that the kids were here, and you took off from here for Cali."

"Yeah, and about the cab ride. Anything that the gangsters could use to threaten or endanger us."

"Uh-huh."

He wasn't quite getting my point. "We don't know who might come after us next. I trust the police here, but damn it, you never know. I don't want you to be in danger. We just don't know how powerful the people are who are after us. In Mexico, they are all-powerful. What I am telling you is that we have to protect ourselves."

"So what do you want me to tell them?"

He was getting it after all.

"Nothing but the truth. I took a cab to the school to try to find Kurt. I didn't find him. And I don't know anything about him being killed. That's all true, and I want to try to keep as much of this as possible away from the school, for the protection of it. I know life isn't this easy, but I would like the criminals and the cops to just forget me, and us, and the school."

"You are sure he was killed?"

"Well, I haven't seen anything about it, but then I've been gone. Google it. Kurt Ainsworth." While he searched I went back to my room to finish unpacking and repacking. I was pretty doubtful as to whether living over there was the right thing to do. But it seemed like there was a path before us now, and wherever the path went was where I would go, with or without logic.

Matt came in. "I can't find anything."

This worried me. "Really?" I pulled out my laptop and repeated Matt's Google search. "No, nothing. Well, I'll look later. It's hard to believe a murder would not be reported."

"Or he was not murdered."

"Yeah," I said. "Of course."

Chapter 20
TEDDIE

We were at my hotel on the beach. Antonio had showed up out of nowhere while we were hanging around the pool with some people. I knew he was there for a reason. As we walked to dinner, he pulled me aside. "Someone kidnapped the Padilla kids."

"What! How'd they find—where?"

"Up in San Francisco last Sunday, I think. It's been in the news."

"Holy crap."

"Yeah," he said. "But they failed. They were intercepted by the police in a boat. There was some kind of shootout. A couple of them were killed, but the kids are alright."

"Who did it?"

"We did."

I was speechless.

"That is, Abella."

"Doesn't he know that makes it—?"

Antonio gave me a level look. "He knows exactly what he's doing."

Obviously the rest of this discussion had to wait until we had some privacy. All through dinner with Michael and some girls we had met, we said very little, and the suspense killed me. Obviously Antonio had not come here just to tell me the news. Something was going to be done about it.

Later, when we were alone, he said, "Abella knows this will blow us up. He knows that you and your father will take the fall."

"How did they find them? Did we know? Did you know?"

He shrugged. "We weren't looking for them, but obviously Abella was."

The bar suddenly filled up with people. Noisy people. We left our drinks on the table and walked out to the concrete promenade along the beach. A mild, damp breeze blew off the sea, and we sat on a wall and looked out at the white foam and the darkness of the water.

"Was the mother with them?"

"She wasn't mentioned. I think they were with some other relatives, an aunt or an uncle. I thought maybe you had seen something about this."

I felt a little buzz of recognition. I had heard something or seen a headline, but the information and the instance had just flitted by because nothing about the place or the incident had seemed familiar. "So what's been happening since then?"

"Well, it's very serious. The pressure we were feeling, now it's worse. Not just the DEA now, but the FBI. And we have a load sitting in Phoenix that we have not been able to deliver. Nobody's been able to get near it. Abella's guys, our guys, have all disappeared. We need to get that to the customer and get the money before Abella does. It could make all the difference."

That's how I got involved in drugs. Up until then I had only known this business as a rumor. My father, naturally taciturn and evasive, described his business as "niche markets"—products or services that people needed but could not obtain through the notoriously hidebound and inefficient Mexican industries. Angel had followed our father's lead, always finding a euphemism for the criminal activities we engaged in. He had a way of framing every conflict and competition as a matter of right and wrong; us against them. Antonio, of course, was much more open about things, but he was basically a thief, a robber, a hijacker—involved in what my father called redistribution. Now he and I had the task of pulling off a major drug delivery under the worst circumstances.

"It's four hundred and forty kilos. Almost ten million dollars' worth."

I resisted the urge to ask if that was a lot of cocaine or a lot of money. Of course it was.

"It's in a Ford pickup in a closed bay at a wheel-alignment shop in Phoenix. Nobody there knows what's in it. They were told the owner would come pick it up in a few days. Well, it's been almost two weeks and nobody has shown up."

"Is the load safe in there? You said four hundred kilos? That must fill up the whole back end, the whole bed of the thing. I assume there's a camper shell or something on it."

Antonio shook his head.

"You mean it's just sitting in the back of the truck, under a tarp?"

"It's really quite ingenious. The floor of the back end, of the box, lifts up. The load is in compartments under there. From underneath it looks normal, and from the top it looks normal, but there's like, a three- or four-inch-deep tray, I guess you might call it. A false floor? They altered the VIN number on the truck so it matches the extra weight. That's one of the ways they catch you, is weigh the vehicle."

"And the kilos are in this tray?"

"Exactly. Looking at the truck, you can't tell. You weigh it, you can't tell."

I felt the thrill you feel when you learn something new and amazing.

"What about dogs?"

"That I don't know. Maybe you can't beat the dogs. But it is ingenious. The only way to open it is with a remote—like a key remote? You hit the remote and the floor of the box unlocks. Then you just swing it up, the whole floor, and there it is: ten million worth of happy dust."

"Ingenious. That pays for all the work on the truck, I guess."

"Yes, I would think it does."

Chapter 21
MALLORY

He had let me take his picture. He had not minded it. He had actually posed. That didn't seem very gangsterish. Weren't they always hiding, ducking and dodging?

Before going to bed last night, I posted his picture for my online crewe: *Anybody know who this guy is? Seen on the beach in California today. Famous like Amos or maybe just Notorious?* This wasn't just idle, brainless, millennial noodling in bed by me. The group who would see this had already found a stolen guitar, stolen cars, missing dogs, and a guy who hijacked a passed-out drunk girl in a parking structure. It's like a crime-fighters collective with snarky comments. Just thought I would throw it out there.

I slept alright for being in a strange bed, but I still felt out of place. And uncomfortable. I guess I have woken up in a strange place before, but always with someone. Parents. A boyfriend. A girlfriend. But Carissa had left me for Michael, so here I was, alone, in a bedroom in a suite that had been rented by who knows who. There hadn't been any noise outside the door so far, and it was 8:17 in the morning and chilly. I didn't want to stay any longer, but I also didn't want to throw clothes on and sneak out. I wasn't worried about Carissa getting home. She was on her own now. So I fluffed up my hair, patted my face, pulled the robe around me a little tighter, and went out into the living area.

Teddie was sitting on the couch in shorts and a Hilfiger sweatshirt, holding an iPad, playing a game, I assumed by the look of sleepy concentration on his face. I had no idea when he'd come in, or when he'd got up, but he was obviously up and at 'em now.

"Hey." He barely looked up from the game.

"Hey."

There was seemingly no one else alive in the room or behind the closed doors—no coffee or tea or food out, and I sure wasn't going to be rustling that stuff up. I wasn't even going to open the refrigerator or pour a glass of water from the faucet. So I did a U-ey for my room, figuring now was the time to get dressed and ghost. But as I turned, Teddie said, "Hey," again, but this time like an actual greeting. He looked at me and rubbed his thick, bristly hair. "I, uh…"

I stopped by the kitchen counter.

He motioned me to come closer. "Listen, I have a question."

My feeling was that I really didn't give a—but not wanting to be rude, I walked back toward where he was sitting half twisted around toward me. Now he did not have to twist, just look up at me standing there.

"Something came up suddenly and I have to go to Phoenix today. Want to go? Just go and spend the night. I've got a little business to do. You can stay at the hotel or go do, y'know, shopping or whatever you want. It's nice and warm there. This ocean fog here gives me shivers."

I almost laughed, this was such a ridiculous question. "How did I get on this train? Spend the night, go to Phoenix at the drop of a—I actually have a life I was leading, y'know?"

"No, it's not a—I just… this thing came up suddenly, and I—Look, if you're thinking I am trying to hook you… no.

When I get back tomorrow I have to split, I've got to go home, and you'll probably never see me again. So it's not like I'm trying to trick you, like I'm going to keep coming up with excuses to keep hanging around."

I didn't know how to take this. "Okay, but beside the point."

"Don't get me wrong! I like you, I like your company. I just don't want you to be uncomfortable."

"You like my company? I've hardly seen you since our little… episode?"

He did not smile. "Yeah, the episode."

I could not believe I was standing there thinking about this idiotic idea. I did have an actual life, but this Saturday morning, that life was pretty empty, as far as activities. "Is Carissa going?"

"No. Not Carissa, not Michael. My uncle is going, but in another car. I just hate driving across the desert with no one to talk to."

"Why don't you fly?"

He gave me a blank look. "I'd rather drive. I have some running around to do in Phoenix. I don't want to have to rent a car or anything."

It occurred to me that he could have several reasons for not wanting to fly. Like having a bag full of cash and cocaine. Like having to produce a real ID. Like making his movements easier to track. "I mean, just go? I have a swimsuit and a wrap and flip-flops. And I assume I have to drive Carissa home, and not just leave my car here."

"We can go to your place. And Miguel can take her home."

I sat down next to him. The braided tail of this weekend kept twisting around and around new corners. I was still wary of him, but he seemed to have calmed down quite a bit since yesterday afternoon, when he was just another needy, hustle-y guy. I saw him differently now.

"What will we do there?"

He gave me a shy grin. "Hang out. Have fun. What would you do today, here at home?"

"Laundry. Vacuum the floor."

"Well, sorry, you won't be able to do those things in Phoenix. Actually, it's Scottsdale. Very nice place. Better than this." Teddie smiled, confident now. "Go in the pool. Get a massage. It's on me. We'll have a really nice dinner. All on me."

"We had a nice dinner last night."

He frowned. "That was bar food. I mean really nice. I know some interesting people there." His look turned from shy to sly. "You can work on your tan."

My tan is more or less Rihanna. I knew he was trying to be funny. I said, "I wasn't going to say anything, but you're kind of pasty for a Mexican dude."

He laughed.

So anyway, I went. Y'see, I'm a college student, and I work at a kiosk in a mall. But I also have aspirations to be a romance novelist. I'd been reading teen romance since slightly before I was officially a teen, and worked my way up in age and back in time to historical romance, where the heroines don't just deal with jobs and families and society's expectations blah blah, but have adventures. They stow away on ships, cross the prairie, spy on the French commander.

And I, at my kiosk… try to convince a guy to buy the Ray Bans I actually get a commission on, rather than the $9.99 knockoffs.

So anyway, I went.

Chapter 22
BRENDA

We got home around noon. Frank dropped us off, and went home to get his stuff, as he would be staying at my house.

We had been asked to check in with the FBI when we arrived, and I did so, and ended up having a pretty long chat with an agent named Benton. He asked questions about the night of the two thugs. I was careful about my answers, my main goal being not to go off on any tangent that might cause trouble, that they might use when they talked to Frank and cross him up. We agreed that Frank and I would meet him and some Phoenix police detectives at the school tomorrow and go over the incident in detail.

I was not sure if our adventure in California had been reported here in Phoenix. I didn't really have time to think about it, unpacking from the trip and getting the house ready for guests I had not expected. Whatever the boys had had at their *tía*'s house would have to stay there, and I got the impression that was not much anyway. Gemma had bought them some new clothes when we were there Monday, so they could get rid of the wet and bloody things they wore on the boat. But those clothes now needed washing so they could—so we all could—go back to school tomorrow. We would need to go shopping again soon.

Frank got to my place about six. He had barely walked in when a man and woman came up the short driveway. They were dressed like, and looked like, a couple of middle-school teachers, but they were actually Phoenix police detectives. The edgy-looking man was Greg and the friendly, jokey woman was Carola.

"We're here to talk about protecting you." said Carola.

I had them sit on the couch and offered water, which they accepted.

"The DEA," said Carola, "have a lot of info on this gang. The Mangos, they call them. So we'll have good intelligence. They have this group thoroughly penetrated."

"Who do?" Frank asked.

"The feds."

"Do you really believe that?" I asked.

Greg looked like he wanted to say something, maybe agree with me that it was not all cut and dried. But Carola spoke first. "As much as we can be sure of anything in these circumstances."

In other words, it was not all cut and dried. That made me more nervous. How long would this go on? We were about ten weeks from the end of the school year. Would this tension and suspense last that long? Would we? In other words, I was having daily and hourly regrets for not coming clean with the police in the first place. But of course there was a good reason for that.

I tried to focus. Carola was still talking in her calm, bright manner. "We're going to be working with them—" I guessed she meant the feds—"and we'll have primary responsibility for protecting you. We are going to have plainclothes and uniformed presence in the neighborhood. And at the school. We also have placed monitored security cameras at several places overlooking the house."

I wasn't sure what she meant. "What? This house? When did you do that?"

"Just now," said Carola. "Before we came in. It's easy now with the remote tech we have. There's one in the alley and one on the streetlight across the street. C'mere."

She stood up and went to the front door. The rest of us followed her out onto the porch.

"See." She pointed to the wooden streetlight pole across the street. A small strip of shiny black plastic or metal was attached to the pole about eight feet off the ground.

I couldn't see it very well, but it definitely did not look like a camera. "That little strip is a camera?"

Carola nodded. "It has two hundred-twenty-degree coverage. Anyone comes up the street from either direction, we can see them. We can even read license numbers."

"Sometimes," said Greg.

"Most of the time," said Carola.

Frank put on an extra-serious face. "But you're just talking about outside, right? Nothing in the house. I can still walk around in my underwear?"

This little joke seemed to break the tension. I was afraid they were going to question us, but they were talking about how we would be protected.

We shuffled back into the living room, but I left the front door open and the screen door closed. It was a pleasant evening. Greg said, "We're mainly interested in the street and the alley. And we are going to be setting up a similar situation at the school. Probably tomorrow. And we will be following you to school."

"Mary had a little lamb," I said. It just came out.

When the detectives left, we just sat there. I said, "You want a tour?"

"Sure."

So we walked through the house. Didn't take long. There had never been a man living in this house. It had always seemed big enough for me and Nicole. Suddenly I felt very self-conscious about that. I had already told him I divorced a long time ago. But I hadn't told him—I never tell anyone—how tough that had been.

I met Shawn Lopez right after I moved to Phoenix. A friend of mine from UC Davis had gotten a job at Phoenix Elementary district the year before, and when I graduated, I applied there, among other places. It paid less than California, but I was looking for a change, and there were certain compensations: Gas was cheaper, restaurants were cheaper, and rent was quite a bit lower.

I moved in with my classmate at first, while I looked for my own place. She was from Phoenix, so she had a lot of friends, and I knew nobody. Shawn was one of those friends, and I met him within the first two weeks I was here. It was with a group of teachers out on Friday night at a little bar that was our hangout. After forty-five minutes, I found myself having this deep, interesting discussion with this tall, well-built guy about personal responsibility, families, and why I don't want to be buried when I die, and he does. He was an interesting person, and he inspired creative thoughts in me, things I thought of almost as I was saying them.

We didn't come together right away. It took a couple of months before we really made a commitment, and six months after that we were married. Another eleven months and we had a daughter. And by twenty-four months, I knew that marrying him had been a mistake, except for our daughter. But oh, I loved that first year.

The problem was that he was never really married. He was a lawyer, he worked long hours, went to the gym, to the bar, to play golf. He expected me to have my own independent life, my own activities, and I did not want that. We had a baby girl, and I wanted him to be home with us, to be a family, with the warmth that you feel at unexpected moments, the closeness that stays with you day and night. That is meant to be shared with your mate.

I tried to be patient—there are all kinds of families in the world, all kinds of husbands, all kinds of relationships. And I questioned my own view of marriage, my motivations. Why couldn't I be happy with what I had? Finally it dawned on me that all I had was loneliness, and a man who would fairly often come home high and rowdy and wanting sex. A real country song.

So I shot him. I shot him right out of my life. And then I was as happy as I've ever been. For the first time in my life I was the adult in the room. The one and only adult, responsible for a child I did not know how to raise. But I knew I would be able to figure it out. I was afraid sometimes, and lonely, but the absolute independence was thrilling.

Maybe I loved it too much.

My job was all-consuming, and teaching was almost the least of it. We were nurses, counselors, social workers, referees, den mothers, nutritionists, and cops. And I did after-school activities—sports, recreation center, tutoring, drama. Truthfully there was so much to do I usually felt like most nights were a race to get to bed by ten.

And there was Nicole.

And especially Nicole. She was with me all the time, at those after-school things, first as a mascot, later as one of the kids, and the last few years as a sort of apprentice. There came a point, a couple years after the divorce, when Nicole was in third grade, and I had to decide whether I would get a master's degree. It was pretty much expected by the district and my peer group. It would mean less time at home, paying less attention to her. And there was no husband to take up the slack. I had already considered, many times, moving to Tracy, where my oldest brother lived, or back to Modesto, where my parents and sister were.

So this time the pull was very strong. But it made me so sad, almost desperate, when I thought about leaving Phoenix. It had become my home, and it was the only home Nicole knew. Now I think that what I was feeling was that going home was giving up on a hope. I don't know what the hope was, and there's no logical reason moving should have really changed my life. I would argue this to myself, try to talk myself into it. But it wasn't just an emotional thing. I had friends here, people from work and from the neighborhood, who I really liked. The high school girl across the street was my best babysitter, and Nicole had playmates up and down the street.

So I found a place for her to go after school and had Carly come in every Wednesday night, when I had my methods class, and I got started. And in a few months, my whole life seemed to blossom. I had escaped from the nameless dread of failure and loneliness. Outwardly, nothing changed. Inwardly, I had reached a mountaintop, and I liked the view.

Chapter 23
FRANK

The first night at Brenda's, I slept on the couch. The boys were next to me on an air mattress on the floor. I slid the 9 mm into the space under the couch, within reach. I woke up early the next morning and put the gun in my clothes bag in the hall closet. The clip went into my shaving kit. Then I went for a walk around the block, trying to get oriented to the neighborhood. When I got back, Cris was already up and getting dressed. Adam was still asleep, but wearing pants and shoes. Had he gotten dressed and then fallen back asleep? Or slept in his clothes all night? Who knew? His Tía Aida, sure qualified as eccentric. Maybe it ran in the family.

He would not wake up. His eyes opened, but there was no recognition, and he did not move. When he finally got to the table, he ate only a couple of spoonfuls of the Trix that Brenda had made a point of buying.

And so we went back to school for the first time since the previous Friday. Everyone, of course, knew about Kurt. It hadn't been on the news, but the cops had been there, and the rumor mill had been working. The few friends I talked to knew that the men who had killed him had also come into the school, and Brenda and I were maybe in there? And what happened? I just said I didn't know about Kurt at that time and thought about calling the police, but the men went away. No harm to us. Regrets and sorrow about Kurt. Few really knew him, none as well as I, so sympathy was directed at me. I felt funny about it, since I knew so much more than anyone else. But I was happy to sort of stand up for him.

Right after classes let out, one of the Phoenix PD detectives and an FBI agent whose name I did not catch came in, and Brenda and I walked them through the incident, from the door that the two killers came through, to the classroom, to the bathroom, through the gym, and out the side door. We told them what we had learned from the boys and from Aida about who the two men might be, and about the conflict in Mexico that had led the kids, and seemingly the strangers, to be here. Then Brenda took them to talk to Adam and Cris. The cops were investigating the murder of Kurt, of course, trying to fit the pieces to that, not what the two thugs did when they were chasing us. We got away. Kurt didn't.

The detective was very interested in how and why Kurt ended up in the trunk of his own car, five miles from the school. I had already realized that finding Kurt and moving his car had been a mistake, one from which I probably would not escape. I had tried to touch only what I had to and wipe what I touched. But surely there was DNA evidence from his clothes, or the driver's seat, or something. At the time I did it, I was thinking of how to protect Brenda, the kids, myself, and the school, and did not see how it mattered to the police or anyone else where he was found.

But of course it mattered. Moving the body was a crime, though I couldn't think what the crime was called.

Anyway, we went through all that, then everybody left and I went back to work.

By the time I finished up it was six-thirty. As I was leaving to go home—that is to Brenda's—I found the FBI guy standing in the parking lot, looking at the surrounding neighborhood. The street that runs past the school, Twenty-Third Avenue, has two streets that butt into it, one near the office, another up near the end of the ball field. They both run east into residential neighborhoods. He seemed to be studying these streets, his back to the school, but he turned and looked at me as I approached. The agent was a tall man in his mid-thirties with short, sandy-blond hair and pink cheeks.

I already had my keys out, ready to hop in the truck. But I had to say something. Had he been out here the whole time? I calculated that would be nearly two hours. "Still lookin'?"

"Yeah." He turned toward me. "Uh…"

So I had to stop.

"Did you notice a strange car that night in the parking lot or whatever?" He had a sweater on. Maybe he had been out here the whole time.

"No. Really, I had tunnel vision. I only saw my truck." This was true—I hadn't noticed Kurt's car, or any other cars that night.

"There was a car here, though." He pointed. "Parked right on that corner. You didn't see it?

"Do you think it belonged to—?"

"Oh, we know it did. Our man was sitting in it."

I didn't understand. "You had a cop in the guy's car?"

"Let me clarify. We had an informer. Actually, the DEA had an informer. One of the gang who was working with them."

"Really! But the officer said—" I felt suddenly short of breath.

"No one knows about him except the DEA and me. Phoenix PD doesn't know because he's part of a DEA infiltration of the gang."

"But you just told me."

He closed the distance between us. "I want you to understand the situation."

He sort of turned to the side and looked down the street. It struck me that this was an intentional action, and my uneasiness increased.

"He heard shots."

"Who?" I said. "The guy? The agent?"

"The informant. Yeah." The FBI guy turned again and looked toward the gym.

This was the first time any official had shown more than a passing interest in what we did that night. So I would have to be very careful. I tried a small diversion. "You mean when they got Kurt?"

"No, he wasn't shot. He was, well…"

He obviously did not want to say anything about that.

"So, you hear any shots?" he asked. He had a slight smile. I was getting used to the fact that he usually had the same slight smile on his face.

I had been holding my keys in my hand without moving or jingling them. Now I felt like I should put them in my pocket casually because my fear was spiking, my heart was racing, and I really needed to do something with my hands. But I fumbled the movement and the keys dropped to the ground. I stooped to pick them up, trying to calm myself.

I straightened up and got the keys into my pocket on the second try. "No. Maybe the shots came from, you know, the neighborhood. It's pretty rough down there." I pointed southwest, where a trailer park and some grungy stores stand across from the railroad tracks. It was possible that the boys had told him about the guns and the shots. I thought we had an understanding among the four of us not to mention guns or shooting. This was the narrative—alright, the lie: We never saw guns, never had direct contact with them, and the two men had left, which was why we never called the police. Because we were never actually threatened. And we did not know then that Kurt had been killed. That part at least, was really true.

Another thing was that Brenda had been outside when the shots were fired, and she did not hear them. How could the informant have heard them? That thought led, of course, to the possibility that this FBI guy was just fishing, trying to trick me.

He considered my attempt to blame the neighborhood.

"Well maybe," he said. "Our man called the two guys and got no answer. He waited, and no one came out, and no one answered the phone. Did you hear their phones go off?"

While we talked, while I played defense, I had been mulling something else. "You knew they were coming here."

Same slight smile.

"You knew. Your man was a member of a criminal gang, and you knew they were coming here to threaten us. And that led to Kurt being killed."

"No," he said. "That's incorrect."

"Really? Then explain. You just said your man was in the car, and you knew it."

"I didn't know. The DEA had this guy working with associates of a Mexican cartel. You see, undercover is, it goes weeks or months and nothing happens. Nobody was alerted, the informant was brought along as a driver. He thought it was a drug deal. The guys come over here," he made a circle with his hand to indicate the parking lot where we stood, "out of sight of the informant. They get the keys from Mr. Ainsworth and do what they do, put him in the trunk, and go in. Then, a little while later, the informant hears shots. He tries to call the guys. No answer. So he calls his DEA control. That's the first time we knew, or rather the DEA agent knew, that something unusual was up. You didn't hear their cell phones go off?"

"Other than the few minutes in the bathroom, we were never close enough to them." At this point a train that I had been hearing for a while without noticing it let loose a long blast on its horn. The track is only a couple hundred yards away, though you can't see it from the school. I had long ago tuned out most of the noise that comes from there.

"And you did not call the police to report that strange men were in your school? Men with guns?"

He had slipped that in. I had been very careful not to mention guns. "Well, I'm getting a little caught up in your story. Your informant maybe said they had guns. I didn't."

"Well, did they?"

"Actually, I don't know. I assumed they were dangerous. But as to actual guns? I cannot say that I saw guns."

The train horn blasted again, but farther away now.

"Then you all went home. To your house?"

"Yeah." This part needed a little quick thinking. We hadn't really rehearsed it. "There had been a social worker supposed to come and get the boys. But we missed her. And everybody was a little, uh, nervous and upset, so I said, let's all just go to my house and eat and figure things out."

"And what did you figure out?"

"Well, we decided that it wasn't safe at the school for the boys." And Brenda and I, you know, talked to their aunt and we decided we would take them to California to stay with Brenda's brother—"

He nodded. "Who is a police officer."

"Right. So we made plans to do that. Their aunt was agreeable. In fact she went with us."

He scratched the back of his hand. Not exactly bored, but pretty low key.

In fact, he was not bored at all. "Then you went out at, what, about ten?"

This was definitely not a casual conversation. The informant had apparently followed us. "So you were watching us." My voice rose more than I intended. "Why were you watching us?"

"We weren't. The informant was."

"A member of the gang followed us home? Or all three of them?" My anger threatened to overwhelm my fear of saying something stupid.

"Not all of them. The two who went in the school have not been seen. The DEA informant was the driver. It's possible they went out the other side of the school and left from there. We're not sure why. Maybe they were suspicious of the driver or were intercepted by some rival faction. All we know is shots heard, two men disappeared."

Had the man really heard shots or was this a trick? Filed away for future reference. "So why did he follow us?"

"He didn't know what to do. He assumed the other two had somehow been arrested, so he didn't want to hang around the school. So he followed you for a while. He was still trying to make phone contact with the other two. So you went out again?"

"Yes. We got the boys settled in, which took quite a while, as you can imagine. We both needed to unwind, so we went out for a drink."

"But not somewhere nearby."

"No, I wanted to go to a place I know that's crowded and noisy on Friday night. We went to the Yucca Flats, in Tempe." This is a funky sort of bar that is popular with old farts early, but has bands at nine o'clock and gets invaded by college kids. But the old farts don't necessarily leave. It's a place I rarely go. Hopefully no one would be able to say I positively wasn't there. Of course, I wasn't.

"Yucca Flats," he said. "Okay."

"Didn't your guy follow us?"

"No. He went home."

That was good if it was true. I had to get back on offense. "I want to know. Was that man a threat to us? Is he a gang member?"

"He is a member of the gang, but he is not a threat to you. We have him on a very tight leash. He knows that if he plays games with us, he will die. As certain as sunrise."

Again I wondered if he was bullshitting me, trying to get me to make a mistake. "Where is he now? Is he around here? Is he still spying on us?"

The FBI man pinched the skin under his jaw. His name was Benton, I remembered now. "No, he's not around. He followed you to California."

This was like a whack with a two-by-four. "What?"

"Yeah."

"So he followed us because he's an informer, or because he's a gang member?"

"He followed you on his own, but he informed his handler at DEA."

I felt dizzy. How many betrayals were we dealing with here? "He follows us all the way up there and then leads the kidnappers right to us."

"No, he had already been picked up, remember?"

"That seems irrelevant, if you ask me." I was getting hot again. "He led the gang to us. He set us up."

"This was not a deal where somebody had to be physically led. No, the gang or group or whatever it was up there was not informed by our informant, okay? Only we were. But that seemingly had nothing to do with what happened at the airport."

"That sounds like bullshit. Your man gave us up."

"He says he didn't." The smile was gone.

"And you believe him? They found out that I was taking a sudden, unexplained trip to a place I've never been, and he just followed us up there. And then we're kidnapped by people who knew we were going to the airport. And you believe the informant?"

It was very strange to learn that our mortal souls had been just a chip in some power struggle among evil and ruthless people. I felt a very strong urge to tell him about killing the two guys. But I had to fend him off somehow. For all I knew, the gangs had informants every bit as good as the cops' informants. And admitting I had killed them might bring them back instead of keeping them away. So I said nothing.

And, in other news, I was scared.

Benton turned and walked away, got into a car and left, leaving me standing there, free and unharmed in the purple twilight. I had expected doom to fall on me like an iron house. Like a penitentiary. And he just walked away, as calm and unimpressed as anything. He hadn't said a word about the stuff I thought was suspicious, and he hadn't even blinked on Yucca Flats Out for A Drink After the Attempted Kidnapping, shaky as that had to seem.

Either the spy actually stopped following us at some point that night, or he was lying to the feds. If he was lying, if he was secretly reporting to the narcos, then they knew what had happened to the two hit men, and we were probably doomed. I didn't want to discount their capabilities. It was possible someone could have followed me or Brenda home. I was looking for someone the whole way, but traffic was just busy enough that it would have been pretty easy to tail us. But where we went after we got home—I was very sure no one had followed us, and only Brenda and I knew. So as long as we told no one that part—the part at the end of a long, dark road, far from town—it was still a secret.

Chapter 24
MIRANDA

Adam is the good and quiet one. But that means sometimes quietly stubborn, even insistent. When he thought he was right he would—calmly and quietly (usually)—argue a point. In order to prevail he would even go away, do research, and bring back written proof.

He never wanted to eat breakfast, or at least the breakfast he was served. He would eat half an egg, one pancake, three spoonfuls of cereal, then try to rush away from the table. And it wouldn't do much good to make him sit there longer. I would tell him—it's such a cliché, but clichés come from the truth—that breakfast is the most important meal of the day. He said it did not matter if he ate a little or a lot, he was still just as hungry by lunchtime. So might as well eat just a little.

I suspected some kind of neurotic problem. God knows, just on *Cristina* alone I have seen so many heartbreaking stories about kids' and teenagers' problems. But Adam went out and found articles and videos that backed him up. They said it is okay, and maybe even preferable for those on a diet, to eat a small breakfast combined with a normal lunch and dinner. He definitely was not on a diet, as he ate like a horse at dinner, so that demolished my argument. And since I am always watching my weight, his argument even gave me something to think about for myself. Maybe that was his secret plan all along. Anyway, that became the compromise. At least one small serving, and I will get off his case. But it has to be a whole egg.

Cris is different. Second children always are. He was not exactly the opposite of Adam, but he was neither too serious nor too stubborn. He always seemed grateful and appreciative of almost everything. Cheerful. Willing. The danger with that type of personality in a child is that it is easy to overlook something serious. Maybe he's laughing it off, or maybe he's burying it.

He was a slow developer in primary school, especially in reading. We did not ignore that, of course. I made sure he got extra help, especially after he really floundered in second grade. And he quickly caught up after that.

What I did not realize for years was his deep resentment of the second-grade teacher. He felt, still feels, she pressured him and shamed him and made him feel stupid, if not mentally defective. But at the time he gave no sign of such emotion, at least that I could see.

He laughed it off. Buried it. No long-term harm done, I suppose. But that was the kind of kid he is.

And Vicente, their father, my husband. I am still in awe of him. He was above the level of the rest of us, and sometimes that was hard to deal with. But now that he is gone, I see him in an even more glorious light. He cared about Mexico, about our state, and our city, and our neighborhood. As a young man Vicente had been part of the rising middle class—the Young Turks—that we all thought was going to spring us out of poverty and corruption. And then he saw the country overtaken by the narcos.

We of the Mexican middle class are like anyone. We have something, not nothing, and we want to improve our lives. The middle class will tolerate an oligarchy and corruption so long as we are treated fairly and given opportunities to have good jobs and businesses, a fair financial system, and a good education for our children. And Vicente, a businessman and father, wanted those things.

He didn't care if the narcos did their business quietly, as long as they made a show, however hollow, of respect for law and society. Before the narcos, northern Mexico—at least Sonora, Sinaloa and Baja—had a small but growing commercial class. We had peace and order. There was a certain level of graft and corruption, but like other parts of life, it was predictable, and orderly, really just a form of cooperation among equals. The law could be oppressive or permissive, depending on who you were, who you were dealing with, the circumstances of the infraction, the phases of the moon. That capriciousness tended to make most people very careful about what they did and what they said.

But since the 1990s, drug traffic and human traffic across the border become bigger and more lucrative businesses. And the people doing this business are not part of the established business class. They are outsiders, low-class uneducated hicks and street kids who hide their lack of education and upbringing behind their aggressive attitude, and their money. They have a lot of money, which is fine because it actually represents an expansion of the economy. But they also usurp political and bureaucratic power and pervert the legal system with their trunks of dollars and their threat of violence. They assume they can get or have anything they want, from a private jet to a municipal project.

Most disturbing is their dominance of the police and the courts. What had been before an understanding, a give and take, now is very open and brazen. The narcos demand a justice system that is on its knees to them. Before, a judge, a police chief, a mayor, was a person of some dignity and accomplishment who commanded respect. Yes, there were grafters, but that was a marginal activity. Now it is different. There is no dignity when you are humiliated in the most public way, when your choices are take the bribe or be found dead in a ditch.

This exercise of absolute power, more than the criminal activity itself, brought shame to the country. If you own a business, you cannot protect your employees, or guide them. Really, you cannot even trust them, because any one of them might have a brother-in-law who is a triggerman or a coyote; any one of them might be the girlfriend of a thug. Anyone who walks into your store might be checking you out as a target for extortion or kidnapping, or "protection," as they call it. He might take something from you and dare you to stop him.

Vicente's first business was in shipping and trucking, so there was no way for him not to be involved with narcos. He was quite sure that in the past, a certain number of his customers had shipped drugs. Never with his knowledge or consent, but perhaps with the cooperation of a driver or a warehouse worker. Vicente did not worry too much. His trucks always met all the requirements of the law, and if a driver was caught with drugs, Vicente cut his ties and disowned the man. This had happened twice since 1990. Each time the driver was prosecuted, and Vicente cooperated fully with the police.

As time went on, however, the balance changed. Now if they wanted to, the narcos could commandeer one of his trucks, stuff it with whatever—or whoever—they wanted, and if the truck ran afoul of the law, it would be Vicente who was liable for whatever cost or penalty might ensue. Because now the policemen and the judges and administrators who had been of a piece with the businessmen and bureaucrats are under the influence of bribery or threat that law-abiding citizens cannot match or counteract.

That happened to us in 2010, and nearly ruined Vicente. He lost a good truck, paid a fine, and was threatened with being sent to prison—a prison that he knew was largely controlled by drug gangs. He survived this incident, but knew he could not afford another like it. So he decided to do something.

Vicente had no desire to enter politics himself, but he supported the mayor and the police officers of his town who were trying to fight the narcos, or at least curb their most egregious behavior. Not all the police could be said to be opposed to the narcos, but a good number of them were, and the mayor and other city government leaders were considered much stronger on that score than the judges and court officers, who could be assumed to all be on the take.

In a typical example, one of the underlings of the narco gang, the Mangos, was accused by a bar owner of pulling a gun and threatening patrons. When patrol officers arrived, the narco gave up his gun, but ended up in the hospital anyway. He said the officers had beaten him. The police inspector who investigated the situation, Saenz, exonerated the officers and arrested the narco, but a judge freed him. The mayor, Díaz, tried to have the judge replaced and met with resistance from the judicial administration and threats from the local thugs.

That is what started the fire burning: the official judicial hierarchy of the state and federal government siding with a corrupt judge and criminals over the town government and its police. What had been an incident turned into a struggle, and then a crusade. Vicente decided to join the crusade because the owner of the bar and restaurant where the incident took place, who now felt threatened by the Mangos, was a friend of his. And Vicente, too, was tired of dealing with *ponces*, as he called them—referring to the corrupt officials as much as the criminals. And he saw the power and influence of his liberal, educated generation draining away. They had been the ones, in the era of reform in the 1980s, who had pushed out the old PRI fucks and their stories of the revolution and import-substituting development which made them rich by selling Singer sewing machines and Florsheim shoes—*hecho en México*! But substandard and overpriced. Vicente and his generation had created a modern economy based on free trade, on manufacturing and exporting, to supplement tourism. And now these criminals were destroying all of it.

There was another branch of society that played a role in all this. That was the press, the media. When I met Vicente I was a young journalist full of university ideas about the need for a free and unbiased and progressive press. Just like in the business world, in the press you had to live with a certain amount of corruption and hypocrisy, and reformers were channeled into certain safe areas. You could write about the cultural activities or some new technical success of the local communal farm, but not about abuses of the land tenure system by the rich landowners and their political allies. You could discuss the new factory in town and the high-wage jobs it would bring, but not the sweetheart deal given to the factory owner, which was worth years of those good wages.

But we could also see progress being made, and so what if some asshole was made undeservingly rich, when hundreds of people got a drastic upgrade in their standard of living because of those jobs? Who cared if the communal farmers leased their land to the rich landowner, if the money from that lease was guaranteed and almost as much as the small farmers could have made from a year's labor? With some brains and some luck, the average citizen could improve his finances, help his son get one of those factory jobs, his daughter a college admission, his wife a vacation.

Yes, to some this may all sound so old-fashioned, paternalistic. This is Mexico I am talking about. Mexico twenty, thirty years ago. And old-fashioned as it may seem, I believe most middle-class men had aspirations for their daughters as well as for their sons, and a sensitivity to the difficulties of being a working woman. And even if they didn't have those things, they might know that certain women—either because of their wealth, their class, their upbringing, or simply their attitude—were not to be messed with. In other words, certain women were not only protected by the patriarchy, they were actually interpreters of it, beneficiaries of it, almost co-owners.

Vicente was certainly one of those men with aspirations. In fact in some things he was more radical or vociferous than I was. And I was one of those women, I had my job at *La Voz* partly because I started with a degree from the Autonomous University, and because I carried my class identifiers with me, even when I was working for the left-wing independent weekly paper. So when Sr. Sandoval met me, he could be confident that I would adapt to the orthodox progressive stance of *La Voz*.

But even as I was being hired there in 1999, that modern progressivism was under attack by the narcos, and the human traffickers. And very specifically, by the Mangos. They had been in a turf war with another gang for the better part of a decade, but around 2000, that war turned into a route as the Mangos sent most of their rivals into hiding or, with help from their friends, to prison. Then their power, and their ruthlessness grew unchecked. Sandoval fought them for a while, and though I doubt he ever really felt threatened—he wasn't the type of man you could threaten—he eventually decided that rooting out political corruption was a thankless task, or the task of a generation, not of a six-part newspaper series.

I had a conversation with him in which I reminded him that Hitler could not have taken power without the help of a compliant press. He denied the relevance of that example. But I could see that things were changing, and I decided that the time had come for me to be a full-time wife and mother. As such I was free and able to help my husband in his business and protect my children.

Then they came after us. The city had received a grant to expand the recycling program. The Mangos somehow got their hooks into this business and tried to take it over. My husband stood up to them and they hijacked one of his trucks. And then they killed him, and I knew it wouldn't stop there. They knew that I was full of vengeance and had the strength and connections to hurt them. I sent the kids to my cousin in Phoenix and went to Puerto Rico, where I contacted the FBI. I thought I could get asylum as a victim of the drug war. They recommended an attorney, and they helped me get a visitor's visa. And they started a file on my awareness about the Mangos and their activities.

My only prayer is that I get to see and hug my boys again. They are the world, and everything else can go to hell.

Chapter 25
FRANK

I went home for the second night to my new, possibly temporary family at a new, definitely not my, place. Brenda's house is almost to Scottsdale, near Papago Park. You can't see the park from there, but you can see the two big round-shouldered buttes that rise up on either side of McDowell Road. Round as clouds but solid boulders of sandstone or granite, with a few tiny shrubs growing in the cracks, otherwise bare. Sometimes the buttes seem gray, other times dusky red or pink. Wind has carved caves into the rock, irregular holes, like the mouths and eyes of cartoon ghosts or the corpses of dead soldiers left out in the sun or snow too long. On the other side of those buttes, Phoenix becomes Scottsdale. The buttes don't mind. They've seen it all and say nothing.

Before I got home, the three of them had cleaned and organized the bedroom that Brenda called the junk room and a couple of twin beds had been revealed. So the boys would be in there now. We had dinner. My son called and we talked for a while about him getting his own car insurance and getting off my policy. He was eighteen when he went in the army, and had an old beater. Now he's out and has some cash, and he's looking for a nice car. And he's doing it on his own; hasn't even mentioned any other way. Including insurance.

The boys were in their room, and I was sitting on the couch, facing the TV but not really watching it. Brenda sat down next to me. In a low voice she said, "Cris wet his pants in school today."

"It happens." But I was calculating: Sixth grade? Kind of late for that.

"No, it doesn't." She confirmed my thought.

She was sitting pretty close to me and speaking carefully, in a low voice. We were very conscious now of where and when we spoke about serious things, and nearly everything we said to each other was a serious thing.

"There's a reason," she said. Regardless of the warm, homey setting, she looked strained and tired. "He doesn't want to go in the bathroom. That bathroom."

"Can he go somewhere else?"

"He won't."

The boys emerged from the hall. Adam said, "Can we play our game now?"

"Alright," said Brenda. "Fifteen minutes."

They fished the controllers out of the drawer, and Adam switched the TV to the game screen. They both kneeled on the carpet, playing. The game player was an out-of-date PlayStation that had remained behind when Brenda's daughter went to college. The sound on the game was low. That was a requirement. I watched them, trying to figure out the game. Brenda leafed through a magazine. Finally she said, "Time, boys."

As they sat there on the carpet while the game logged off, I said, "Cris, Did you have a problem at school today?"

"No."

"Do you want to talk to me about it?"

"No."

"You know, what happened to us at school that night was not a bad thing. I mean, it was horrible. But we survived, and we're safe now. The police are there to protect us. They've already arrested most of those men."

He gave me a peeved glance. "I don't want to talk about it."

"It was scary, for sure. And on the boat you two were goddamn heroes. It's unbelievable to me."

"I don't want to—"

"But I do. Give me five minutes."

Adam turned toward me. Cris continued to stare at the TV screen.

"I know this is very hard for you. I'm older. I've seen some blood and violence, I guess. Never like what we've just been through, but anyway, you learn things. You guys are more, I don't know—" Tender? Innocent? I wanted to empathize, but not insult them by presuming too much. After all, we were still really strangers to each other.

Adam gave me a hard, level look. "We're not afraid."

"I'm not saying that."

Brenda said, "We want you boys to be able to express your feelings because it is very hard to go through what we've all been through, and what we've seen. I know we are not your parents, but we are not strangers anymore."

Cris bent over and sagged to the floor, shaking with sobs. Adam stared at him with haunted eyes but a clear determination not to break down. Cris crawled toward the couch and, unexpectedly, right into my arms and onto my lap. I was surprised, but I immediately understood. He bawled quietly for a few minutes.

"It's alright, Cris." Adam laid a hand gently on his shoulder.

After a while, Cris said, "I'm not afraid to go there. I am not afraid of those men for myself. I'm just afraid that they will come back and hurt everyone else. And hurt my friends and the teachers and little kids."

"If you go in that bathroom?" I said.

"Yes. That's what I'm afraid of. Going in there will bring them back again."

"But you know that's not really true, don't you?" Brenda was also leaning over, touching his head.

"I know. But I can't help it." He was calm now.

"Yes," I said. "You know that. But it's hard. We understand. Do you miss your dad?"

He nodded against my chest.

Adam said. "He just wanted to do his business and take care of our family. He wanted to help people and make the place better. That's all."

I was a pleasantly surprised at his ability to express himself. "You know something about this."

"He just wanted things to be fair. The country was doing well. Then they came. The criminals, the gangsters. Narcos. Coyotes. They weren't anybody special at all. They just had a lot of money."

"So your father fought back."

"He didn't fight. He was peaceful and legal. But they stole one of his trucks, and the law blamed my father. He lost the truck and had to pay a fine and even maybe he goes to jail. And yet the men who stole the truck, who had the drugs in it, they just walked away."

"You know a lot," I said. "You're very sharp."

"It's all my parents talked about for the last whatever."

"Well," I said. "There will be no bad guys coming here. Anymore. I am here. Ms. Castellon is here, and if we have to leave, Matt will come over, and he was in the army."

Cris straightened up a little in my lap. "Did he kill people?"

"No. There's not going to be any more killing. He's just here to help us out. To keep an eye on things. Now, you need to go to bed." I patted his back.

Cris uncurled and found his feet.

"Brush your teeth," said Brenda. "And go to the bathroom."

Cris trotted out of the room, laughing. "Stop telling me to go to the bathroom!"

I had to chuckle. "Well," I said, "he does manage to recover quickly."

Brenda still looked worried. After all, she would be dealing with him in the classroom tomorrow.

Adam crawled forward and put the controllers on the shelf under the TV. Brenda got up and went into the kitchen. I was about to leave the room when Adam said, "Were you in the army?"

"There were no wars in my time. I was too young for one, too old for the other."

"Desert Storm?"

"You are a smart guy. You keep surprising me. You know about wars the U.S. has fought."

"I know a lot. My mom is a journalist."

"Really. I did not know that."

"She and my dad were very strong. They fought together, even though they knew the dangers."

"Where is she now?"

"I don't know. No one knows." He was calm and serious. "And no one should find out, because if it is known, they will go there and kill her. There is no question."

I felt a deep, disturbing agitation, or hopelessness. "I'm sorry."

After a while he said, "But Matt was in the army. Does he have one of those rifles?"

From the kitchen came Brenda's voice. "We've got no milk for the morning."

Adam stood up and hopped on one foot, as if his leg was asleep. "What kind of gun do you have?"

"Whaddya mean? I have several."

"But the one in there." He pointed to the closet.

"You found it. Were you going through everything I have?"

"Show it to me."

"Apparently you've already seen it."

"I was putting something away. We were cleaning up."

"You and I both know the gun is in my bag. You had to look for it. So tell me the truth."

He didn't flinch. "Yeah, I looked in the bag. I don't know why. It was just there. I don't know why I looked."

I thought about this. Maybe it had been more or less

unintended. And now he was just asking about something that he had seen. That's Dealing With Kids 101. Get them to talk to you. Listen. What Brenda had just said.

So deal with the real issue, the gun—not the fake issue of "why did you look in my bag?" Thirteen is certainly old enough to know something about guns.

Brenda snapped off the kitchen light and crossed to the hall. She went into her room and closed the door. I stood up and walked to the closet. I took the pistol out and returned to my seat. "Okay. We can't talk about anything until we talk about safety."

"I know about safety."

"When do you point a gun at somebody?" I was holding it so the barrel pointed at the ceiling.

"When it's not loaded, unless—"

"No," I said. "The answer is never, unless you want to kill them."

"But it can't hurt someone if it's—"

"Thousands of people are killed every year by guns that someone thought were not loaded. The only way to positively not hurt anyone is to never point it at anyone."

He stared at the gun in my hand. I gave it to him. "How many bullets are in there?"

He examined the slot in the handle where the clip goes in. "None."

"Are you sure?" I took the gun, pulled back the slide, and showed him the empty chamber. "There could be one in there as well. Even though the clip is not in place, or is empty. But empty as this gun is right now, you still don't point it at anywhere but at the sky, unless you are aiming."

I handed it back to him. "That's the safety."

"I know. My dad had one. And he had a shotgun. I shot it once. Only once. At a fence. Out in the desert."

"We can go out in the desert if you want, and—"

"That's okay." He shook his head, pointed the gun at the TV and made a gun sound. Then he handed it back to me.

"I am going to leave this in the same spot. I want to be able to trust you. But I do not want you to touch it. And absolutely Cris is not to know anything about this."

He nodded. I had not asked him not to tell Brenda. That was a given, but if not, I wanted to be able to tell her myself. Just not today. I took some comfort from the fact that he had not found the ammo. I would move the clip to a new, safer location.

I put the gun away. Adam went to bed. The TV was on a weather report. A procession of yellow sun symbols marched across the screen—the whole coming week. And temps getting too close to ninety for March. I noticed that anxiety was making my nerves twitch and my hands tremble. Very subtly, but it was there. I guessed the stress was getting to me.

Brenda returned and sat in the chair next to the couch. She had on a chenille robe over her pajamas. "Well, how do you think they are doing?"

I struggle with questions like this even in normal times. The answer is, except for a small percentage of assholes and grifters, everyone is doing the best they can. But I knew what she was really asking: How would they deal with the trauma, the multiple traumatic experiences they had just been through, and the fear of what might be around the corner?

"I think they will be okay," I said. "But we have to help them any way we can. And I don't even know what that might involve. We don't know who might show up tomorrow, good or bad. Will an uncle come and take them away? Will the mother show up? Will they stay here? How will we do that?"

"We have to be very careful about whoever does show up."

"Obviously."

"I want to talk to Mary Ann. I'm sure she'll have some good ideas." Mary Ann was the school psychologist. "In fact, can you carve out some time tomorrow? She'll be in the building, I'm pretty sure. She usually is on Fridays."

"Sure."

Brenda gave me a warm smile, and believe me, it really felt

like a gift. "It's good for you to talk to them and to be, I hate to say it, a father figure."

"Yeah, well."

"You're a good man, Charlie Brown."

I'm sure I blushed. "Please. I'm going to pretend I didn't hear that."

She went in her room, and I picked up the TV remote and flipped through channels with the sound off, looking for anything interesting. I heard a noise. The door to the boys' room stood half open and a light shone out into the hall. I got up and peeked in. Adam lay in bed reading a magazine. The bedside light wasn't bothering Cris, who was turned away and fast asleep.

"Hey, don't you want to go to sleep?"

"No, I'm just reading."

I looked to see what magazine he had, but it was folded open and I could not see the cover. On the nightstand stood a stack of more mags, the top one a copy of Seventeen with a girl I didn't recognize (of course) smiling and swishing her hair. So Adam was just reading anything, probably because he could not sleep. "You read English very well."

"Not really."

Being an eighth grader, Adam is impervious to both praise and joshing. I remember Matt at that age. Cheerful and chatty when he wanted to be, but also sullen and silent around strange adults or in new situations. But that was a normal kid in normal times. Adam and Cris had been subjected to horrors and loss, and maybe not least, they had been forced to leave home and everything he knew and to live now in a makeshift bedroom with people they'd never met until a week ago, with old magazines stacked on the table.

"Is your side hurting you?" Brenda had been changing the dressing as needed. I had not heard much about the injury or the treatment.

"*Déjame*," he mumbled, refusing to take his eyes off the page.

I was not in a position to give orders, only suggestions. "I suggest you turn the light off. You'll thank me in the morning."

"Okay." But he made no move.

I got my pillow and went back to the couch. The light in the boys' room went out, but later on that night I got up, and the light was back on.

I was up early, but not quite early enough. Everything felt a little scattered. I couldn't put off a shower, but made it a quick one, already resigned to the necessity that breakfast would be a piece of toast on the way out the door. As I shaved, I noticed that the injury to my jaw had developed a lavender bruise. One more thing I would prefer to not have to talk about. I also noticed some small pink blotches on my chin and near the corner of my mouth. Was that the psoriasis returning?

At school, the news was out. Kurt's obit was finally in the paper, with, of course, no details about his death. There would be a memorial service on Monday. That would be a difficult day.

Walking through the jabbering swirl of before-school kids, I went to the gym and let myself in. This would be the only time of day that I could count on the place being empty. Once the first bell rang, the PE teachers might bring classes in at any time.

The frosted-glass windows under the roof at each end of the basketball floor let in a cool morning light. This is where my life might have ended, but I went on. And now I had arrived at another day. I did what I could that night. But now I had come to another day. Benton, the FBI agent, had asked about shots. I did not know if that question was as simple as it seemed. But now was the time to find out. When I cleaned up that night, I never thought about bullet holes or slugs in the walls. And I had not thought about them since. Another fatal mistake by me. Cowboy had fired twice toward us as we were crossing the floor, and twice into the folding framework of the stands. Maybe they wouldn't think to look for the two slugs under the stands, but the other two must be buried in the west wall of the gym. I had walked through that area several times since then, furtively surveying the scene, and hadn't even thought about bullet holes, or bullets, or anything like that. Had the FBI guy found them?

Maybe I hadn't thought of bullet holes because there were no shell casings on the floor. Now I remembered that Cowboy had a revolver, a .357 or .38, which keeps the spent casings in the cylinder. Letterman had an automatic, which would have spit out the casings, but he never fired.

I crossed the room, hit the lights, and walked back out onto the empty hardwood floor to the spot where I'd slammed into Cowboy in the dark and grabbed the boys. I retraced our path. He'd fired two shots at us as we ran. I inspected the surface of the folded up bleachers. They were nicked up, scratched, and stained. Could use a complete refinishing or even replacement. But I did not see a bullet hole. I looked at the brick wall above the bleachers, and near the doors, and the doors themselves, and found nothing. Everything in this room is at least twenty-five years old except the vinyl-covered pads which line the brick walls.

I walked up to the pads. Two inches thick, they hang on Velcro strips to allow them to be moved, though they hardly ever are. Kids like to run into them, push each other into them. They are nicked and gouged. Any big tears we repair, and when one gets too torn up, we replace it. I followed the pads along the wall, using my eyes and fingers. A bullet going in here might not make a big hole, and then it would slam into the block wall behind. Would it then shatter? Bounce? Splat?

Twenty-five feet along, I found it. A nick with a thimbleful of stuffing bulged out. I pulled the pad loose, and there I found a silver fingernail melded into a dent in the brick. I picked at it with my pocket knife and it came loose. It was smaller than a dime and weighed almost nothing. Surely this was not the whole bullet? I looked over the wall, the back of the pad, and found some grainy dust, presumably from the impact, but nothing else.

I had feared he would shoot us, even though it was dark,

maybe aiming at the sounds we made running, or at our shadowy forms. But he had missed us by ten yards, I now estimated. I replaced the pad. I did not have time to search for the other bullet. I was satisfied now that the police had not searched for evidence of a gun being fired. Benton's informant had heard shots. That's all they had.

The next thing to deal with was the school counselor. It would mean telling the same story again. I had learned in the first few tellings that it does no good to skip through and leave stuff out. You just end up having to go back and fill in, and the more times you go over it, the more likely you are to make a mistake. I had adopted a strategy of being exact on some things, like the sequence of actions and movements we made, and very hazy on other things, like the time things happened and what was said. The sequence established our innocence. And it was a list, easier to remember. Exact times, on the other hand, could make us look guilty. This was why I worried about the informant in the car outside the school that night. If he knew the exact times things happened, he or someone, like Benton, might realize I was lying about the sequence. There were gaps in the time that the sequence could not explain. That could hang us.

Chapter 26
BRENDA

We were on our way to see Mary Ann, the counselor, who, it turned out was not at Grand Avenue that day, but at Emerson School. It was lunch time, and I had one hour free. I was determined to take this step, and do it today. I didn't think I could wait until next week.

Frank said, "Thank God it was dark when those two men were crushed."

I was driving. A bright, busy day in the heart of Phoenix, but the memory being called up was of pain and terror. I glanced at him. "Really? But they were right in front of you, weren't they?"

"They were pretty close," he said. "But the motor was noisy and the stands were banging. We couldn't see anything, or hear anything except the silence."

"The silence?"

"When the motor stopped and everything was still, the dead silence. Then one of them groaned."

A silence now enveloped us on that noisy street.

"I think we have to tell her the truth," I said. "Tell her everything."

"I don't see how we can."

Since we'd got home—really even on the trip back—our challenge had shifted from survival to how to deal with two boys who were now our responsibility, and who had just been through a harrowing experience. "But if it is a question of the mental health of the kids..." I said.

"That is a tough question." Tough-guy mode.

"Come on!" I lost my temper. "Don't blow me off! We need to really discuss this."

"I'm not blowing you off, but we can't change the plan now. The plan was to say what we had to say. If we change now, well—"

I tried to be calm and convincing. "We did it to save those kids. And to save ourselves and the school. We both believed we had to make those men disappear, and we did."

"I didn't—I really did not know what was the right thing to do."

"Well, I didn't either. And that decision was made under a lot of stress. Maybe things have changed."

He shook his head. "This could be dangerous."

"I only want to tell Mary Ann," I said. "She will keep it confidential."

"I seriously doubt that," he said. "This isn't some kid with ADD. This is covering up killings. She can't sit on that information. No way."

"But Adam and Cris need to be able to process what's happened to them."

"Process!" He turned away and stared out the window. Stared unseeing.

That night, my first reaction had been to call the police, report everything. He had talked me out of that, and we had begun covering up from that moment on. The further we got down that road, the more I believed it was right. But things had changed. "The fear, the pressure, the trauma, the memories—that might be almost as bad as what those thugs would do. I worry that we are using them now just to protect ourselves."

"You think I don't get that? We told them to lie, now we're going to tell them to tell the truth? You think that's not confusing?" He paused to reload. "And the police are going to find out. And they will not be happy."

"I think we can trust Mary Ann, and trust the kids. But even if the truth becomes known to someone else, I'm not going to hide from it. We swore we would do what it takes. But I didn't know what that would mean. I don't think you did either. So now maybe it means something different. I don't know."

"But if I or we go to jail, or get charged with a crime, do they get sent to Mexico? And if what we did becomes a big story, how can that gang not come back at us?"

"The police are protecting us. Benton said they would give the boys asylum and protection."

"Who?" he asked, impatient.

"Benton!" I slapped the steering wheel. "The FBI guy. Wasn't he Benton? Benson?"

"Temporary asylum and sporadic protection," Frank huffed. "That's not going to be good enough."

"They were outside last night," I said. "I texted them before I went to sleep."

We had arrived at the office. "Alright," he said. "We can tell her the men were there, and they were killed. Adam and Cris know that, so that's fine. And we can tell her why we are trying to cover it up. And we can tell her about Aida. Those are things Adam and Cris need to get off their chest." He held out his hand and I grasped it. "But our secret—that remains our secret. The boys don't know anything about that and don't need to." His voice was husky with emotion. "Nobody does. I will never tell that. I promise it. Never. But you have to make the same oath."

Tears were in my eyes. "I will wrestle with that 'til the day I die."

We sat there for long, slow minutes.

He shook my hand. "I will help you all I can. As long as it stays our secret."

"It will."

Mary Ann, who I barely knew before, said everything we told her would be confidential unless someone was in danger. Then she would have to follow the usual rules. That was before she heard what we actually had to say. We went through it step by step, the two men were both killed accidentally, by Frank trying to defend us.

"And you never reported this?" she said. "What happened to the men?"

We told her as little as possible, but it was still enough to shock her. I was hoping her professional confidentiality would hold up.

After a long pause, she said, "Alright, I won't pursue that. I realize I was not there, so I can't see it the way you did. And I don't really know anything about these gangs, and you may be absolutely right. But would it make sense to you to inform the police of all this and let them help you plan a strategy? Doesn't it seem like they might have the knowledge to come up with a plan that would be better and relieve of the stress of having to carry all this, do all this, on your own?"

We said that made sense, and we would certainly consider it.

As we told our tale Mary Ann remained professional on the surface, but I could sense her withdrawing from us, even, in some sense, rejecting us. She focused on the boys because that's what she should have done, but also because they were not there. It's hard to explain. I just felt like she was listening to the story without really understanding it. But maybe it was the way we—mainly Frank—told it. Even though she agreed she would not call the police or notify anyone, there are rules about that. She might decide to reevaluate that decision over the weekend.

That worried me.

Chapter 27
MALLORY

We left at eleven. He followed me to my apartment. I changed clothes and packed a bag. I said, "The first thing I'm doing when we get to Phoenix is take a shower."

"Take a bubble bath with—"

"Look, I like you fine until you start trying to impress me. Gold plating and champagne don't impress me. I'm not some naphead from back of town. I'm impressed by men who work hard but don't show it. Who watch and wait. Who speak the truth softly, with a smile."

"Sorry," he said, obviously amused.

"Shower. First thing."

He had a BMW M6, which is a whole lotta car. Leather soft as velvet. Before long we were into the hills east of town. On the back seat was a book. I picked it up. World's Greatest Engineering Feats.

"Are you reading this?"

He glanced over. "Finished it."

I was a little impressed. "Are you studying engineering?"

"No. I read that for fun."

"Very nice." My interest increased. "You read for fun. What else do you read?"

"Oh, mysteries, suspense in Spanish."

"Do they have good writers?"

He sent another glance. "You mean Hispanics? Yes, but most Spanish language mysteries are translated from English. Grisham. Sara Paretsky. And, like, speaking of that, was *The Girl with the Dragon Tattoo*, that series, originally written in English?"

"I don't know."

He zipped around a truck doing seventy. "Or Swedish, or what?"

"No clue," I said. "Don't really know it."

"You must be a reader, too. Only a reader asks someone else if they are a reader."

"Yes, I read."

The highway opened up to a broad, flat, empty desert. "What do you mean, I read? Read what, *chica*?"

"Lots of things. I could read an engineering feats book. And romance novels. You'd be surprised how good some of them are." I decided to go for it. "I like historical romance. There's a whole subgenre about black people in the Civil War and Reconstruction, and the west. I especially like stories about the West. Cowboys, ranchers, Indians, Buffalo Soldiers and the teacher at the town's only black school. Stuff like that."

"Uh huh."

"I know, you think romance novels are escapist junk, and they are. But historical romance—a good one—always has details of life that are well-researched and factual. In fact some of the writers get so sidetracked by the historical stuff that they forget about the romance for thirty pages at a time. But I love that stuff."

"To each his own." He laughed. "Her own, that is." He was fairly charming when he let himself be, and not bad looking. I thought about telling him my little secret about romance novels, but decided not to.

"You probably like Isabel Allende," I said.

"No!" He almost shouted. "I hate that stuff! Ghosts and magic and talking toads and curses that last a hundred years."

"No, I don't think you're allowed to hate it. Us ethnic people, we have our standards, even when it comes to highbrow shit. Like I am not allowed to not love *The Color Purple*. Oprah would have my ass."

He chuckled in appreciation of my radical ideas.

What the heck. "I write, too. Romance. Historical."

He gave me a surprised but appreciative look. "Really! Are you good? Have you been published?"

"I'm still learning the craft. I'm not ready to publish. But I'm in a writers' group. I work on it every week.

"Interesting!"

Interesting. He found it interesting. Most people do. They look at amateur writers like they look at other social cripples, like obsessive-compulsives and vegans. "Romance is hard. It's strict."

"I think I've heard that. The girl has to meet the guy on a certain page and kiss on a certain page, and so on."

I said, "Well, some people say that. But it's really a lot simpler than that. The heroine has to be sympathetic, the reader has to care about her. And readers have to fall in love with the hero. But the biggest one is the H.E.A."

"The what? The H—"

"Happily Ever After. Must have it." I did a little cha-cha in my seat. "Cannot be, you know, half-hearted. Can't be maybe yes maybe no, or we just go back to our same old lives. The lovers end up together or there's no reason for the book to exist."

"Sure, that makes sense."

"And that's not easy. You can't just throw any two characters together and it happens. There have to be strong reasons. You can't compromise the woman's integrity, or the man's, uh, masculinity."

"So he has to speak the truth softly and smile." He said it softly, with a smile.

I laughed, and punched his arm. "Exactly. You got it."

"So are you writing something now?"

"I am."

"Tell me about it," he said. "Tell me the story. It'll pass the time. We got a long way to go. Where is it?"

"Where is it set? In Arizona, strangely enough. It's back at the time of the Indian Wars. The Apaches. And some of the Indian fighters are Buffalo Soldiers. Do you know what they are?"

"No."

"Well," I said. "They are black soldiers, they served in the West. So my hero is Frederick, and he is stationed at the Apache reservation in Arizona. And the heroine is Betty. She was a poor seamstress who worked her way up to owning the dry goods store in, I think it's going to be Fort Thomas. Still deciding that. Fort Thomas was a real fort, near the reservation. Betty is smart about business. I use a little of my biz-school knowledge with her, but only a little, because, well, you've got to stick to the romance. But the thing is, she is practically the only respectable single woman in the state, all the others being either servants or prostitutes."

I caught myself saying "all the others being." Talking like a writer. But he didn't seem to notice. He also did not comment about my character's names, which I guess I'm going to have to change at least one of them, though I love them because Frederick, as in Douglass, was a very common black name at that time, and Betty is named for my sweet old aunt. But the people in my writers' group gave me a hard time about them. They asked me if there was a divorce on the Flintstones. I didn't get it because my only Flintstones reference was vitamins. They explained it to me, that in the cartoon Fred and Betty were married to other people. Even Raisa, whose parents are from India, knew more than I did. Then Dean, the only man in the group, said, "Yeah, Betty was the hot one."

They all laughed or shook their heads or both. But I said, "He's right. The Betty of the group in the club is the hot one."

As we approached El Centro I looked at my phone to check for a response from my ppl about my posting last night. There were a couple of not-funny cracks, and from someone I don't pay much attention to: "this guyz banger! watch out!"

So Teddie was at least a little bit of a known quantity. I made a note to do a little searching when he wasn't sitting right next to me. But I wasn't alarmed or anything. We had been together for almost a full day now, and the longer we went on, the more normal he seemed. He had uneven ears, so his sunglasses were always a little crooked when he looked at you. And he had this easy quality when he was not trying to impress a person. I said, "So, you married?"

He laughed. "No. I'm not old enough."

"Who says? How old are you?"

"Twenty-one. I mean, I am old enough, but no way. Not a priority now. Are you married?"

"No," I said.

"No, you're too adventurous. Not like me."

I thought he was being sarcastic. "Whaddya mean? You're not married, you hang out in luxe hotels, take off to different places on short notice. Not to mention bribe young women for favors."

He glanced at me with a sort of sheepish pride. "No, everything you see is about business, about being where I'm supposed to be. I am watched by different groups. I have to appear strong but also hide behind fronts, and seem harmless. And clueless. Everything I do has a real reason and a fake reason. Like this trip to Phoenix. Do you know why I'm going?"

"No." I figured it would be a good idea for me to not be too curious. "As long as it's safe. And you told me it was safe, and I believe you. You're weird, of course, but I don't feel unsafe with you."

"Oh, it's very safe," he said, and this time he definitely had a sarcastic tone. "I'm going to meet with some people from the Plastic Recyclers Association."

"And these are the glitzy people you told me about? Plastic recyclers?"

"No, those are some other people I happen to know. And I

did not say they were glitzy. I said they were fun."

"I don't understand," I said. "Is recycling a real thing to you, or a fake thing?"

He flicked a hand off the steering wheel. "It's both. Like I told you, I have to keep up fronts. But even the fronts have to make money, have to fit into the bigger picture."

"What's the bigger picture?"

"Business," he said. "Capital B."

"Including the drug business?" It just popped out.

He smiled.

"Not talking, eh?" Couldn't help it. Instant regret.

"I'm not in the drug business, though I know people who are. I am in the money business."

This was a good opportunity to change the subject. "You know what's a funny thing? I'm in the money business, too. I am majoring in accounting and finance. That's all about money. Nothing but money. Maybe you should hire me."

"Maybe I should. But that's besides writing novels?"

"Probably because of," I said. "I want to write, but I don't want to starve."

"Of course not. You have to have something coming in."

"And what about your friend? The professor, or your uncle or whatever he really is."

"He's in security," said Teddie.

"Where there's money there has to be security."

"Yes, you are right again."

He had been bold for a moment, but now that closed off. The miles went by. I looked at my phone.

Someone, in response to my post last night, had sent me a link. A story in a Texas newspaper. About a drug gang with a silly name, Mango. They smuggle drugs and people across the border. They are smart and careful and hard to pin down. The supposed leader is named Soto. He sounded like an older man, someone who had been around a lot longer than twenty years. It was a long story, longer than I wanted to read in a car on the phone. A quick scan didn't find any mention of anyone called

Teddie or anything about San Diego. But it sounded like what I had heard from Teddy and the uncle last night at dinner. The article seemed to be a couple of years old. It was posted from a guy I sort of know, a stepbrother of a good friend. I commented: Does this have something to do with my guy?

There was no immediate response. The miles went by. The air in the desert was warm and dry; the gray, jagged mountains in the distance looked like places no one had ever been or would ever go to. I thought about what I was doing. I questioned it from several angles. I was no longer afraid of Teddie, and he had said it would end tomorrow. Would he try to pay me for sex tonight, or some perverse Idunnowhat? If he did I would leave immediately. I had more than enough on my credit card to pay for a taxi and a plane trip home. But I judged that he would not try that. He had not tried to come on to me, even when he was snuzzling my boobs. He seemed like a young man with a lot of conflicts or responsibilities, and many acquaintances, but not many friends. I have known people like that. Their social life is a function of their family or their work life, so friendships are transitory and shallow. That's the way Teddie seemed to me.

Chapter 28
FRANK

On the way out of the shrink's office I got a text from FBI agent Benton asking me to call. So before we got in the car, I called.

"We think we have them," he said.

"Have who?"

"The assailants. The would-be kidnappers. Kurt's killers. I need for you to come down to look at them."

This I did not want to do. "In person? Or photos?"

"You already picked them out of a photo array."

"I don't remember who I picked out."

"That's why," he said. "Why we need to get you down here."

He had brought a file of photos to the meeting yesterday. Brenda and I looked at them, and I remembered making vague comments about some of the men in the pictures. I had not seen Cowboy or Letterman in any of them—they certainly would not be in the lineup. So I would not be able to ID them, and it would be immoral to name anyone else. It would also be suicide. If I picked someone, he would deny it, and he would be telling the truth. And that would hang me.

But standing by the car, phone in hand, I had another thought: What if they had someone who really had done something terrible? Why not put it on a man who they would believe capable of anything? Whose story they would never believe because he always lied? It would be very risky because he would not only be speaking the truth, he would probably, undoubtedly, have an alibi. But at some point it might be his story versus mine. In that case wouldn't my story, the story of an innocent man, be more likely to be believed?

Ah, but that was the rub. I was not innocent. These thoughts all whirled through my head while I considered my response to "get you down here to look at them." Why me? "But what about your informant? The driver? He knows them. He knows them."

"He's still in California. Haven't quite cleared him up there. Besides, we need your ID as much as his. You're the victim."

"Haven't quite cleared him up? That's nicely put. In other words, he's a criminal too. Look, I have no desire to see these hombres unless I have to. Get the driver to look at them first."

"Well, I am going to have to speak to the boys, then."

That, of course, could not be allowed. Feeling backed into a corner, I said, "When do you want me?"

"Tomorrow at ten A.M." he said. "Do you know where the Towers Jail is, in the Durango complex?"

"I'll find it. But I want you to understand, I don't want to do anything that's going to be contradicted by your snitch. I don't trust him to tell the truth. And frankly, I'm not sure you trust him either."

"Ten A.M."

The truth had been lying quietly for a while. Now it was going to bite me.

Chapter 29
BRENDA

This afternoon I had the boys in after-school. I volunteer there one day a week. The after-school program is run by the city, so it's not part of my job. We had the kids out on the field. Cris was involved in a pretty serious soccer game with some kids his age—elevenish. Adam sat at the picnic table under the tree most of the time, writing. Doing homework, I assumed. Some other kids were doing an art project with the rec intern, and others were scattered in ones and twos and small groups around the field.

The thing I remember is the afternoon sky. March is the month the weather warms to perfect, no matter what February has been. It's cool at night, but lovely during most days. This afternoon there were long streaks of high clouds running across the sky, and as the sun got lower, it illuminated these clouds in a bright but diffuse light, tinged with gold. The beauty of it struck me, and oddly enough, it took me back to that night on the boat. The scene and emotion could not have been more different—cold and dark, evil all around, the bridge rising up above us, lit like a monument, the streaks of fog blowing past the towers. That was the moment after I stepped out of the cabin and stood in the doorway, looking at Frank and the boys. I was sure we were all about to die, and I had a fleeting thought that if I died at that moment, my death would somehow be fitting, and significant, in the presence of that huge structure, so beautiful and... not eternal, but full of some kind of meaning—the same sort of meaning that involves pyramids and cathedrals. This feeling only lasted a second in the chaos of that moment, but later, I remembered having that bizarre and sinister feeling about the bridge and the lights and the fog, contemplating my imminent death. And now this beautiful sky took me back there, not because of the image, but because of the feeling. I was not afraid in that moment, I was determined. Fear came later. But when I really thought about what had happened, it was not with fear or horror, but with a feeling of triumph. We had beat them! We had survived! We had won!

Idle thoughts on the playground. A reminder that either I was over the trauma of what had happened a few days ago, or it was buried somewhere deep and safe in my soul, watched over by the angels that have always guided and protected me.

But what about the boys and Frank? I had not faced the terrors they had faced—shot at, thrown into the ocean. As I stood there, Cris ran across a field like all the other boys. But Cris was thrown in the ocean, shot at, and terrorized. And it was all so recently. As I watched him I wondered: What miracle of forgetfulness allows this? How are we not all cowering in fear, afraid to leave our room? But there he ran and laughed. He had not wet his pants today. When we got back from lunch and the halls were quiet, he asked to go to the bathroom. What could I say? I let him go. That had been the only wrinkle. Otherwise he seemed reasonably content, untroubled.

Over the other way, Adam sat staring down at his book, yawning. And here I stood, clipboard in hand, looking up at the sky. All of us peaceful and content in our places.

I wandered over toward Adam. "Don't like soccer? Fútbol?

"Nah, those are little kids."

That was true. "Do you play any other sports?"

He closed his notebook. "I like baseball."

"Really! What position do you like to play?"

"Anything."

"I thought Mexico was mad for soccer."

"Oh, it is, but there's a lot of baseball, too. All year."

"You play anything, but what position do you like?"

"I like first base because I am left handed. I like third base, too. Some people say you can't play third base if you are left handed, but I don't think that's true."

"I see."

"They say you can't throw." Adam pulled his legs out from under the table and stood up. He mimed catching a ground ball. "They say it is too awkward to throw to first base, but..." He raised up and made a throwing motion, quite slow and smooth and graceful, but he winced. "But it's just the same. You just have to have good footwork." He repeated the motion. "See, either way, you turn your body so your front foot is going in the direction you want to throw."

"Your side is hurting you?"

"Oh, it's a little stiff. It's pretty stiff. But I just take it easy."

"Yes, take it easy. We'll keep it clean and keep putting the ointment on it. Do you have a favorite player? A Mexican player? Or someone else?"

"Sure, my favorite first baseman is Adrián González. He was born in San Diego but grew up in Mexico. And as a third baseman, George Brett."

"Who?"

He gave me a look to show that he was being very patient with me. "George Brett, from the 1970s or whatever. He's in the hall of fame. Greatest hitting third baseman ever."

"What is it that attracted your attention to him—so old, and so American?"

"He made instructional videos that I watched. Old ones, but very good. They were on videotape. I still have them. Well..."

"At home."

He shrugged.

I felt a pang. One thing we had not discussed, among many things we had not discussed, was what had happened to his and Cris's home, or where they had lived, or any of the circumstances of their previous life. "You must miss your home. Your parents, of course, but also, I guess, just the comforts. Your own bed, your things."

"Yes, we were rich there. My parents were important."

"Well," I said, "I don't know what it's like to be rich. I've never been rich, but I've never been poor."

"I really want to go back, but I will wait until I hear from my mother. If I do not hear from her again, I will wait and make myself stronger, and then I will go back. I will return. But I may not stay. I am not sure that Mexico has anything left to offer."

I could not miss the determination in his voice, and the implied threat.

A woman came around the corner from the parking lot, and nine-year-old Caitlan saw her from where she was drawing at another picnic table. She ran past me, shouldering her little backpack, calling, "Goodbye Mrs. Casteyo!"

I walked toward the approaching parent and marked Caitlan out on the list on my clipboard. I waved. "Goodbye!"

Right behind the woman came the principal, Mr. Touwsma. Another woman trailed after him. Another parent, I assumed. A boy screamed on the field, one of the soccer players. I turned to look, but the scream turned into a laugh.

Touwsma walked up to me. "So, um, Ms.... the aunt."

The woman behind him was Aida. I thought I might never see her again. She greeted me with a smile and a hug. I responded as warmly as I could, but this woman was really a stranger to me. I immediately recalled my feeling about her; that she was part of something that Adam and Cris needed to stay away from, escape from. I could not say what that was, it was just a general feeling—not even of suspicion, just caution.

Touwsma said, "Miss Rodriguez has some good news. She is going to be able to take the boys in."

I glanced back. Cris was still playing, unaware of us. Adam had his nose in the book again, writing something with his near hand. The left.

I understood that Touwsma would be happy if the boys went away. Having them here at the school made him uncomfortable. Understandably. Most of the staff knew about the attempted kidnapping in California. Most did not know even the sketchy details of what happened here at our school a few days earlier. But they could certainly see the increased police presence, and a number of people were sort of on eggshells about it. As principal, Touwsma was the person of ultimate responsibility for the whole school. And the police had made him aware of the threat of cartel retaliation. Of course he would rather not deal with any of that.

And now here was a solution, an easy solution, it must have seemed to him.

"It was their mother's wish," said Aida.

"Well," I replied, "I really think things have changed."

"Yes, there's been a lot of trouble." Aida shifted on her feet. I could tell she had spotted Adam.

I took a half-step to my right to, not to block her exactly, but to stake a claim. "You're talking about taking them back to Tracy? They did not want to stay there."

She smiled with sweet reason. "Yes, but things have changed, for me, too. I was all unsettled. Now I have a job and a place. I work in the call center. I make twice as much as here. Your brother has helped me out a lot. He and Gemma want the kids up there. He's a really good guy; he'd be great for them."

I did not know what to say to this. For one thing, Willy had been helpful, but *my* good guy had saved the lives of these kids! Twice! "I, just… it's not going to happen. It can't be allowed. If the mother shows up, of course I will give them up. But short of that, no."

I could see Touwsma's disappointment, but only because I've learned how to read him. He would politely but firmly support me.

"Why not?" Aida argued. "The boys need to be with their family and away from here. If I had known you were going to bring them back here, I would have said no way."

I had serious doubts that the welfare of the boys played any part in her decision to stay in California. "Well, I know what the boys will say, but let's not even go there. No. I'm making the decision. They're staying with me."

"But...," she gestured toward Adam and moved to step around me. Again I shifted right to block her, this time not subtly.

Touwsma said, "Well, if she's their guardian, we—"

"She is not."

Aida glared at me. "No, I am."

I remained calm. "The legal guardian, under Arizona law? No."

"How do you know I'm not?

"Have you been to family court?"

She cocked her head.

I said, "We deal with immigration issues all the time, with kids who are in custody of relatives or whatever."

"Well, Willy said that the law says—"

My words, or my attitude, had convinced Touwsma. He chimed in. "Well it does seem like stability is a very desirable thing for these boys. And as for safety—we are well protected."

She was cagey. "But who makes this decision? Isn't it the court? You're not their mother, no relation, and Miranda put them in my care."

"That's not really a school matter," said Touwsma. "It may be this has to be decided in the legal system. But we have no authority like that. If they remain here, we'll take good care of them."

I could have hugged him. That well-practiced delivery. He turns parents and employees and students down on various issues every day. This was not that different. "I have to agree," I said. "We can't make that decision, so the boys have to make it. And they've made it."

She gave up, but I could see her planning her next move. She would be talking to her "lawyer." My brother. What exactly was possessing him about these kids or this situation I did not know. But I knew the source—his well-cultivated sense of superiority. By age, by gender, and by tradition, he was the don of the rancho, and I was the unmarried younger sister. And he was asserting that authority. I, of course had not accepted that BS since early childhood, and would not be starting now. This had always been a challenge for me and him—to find a compromise, a way to satisfy our own sense of self and yet get along with each other.

So I might call him this evening. Or I might not. But I would certainly be talking to Frank about it. "Call me tonight," I said. "You can come over and see them." I looked at Touwsma. A tiny wrinkle in his cheek told me this was a reasonable compromise, and a way to end the current conversation. I gave her the number. My home number. No way my cell.

She turned around and Touwsma walked her back toward the parking lot. I followed them far enough to see her get into her car, and it occurred to me: She came back to get her car. And her stuff. She was here anyway, to get her car and her stuff, and the boys if she could. Kill two birds.

On the way home Adam, in the back seat, fell asleep before we were out of the parking lot and rode the whole way home with his chin on his chest.

I said to Cris, "Your Tía Aida has come back to get some stuff."

"Can we get pizza tonight?"

"Sure. And she might call my house to talk to you and Adam, or come to see you."

"I don't want to see her."

I was a little surprised at the response, delivered quickly and with firmness. "I'm sure she just wants to see you're okay. I'm sure she misses you."

"I don't care. I hate her."

This surprised me even more. It was contrary to every

interaction I had seen between Aida and Cris. In fact when we left her behind in Tracy, he had been very emotional, giving her a fervent hug and even crying. I said, "I'm sure you don't mean that."

"I mean it. She wouldn't let us play or do anything. She slapped me. And she and her boyfriend did drugs. She molested me."

"She molested you?"

"Yes, very much."

This set me back on my heels. As a teacher, you never want to hear a child use that word because it means that you are about to dive into a very sad and dark hole. "In what way did she molest you?"

"In every way. *Fue muy pendeja.*"

His switching to Spanish to call her a bitch was another kind of warning. The most common word in Spanish, at least Mexican Spanish, for to bother is *molestar*. I think *molest* also used to mean something like bother or annoy or intrude in English, but of course, it has come to mean one specific thing. So I switched to Spanish, also, to ask him, *¿En que sentido te molestió?*

He switched back to English. "Her apartment stinks, and her boyfriend stinks. She wouldn't even let us watch a TV show."

I let it drop for the time being. But this was something else I would be discussing with Frank, or Mary Ann, or, maybe soon, a lawyer.

We got home and I shut off the car. Cris got out and headed into the house.

Adam still sat slumped against the door. "Adam? A-d-a-m. Wake up. We're home." No response. I nudged him. "Adam!"

He snapped right awake, almost as if he had been faking it, blinking the sleep out of his eyes in a couple of seconds. "Okay."

"What are you up to? Are you not getting enough sleep at night?"

"Nope. Not at all."

"Oh my." A new worry.

"My system's screwed up, but what can you do?" I wondered

if he had really wakened, or just opened his eyes. He seemed to be talking in a dream.

"But you've got to get enough sleep."

"Apparently not. I'm actually doing great. That little nap was perfect."

He got out of the car and went into the house. I followed him in. Frank was already home, and letting them order a pizza seemed like a good idea. I wanted some space from everything for at least an hour or two. So I quickly decided to go to Applebee's for the Friday happy hour that is a regular thing for some of the teachers. This was the rowdy, fun group of teachers who honestly might not have been the best teachers, but at happy hour, who cares? We complained and gossiped, and I drank two Moscow mules and laughed until my sides hurt.

Frank sat on the couch watching TV. I could hear the boys talking in their room. I had something I'd been wanting to talk to him about.

"Frank?"

He looked over at me.

"Come here, please."

I walked into Nicole's room and turned on the bedside lamp. I had cleaned it up yesterday. All of Nicole's personal stuff I put on the shelves at the end of the room. The bed had been made with fresh linens. I waited as he walked in wearing that vague, uncomfortable look that seems to be his natural expression.

"So it's ready for you."

"Gee… you know…" Pause. "I'm good out there on the couch, really. I am very comfortable there."

I already knew that. "But I'm not. Where I'm from, we don't do that."

"You slept on the couch at your brother's."

"That was because there were eight people in the house. And it was temporary."

"So is this."

I did not want to get into that whole aspect of the discussion at this point. "Maybe it is. But who knows? As long as you are here, I want you to be comfortable here."

"I see."

"Look." I opened the closet door. "This half is yours. The dresser is completely empty."

I pointed. "Here's a dirty-clothes hamper. You do your own laundry. We'll decide between us what to eat, and split the groceries and the TV remote. We're roommates. I haven't been roommates in a long time, but I'm starting to remember how it's done."

"I feel awkward."

I sat down on the bed. "Tell me about it."

He rubbed the stubble on the top of his head. "I like you, and I feel very close to you. But I don't want to presume something that isn't there. I think you are a wonderful woman, but I don't want it to be like we were thrown together by fate, like we were strangers from a ship that sank, and we both washed up on the same desert island."

I knew exactly what he meant, though I could not have said it half so well. "One reason I want you to sleep in here is just to avoid that very thing. Like I said: roommates. I like you, too, but I haven't got time for a personal life right now, for a new relationship. There's not enough space in my brain. I like you. I might even love you. But this is just about housekeeping. So this room is where you sleep, and that—" I pointed in the direction of my bedroom "—is where I sleep."

"I get that. But Nicole will come home from school, and she'll want her room back."

"Yes, in May. So we'll change the sheets and figure something out. Who knows what will be happening with us in May?" I reached for his hand. "I want you here. I feel safer with you here. And I need help with the boys. I can't do it all."

He took a hesitant half step toward me, and I rose into his embrace. He was taking big, slow breaths, but he didn't say anything. Despite what we'd just agreed on, it was like we'd been thrown up by the sea together on a small island, strangers forced to depend on one another for survival. It was exactly like that.

When Shawn and I divorced, Nicole was seven years old. We were living in a nice three bedroom, two bath house in a nice area called Arrowhead in Glendale. Because Shawn had saved some money, we were able to make a large down payment. But Shawn was only minimally involved in being married to me, so when I suspected him of cheating, I confronted him. He denied it, but he made it clear he did not care if I believed him or not. His life was what he said it was, and that was it. So I divorced him as much for his aloofness and arrogance as for the affair.

I was determined, and backed by my lawyer, that I was going to keep the house, with its affordable payments, nice amenities, and nice neighborhood. And get child support. After all, I was making thirty thousand a year, a fraction of what he made.

I met with Shawn's lawyer one day, and he presented me with a paper: a lease on the house.

I said, "I don't want to lease the house. I want to live in it."

"Yes," he said. "This is a lease, so you can do that."

"No, you don't understand. As part of the settlement, I want to own the house myself. I certainly don't want to lease it from him."

The lawyer managed to look at least a little sympathetic as he told me that neither Shawn, nor I, nor the two of us together, owned the house. Shawn had sold it the previous year without my knowledge and leased it back. As this realization hit me, I felt a wave of nausea so intense, I thought I might vomit. I was instantly covered in sweat. My hands and legs shook, the light of the desk lamp blinded me. How he was able to sell it without me knowing was a mystery to me. He had taken the money from the sale and used it to invest in other properties. Now he claimed that the proceeds from the house and other assets were lost in bad investments. My lawyer did a wonderful job of shredding that story. Mainly because of the deception, I ended up getting $150,000 from him in the settlement, along with the child support.

I moved into an apartment and did not do anything about a house for a year—I didn't do anything about anything for a year. In the meantime, the financial collapse began and real estate prices crashed. It took me another year to decide if it was still smart to buy a house, and then I bought this one, in foreclosure. Much smaller, but the neighborhood was nice and down-to-earth. Meanwhile, Shawn really was losing it all. His investments, his job at the law firm. He sold RVs and trailers for three years. I was alright. I had also used some of the settlement to buy some IRAs and annuities at a very good time. When Shawn stopped paying child support, I got a judgement against him and sold his car.

He's doing better now. He's got a new lawyer job. And Nicole's child support ended last August.

And now I had a man in my house, and two boys. Frank said he liked me and felt close to me, but he didn't want to presume. I felt some of that, too. But I also felt something more. That first night, he had shown a tenderness toward the boys, toward me, and even, I would say, an almost grudging tenderness toward the injured man who lay on the floor there, breathing his last.

But I had also seen him act creatively and decisively to save us. Attacking the men on the boat, almost drowning—he still had an occasional deep, wet cough that sounded like he was trying to push out some remnant of the seawater he had inhaled. He wasn't shy, but he was careful, and nothing seemed to shock or faze him. Frank had a few qualities I really like in a man. And a few I had rarely seen in anybody. And I wanted to get to know him, to see if we could make a real love on this desert island.

But not right now.

Chapter 30
MALLORY

We came to Phoenix, drove through town to Scottsdale, to the resort—not a hotel. Unlike the place on the beach, this seemed like a mansion, or a series of mansions, with perfect lawns, bubbling stone fountains, yards and yards of beautiful pink and yellow flowers and bushes, all flawless and perfectly trimmed. You could see a golf course from the terrace, and the resort had all the expensive amenities. I thought I might get a massage, but we arrived too late to do much more than take a slow shower and get dressed for the evening out. We went to the hotel's white-tablecloth restaurant—a pretty popular place, but the prices kept out the riffraff.

His interesting friends turned out to be somewhat vacant. The professor/uncle, Antonio, was not there. A pretty woman with watery eyes in the kind of loose but tight halter dress I could never wear seemed to want to squirm into Teddie's embrace, but he was standoffish, mostly talking to the two other guys there about his railroad dreams.

"...a triangle from Phoenix to Las Vegas to L.A., with spurs to the border, to the Grand Canyon, to San Diego. It will connect to the Mexican lines at Tijuana and Nogales. The problem is getting dedicated lines. There are miles and miles of right-of-ways for all kinds of things—power lines, highways—that are just being held on to for no good reason other than greed. We just need to be able to get ahold of them…"

And suchlike.

It became obvious to me that Teddie and his pals were planning to make a long night of it. I did not want to do that, so after we'd finished the dinner and coffee—by now it was almost nine anyway—I pleaded to weariness and went to my room, my own room. I hung out DO NOT DISTURB, closed the curtains, and clicked through the cable channels a couple of times. Contrary to my excuse, I wasn't sleepy, so I picked up Desert Rendezvous, the contemporary romance I'd brought. I remembered Cory and Lita were about to launch an act-two sex scene. They had a little bit of history between them, but of course, each misunderstood the other. But that was changing. Cory started it off:

"Your body is telling me you want it, but I have to hear it from your…" He reached out and drew a finger across her lips and down to her chin. His own lips closed on hers, soft at first, but with an urgency that would not be denied.

"You're not playing fair," she whispered.

"All is fair in passion, my love." Now he was moving slowly over her, his fingers playing on the tight, slowly flexing planes of her back and shoulders, where they found the rough cord of her bikini top. He pulled, and as if by magic, the fabric flew away. She arched her back, presenting her breasts to his view, and he received the gift with pleasure, flicking the fat, hard nipples with the thumbs of each hand.

I set the book aside. The sex scene would be over quickly now. For all the bitching women do about quickie sex, impatient lovers, and tardy orgasms, the sex scenes in romantic novels usually expire within three or four pages. Just enough to be titillating. It's another one of the rules. After all, if the sex is too long or too descriptive, you aren't doing romance anymore; you've crossed over into porn. Or erotica, or hot, as the industry calls it.

I thought about how I could use the experience of this weekend in a story. And the answer was: I couldn't. All the characters and motivations were wrong. Teddie was surely troubled enough, but not in a dramatic way. And the cocaine sniffing bit wouldn't fly at all. And most of all the heroine was simply not romance-novel-worthy. Too confused, too dithery.

That's why I like fiction. That's why I like historical. I picked up my notebook.

Fred and Betty are out there at Fort Thomas. One of the biggest jobs on the reservation is getting rations to the Indians, who need basic food because they are not allowed to roam freely anymore. They are supposed to learn to farm, but that takes a while. In the meantime the government supports them with rations, etc.

The plot begins when a kindly Indian agent is killed by a proud and vengeful Apache. The dead agent's successor vows revenge on the tribe. Frederick discovers that the murderous Indian has already been killed in an ambush set up by the new agent, who also had the body secretly buried—facts that have been covered up to justify laying retribution on the tribe.

Betty knows that the new agent has been stealing from the Indian rations, a fact which she has been extorted to keep concealed. After all, she has a lot to lose—and being a single black woman, a lot of ways to lose it. Fred discovers this secret and threatens to expose the agent. The agent in turn threatens Betty. Betty blames Fred for causing this dangerous disruption in her life, but, fire-and-ice, she is also attracted to him and admires his courage.

And that's as far into the main storyline that I've got. Gotten? Is gotten even a word? Quick check of Grammarist. Either works; got preferred in most of the English world. Anyway....

I need to understand more about Indians and reservations, about business and social relationships, and class, and prejudice, and law in the nineteenth-century West. These are things that Kianna Alexander and Beverly Jenkins understand so well they can refer to them casually, in passing. I do not have that self-assurance.

But my biggest problem is much more basic. This is a romance novel, but I can't seem to get Fred and Betty together with some spark. So far all it's all just interested glances and passing thoughts. This is a classic romance-writing challenge. Both Fred and Betty are strong characters, but he's old school and cowboyish, she's a highly unusual woman—just as strong and even more clever, determined to keep what she's got… ten. I keep thinking of hot scenes between them for later, but I can't get them past shaking hands at the beginning.

I try, but I just can't seem to pull it off—much like my personal romantic life. Here's one scene:

As she watched Melinda and the children drive away in the surrey, Betty felt a fluttering of hope in the clouds of uncertainty that had fogged the last few days. The dust kicked up by the horses drifted across the small street of quiet houses. "God, I hope they are going to be alright."

His gray eyes revealed he also shared her hope, bordering on fear. "God, I hope so."

Betty turned to go back into the house. The kids hadn't been gone five minutes, but the time had come. Frederick followed her in. She walked over to the couch [note: could be "settee"] and sat down. "So."

He closed the door, and turned toward her. "So. So, indeed."

"It seems we are suddenly free."

"Yes." He crossed the short space between them, then seemed to hesitate.

"Sit down. Let's talk." She patted the sofa.

He sat next to her. "You're probably wondering what's next. Where do we go from here?"

"It did cross my mind." The import of what she was about to say stopped her.

He leaned a little closer, and with a gentle finger raised her chin.

"Do you think..." Her voice held the slightest, sweetest tremble. *"Do you think we've found something?"*

"Found something for ourselves?" He finished her thought again. It was a question he had been pondering very seriously. But he wanted her to answer it first.

"Yes," she said, shyly. The reason for her bashfulness was not doubt about him as much as her own self-doubt. Intimacy between them had been soaked in drama, buried in crisis. What would it be like to sit down, have a nice dinner, a long chat, a glass of wine? Was there anything normal they could possibly talk about? *"Yes, but what will we find? Am I real to you? As a person, as a middle-aged mother with a grown child...?"*

"Go ahead and say it."

"Say what?"

Frederick's heart leapt. Before the words were out of his mouth, he knew what her answer would be. *"As a woman. The answer is: I want to find out."* He reached for her hand. *"It's very important to me."*

It had been a slow process, coming to her. Opening up. But during that confusion, he realized now, he had been circling closer and closer to her. And now he had shot past confidence to certainty.

Just like that.

Betty looked at their clasped hands, hers olive tan, his a darker shade. She remained uncertain despite his encouraging words. *"You know, when I'm walking around here, alone, I talk to myself. I tell my history to the walls. What it was like for me as a kid in this way or that way. Or replay something that happened at the store. And of course, I give wonderful speeches on all topics. Orations."* She chuckled. *"You should hear them."*

Fred laughed, too. *"I would love to."*

He brushed his lips against hers, but she was still shy. He let go of her hand and embraced her with both arms, leaning her back on the sofa. Gently. They had nothing but time now. And an empty house.

Betty was swaying backward, but felt no fear. His arm enclosed her shoulders, and his other hand lifted her thigh, pulling her closer. He was above her now, his dark eyes staring into hers with a kind of intensity she'd not seen from him before. For all the emotional moments they'd *shared—moments of terror, of trauma, of relief, of hope—this moment was different. Was this what she wanted? She still wasn't sure. But it felt so right.*

As his hand began to stroke the back of her leg...

But when I was writing that I suddenly found myself wondering what Betty was wearing? That should have been described, or at least mentioned, twenty pages ago. Obviously a skirt of some kind, but what exactly? And he won't be stroking the back of her leg in a nineteenth-century Old West dress. He'd be lucky if he could find her leg.

And then I remembered something even more important. As now written, the scene would have to end like this:

Something made her look up, and she saw the sheriff standing in the kitchen doorway.

She patted Frederick lightly on the shoulder. "We have company."

He nuzzled his face between her breasts, sending jolts of desire the entire length of her body. "I don't care."

The sheriff said, "I'm still here. You left me standing here after the big reunion scene. Everyone else hugged and cried and saddled up, and here I stood with, I assume, the look of astonishment that you left me with."

So I had some rewriting to do. That's what I was really planning for this weekend. Maybe in the morning I could get a latte and sit by the pool and do that.

Tomorrow. I clicked off the light, clicked on the TV, and settled into the pillow. What a crazy weekend this had turned into. I already knew that by the time I got home on Sunday night I would be tired, my head full of jumbled impressions and memories. But one thing I would not be doing was gazing at the setting Sunday sun, regretting another pointless, boring weekend.

Chapter 31
TEDDIE

She went to her room early. Everyone else left by eleven thirty. Except Ana. I thought she was leaving with the others and went to the men's room. When I came out, she was back, sitting at the table. I ducked around a corner and walked out through the kitchen hall. Then I called her a cab and told them to look for a woman wearing a silver dress in the bar.

But I did not want to be alone. Her room was next to mine, and as I walked down the hall I heard a TV on in there, so I knocked.

There was no answer. I checked the room number and knocked again.

Through the door she said, "Yes?"

"Can I talk to you?" I whisper-shouted.

"What about?"

What about? "Tomorrow."

"What about it?"

"Can you open the door?"

The TV sound went away. I waited several minutes. I would not knock again. If she didn't respond in some way, I would just leave. But then I heard a metal sound, and the bolt turned, and the door inched open until the security bar stopped it. At first I only heard her voice.

"What about?"

"Don't want to let me in?"

Her face appeared. "This is good right here. What are we discussing?"

"Well, tomorrow, I was just wondering." What was I wondering? "What you have planned?"

"Nothing too strenuous. I was thinking I might get a massage, if that's alright. Maybe hang around the pool if it's nice. You're going to a meeting, right?"

I was getting self-conscious about talking in this public place, even though there was no one else there and nothing around me but locked doors, carpet, and a potted plant. It just felt odd to be out in the hall talking through a crack in the door. "You don't want to let me in?"

"No. Tomorrow, meeting?"

"Yes." I blurted it out. "But I don't want to go."

"Really."

The fear that I'd been fighting suddenly overwhelmed me. I could not speak. I shook my head.

"What's wrong?"

Through the three-inch crack I could see one eye and part of her mouth. It suddenly reminded me of being in a confessional. "I've come here, I mean to *los estados*, and I don't know why. I mean, I know the business reason, the duty to my father and my family, but I don't know why I am here, really." My voice had grown hoarse, and I could not control my breath, which was coming in sobs. "My oldest brother went to the university to study. He's not really part of… he left us behind. My next oldest was killed right in front of me." My voice caught, and I had to wait a moment before I could go on. "And now it's my turn. I'm not ready."

"Good Lord," she whispered.

I stared at the floor. I was sure the next sound I would hear would be her undoing the security bar and opening the door. Then she would give me a warm, motherly hug and let me come in.

But she just stood there, looking at me through the gap. One blinking eye. "That must be very hard. But I am sure you can make a good decision if you think about it the right way."

She moved a little closer to the opening so I mainly saw her mouth now, telling me something in a husky whisper. Something I did not understand. At first I could not follow, because I was translating. But then I just listened.

"...learned from trying to write real human characters. We all have an inner conflict and an outer conflict. The thing is, we concentrate on the outer conflict, but what we really need to do is solve the inner... Does that make sense?" The eye appeared again. It was a sympathetic and serious eye and eyebrow, and there was half an encouraging smile below it. Below the security bar.

I had no idea what to say. I nodded.

"For example," she continued, "in the book I am writing, Betty, the heroine, is facing many problems, and she has to respond with strength and courage to solve them. But what she doesn't understand very well is that those outer conflicts, those battles, are not the real her. Not the essence. So Betty's inner conflict is that in this constant effort to show strength, and watching for people who are trying to trick her or trap her, she can never let her guard down, even to herself or the people who love her. So at the end of the day she does not let go and refill herself. She feels used up, totally alone, like she can't go on. You can't live like that."

The eye searched for understanding. I did not know what I was looking for when I knocked on this door, or what I had found. But the eye, the lips, the dark slot in the white door, the calm, caring voice had me sort of hypnotized.

"Maybe if you can resolve that inner conflict, you'll have a better idea of what to do, or at least why you are doing it. Does that make sense to you?"

"Yes," I said. "How does she, you know, get out of that? Find happiness."

The corner of her mouth turned up. "Betty? Well, I'm not totally sure. But it has to do with understanding that she was formed and shaped by her past experiences—by being abandoned by a father and trusting a man who betrayed her."

"Were you betrayed by someone? Were you abandoned?"

"My father died when I was twelve. I definitely felt lost for a long time."

When she said my father died I felt a jolt. I wanted to tell her my mother died. But it seemed profane to say it. "What about now?"

"Oh, sweetie, I'm alright. I have my mother and my sister, up in Long Beach. And I have goals. My goals keep me company."

"Even when you're alone at night?"

"Well, maybe not then. But I have friends I can call. And I have a boyfriend."

"But he's last on your list."

She reached through the gap, and I took her hand. "So what's your inner conflict?" she said. "That's what you need to figure out."

Chapter 32
FRANK

The next morning I was at the lineup. I knew, vaguely, where the jail was, but it took multiple tries driving around that big county complex down there to find my actual destination. I had slept poorly and woke up groggy. The so-called lineup was just video of several men, four or five, all Mexican-ish, different shades, different shapes of faces. To me they looked like two landscapers, a teacher, a bartender, and one sort of like Ivan Rodriguez, the ballplayer. Benton was there, but he seemed to have lost interest in me as a witness.

He said, "I actually don't like any of these guys. But we may try again in a few days. We're working on a lead."

I was out of there in fifteen minutes.

Nothing had been said or implied but that I was a victim, a witness. Not a whiff of suspicion or distrust was breathed toward me. I walked out elated, but only for a moment. Benton's statement made me wonder if there was a game going on—charades?—over my head or behind the scenes. Was he being truthful with me or trying to entrap me? What had I done—hide evidence and lie to the police? Not good, but also not murder. I couldn't seem to shake that sort of grogginess, or dizziness, I'd woken up with. For the rest of the day I felt like I was leaning or swaying, top-heavy. Not in a physical or noticeable way. Just kind of constantly catching myself.

Brenda and I had talked about whether we should take the boys to church, if they wanted to go. I brought it up, even though I never go to church. She, it turns out, is Catholic.

"I don't go as much, though, anymore," she said. "Nicole stopped going, and I've dropped off myself. But Cris said they were Catholic. Do you think it'll help them to pray for their father? And their mother?"

"Is that what happens?"

"Well, not as part of the, you know, service. But I cannot go to Mass and not think of my mother."

"I never went to church as a kid, and I never took Matt. But my family read the Bible. The old one, you know. The King James. And I read Bible stories to my son. The ones in children's books. I believe in spiritual education. The human being has a need for a spiritual life. It's as much a part of us as the sense of touch or smell. We talked about that stuff, Matt and I. Those were some of my favorite talks with him. And his mother was a sort of half-assed Buddhist, and he was exposed to that."

Conveniently enough, that's when Matt and the boys walked in. They had gone for ice cream and were still licking the cones. Matt has a way with kids, and they had formed an easy bond right from the start, from that first morning at my house.

"We got gelatos," said Cris.

"Very nice. Where'd you get those?"

"It's that coffee and bakery place up on Indian School, by Chicago Hamburgers."

"What's the difference between gelato and regular ice cream?" I asked.

"Oh," said Adam. "It's a lot creamier. Awesome flavor. I got toffee."

Brenda laughed. "Sounds very good! You didn't bring

me any?"

"I tol' you we shoulda!" said Cris. He offered his to Brenda, who waved it off.

"That's another thing," I said. "What is toffee? I've never figured this out. Is it taffy? Is it coffee? A combination?"

"Jeez, Dad," said Matt.

"Yeah, Dad." Adam shook his head. "It's just an awesome flavor."

After Matt left, Brenda corralled the boys in the kitchen. "So I've got a question: Tomorrow is Sunday. Do you boys want to go to church? ¿Á la misa?"

Cris shook his head. "Nope."

"Are you sure? We could go to my church. It's a... friendly place, I guess I would say. And we can get donuts on the way home."

"Let's just get the donuts," said Cris.

Adam nodded. "Church sucks."

I basically agreed with that sentiment, but I also saw Brenda's point. "We're just trying to get to know you guys. Looks like we're going to be together for a while. And we want to try to give you any help we—"

"Oh," Adam snarled. "So if we go see Jesus and pray for our dear father, everything will be fine."

"No, of course not." He had caught me by surprise. "But there's nothing wrong with praying."

"I just don't see the point." His flushed face belied the cynical words and cool attitude. "What's done is done, and there's nothing we can do about it now. He's gone, she's gone, and here we are, living with strangers. And pretty soon you'll be gone, too. And we'll move on. It's not a big deal."

I said, "It is a big deal."

"And we're not going anywhere." Brenda had an edge in her voice. "Aida wanted to take you back to Tracy. I told her I would give you up to your mother and no one else. So pray for your mother, but save one for me."

"Donuts," said Adam, seemingly oblivious to Brenda's

heartfelt request. Cris wagged his head and laughed. The warm family feeling of a few minutes ago was completely gone.

"Alright. We're just making this up as we go along. Just trying…" Brenda's voice trailed off.

And speaking of making it up as we go along… after dinner we watched a cartoon movie that Cris had asked to see. I thought I was done with cartoon movies when Matt grew up, but I watched it too.

After a while I noticed Adam wasn't in the room. He had gone into the kitchen, but the lights in there were off. I got up and looked in, then went back to the boys' bedroom. He was not in the house. Brenda noticed me crossing the room again, but she didn't say anything. Adam was not in the backyard, and not out front. I walked to the end of the short driveway and didn't see anything that looked like a surveillance car parked in the street, but I knew the front of the house was visible to the camera on the streetlight pole. I wondered if I would soon be calling the contact number to ask if they had seen Adam leave.

Where could he have gone? Why leave? Just blowing off steam, needing some privacy, probably. That would mean a walk around the block, or down to the 7-11 on the corner of Forty-Eighth and McDowell. Or the Jack in the Box. If so, he would be back before long. I waited by the car, wondering where that police protection was that I had heard about but not really seen.

After ten minutes I couldn't stand there anymore. I went into the house, grabbed my keys off the top of the fridge, and skipped out, as Adam had obviously done. I drove slowly down to Forty-Eighth, looking around, and parked at the 7-11 for a while, but he wasn't there. I thought about going in to ask the clerk if she'd seen him, but what would I say? I wasn't even sure what he was wearing. And the place was busy. She didn't have time for me. I drove back, circled Brenda's block, then the next block up, then the next block down, then two of the three, then all three and passed the 7-ll again. I went down Forty-Eighth to the freeway, and up and down McDowell. I came back and sat in the truck on the street in front of the house.

And my thoughts were circling just as pointlessly. Had he gone for a simple walk and been grabbed by waiting men? As scary as it was, that seemed the most likely answer. But then this was a thirteen-year-old boy. Why wouldn't he want to get away from us? I would've at that age—I still would now. But where to? Maybe he had friends—he'd been at the school for almost a month now. But how would he get to them? We were clear across town from Grand Avenue's district. Had he used Brenda's phone in the kitchen to text somebody to come pick him up? But then why not just tell us? He could take a bus over there, I suppose, though I couldn't say which bus you would take to get from here to Twenty-Third Avenue and Thomas.

Every road to a reasonable harmless answer closed off as the time stretched past one hour and toward a second. Brenda did not come out, by great force of will, I was sure—determined to stay calm and stay with Cris, who would surely react to any sign of panic or disturbance. Let the kid watch his movie like a normal kid at home on a normal Saturday night. Adam had been taken, or he had gone somewhere with a purpose—a purpose I could not guess. Did he know something I did not know? Or know someone? Maybe he had gone to Aida's neighborhood. Maybe he knew someone there. But again, that was miles away.

As ten o'clock approached, I realized that there was someone in a car that had been sitting at a house a couple of doors down, on the other side of the street. I didn't know this street, so didn't know if this was one of the neighbors or what. But there was a dark head visible through the window. I tried to recall if I had seen the car pull up or someone come out of the house there. I could not be certain. But regardless, they might have seen something. They might have seen Adam. Or maybe, very probably now that I thought about it, this was the cops watching the house. Of course they would be sneaky about.

Or maybe this was the gangsters, who had found us and now were moving in and had already grabbed Adam. I got out of my truck. I was too frustrated to be cautious. Besides, the night was quiet and calm, the car looked innocuous. A Nissan four-door—a Sentra, I guess.

Walking up to it, I realized the engine was running, and as I sort of came around the rear of it and was just about to say, "Hey," or "Excuse me," or something, the car suddenly revved loudly and squealed away down the street, fishtailing slightly, pulling around the corner without even slowing down.

The noise and sudden movement startled me and I froze. Again I felt that spike of terror, like a bolt out of nowhere. My unbidden reaction was to yell, "Shit!"

My heart pounded. What was going on? Who was who, what was I doing, or what was being done to me? I sat down right there on the curb. The street remained as it was, quiet and warm, but now it seemed threatening, not comforting. I sat there for quite a while.

And by the way, Adam did not come trotting up and say, "Hi, Pops, what's happening?"

I finally stood up. I would have to call someone, but first I needed to talk to Brenda. I walked to the house and into the living room, hoping Adam would somehow be there. By some miracle. Brenda still sat in the same spot, alone now. She pointed to the bedroom.

And there he was. He had skipped past me somehow, or maybe never left? How long had he been back? Probably since before I pulled up in front of the house, twenty or thirty minutes ago. Or had it only been ten? I was still trembling from shock and what seemed like a kind of grief.

He was lying on the bed playing with a toy plastic guitar he had found, only a foot long, painted bright pink, with nylon strings.

I stood there looking at him for a minute, mostly just relieved. He plucked at the rattly strings.

"Where have you been?"

"Nowhere, *chavalo*. Just hangin' with the homies, as they say."

"No, seriously."

"Seriously." Rattle. Scratch.

As calmly as I could I said, "I need to know."

"Well, y'know, I need to not tell you. You won't believe me anyway."

Clearly trying to rile me. "Try me."

He shook his head and plucked the guitar. He turned the tuning knob of one of the strings to wobble the pitch.

I fought off a strong desire to yank the thing from his hands. "I've been out looking for you for the last two hours."

"You shouldn't waste your time like that."

"Where were you? Do you realize we don't know who—" I was torn between the need to talk some sense into him versus the need to continue the narrative of normal life we'd been trying to create, that he and Cris were safe now. Especially since Cris was lying there on the other bed watching me. "—who could be out there?"

"Out there!" He threw the little guitar against the wall. "I'm more worried about who is in here! But of course, it's your room, not mine. Your school, not mine. You have a family, I have guys who want to kill me. They are probably closer to me than anyone I will ever meet again. Y'know, killing someone face-to-face, well that's a pretty personal thing. You really get to know someone when they're—" He mimed shooting a pistol.

"We're all afraid. We were all on the boat. We were all in the gym—"

"But I'm the one," he shouted.

Cris, who had been pretending to read a book, stared wide-eyed at his brother.

Adam rolled over to face the wall. Quietly: "I'm the one."

Not knowing what to say and torn by uncertainty myself, I left the room. He was being irrational, but it was brought on by fear, stress, trauma. And I knew there wasn't a fucking thing I could do about it. At least not tonight.

Another question was: How was I in the middle of this? How was this my problem? I had been up and down with this new family, trying to figure out if this would be a long-term thing, or if it should somehow be put out of its misery. Was I seriously thinking of adopting this woman and these kids? Or was I more like the goofy unexplained housemate in a sitcom? Was I the man of the house or irrelevant?

Brenda looked up at me. She had heard everything, of course. She wanted to talk.

"Frank—"

Sorry, but I didn't feel like it. I whispered "We gotta get that kid some help," and continued toward "my" bedroom. I turned back. "Soon."

Brenda let me go. It had been enough for one day.

Chapter 33
TEDDIE

On Sunday morning, Antonio met me at the Starbucks on Scottsdale Road. He had driven over separately and stayed in a hotel in another part of town.

"So the shop is in central Phoenix. Our man is going to meet us and take us there. The buyer will be there. We open the truck, he does a remote payment from an app. We get a verification from our account. We give him the keys to the truck, and we leave."

We sipped our coffees. With Antonio leading, I felt ready to do what we had to do, despite the risk. Still, I needed the strength and the warmth of coffee before starting.

"Do you want something to eat?" Antonio asked. "We've got plenty of time."

"Nah. There's nothing good here. I'm not hungry anyway."

People came and went. The sun outside was already bright.

"This is new for me, too," he said. "Maybe it's the last time we do it. I hope it's the last time."

"Yeah," I said. "No shit."

He tapped my sleeve with a finger. "Don't worry. What's the

worst that could happen? It's just business."

I had to smile at this comment, and the old-school attitude. He really was older than me, and not just in years. I said, "Who's our man here?"

"His name is Carlos. He's one of Abella's guys."

"Wasn't this Abella's load?"

"It was his to deliver. But it was financed, like all purchases, by our bank. It is ours—that is, it belongs to your father, like everything else. Everyone gets their cut, but the leaders say what happens. So it never belonged to Abella, or any other individual. But he would grab it if he could."

"But this Carlos, he was attached to Abella? What got into him? How can we trust him?"

"He's the one who told me about the San Francisco job. And it was not their first try. They also hired a couple of contract men to do the same thing here in Phoenix. Carlos was the contact for that job, but the two guys were arrested. Guess they didn't know that here, someone tries to kidnap you, you call 911, and the cops come."

"But you're sure we can trust him?"

"I'm never sure." He shook his head. "Your father trusts him."

"And he's not being followed? He's not setting us up?"

"I'm very sure of that. No one else knows I'm even in the country."

"Well," I said. "Anyway, I'm glad we're getting out of… you know."

"Well…," said Antonio.

I looked at him. "What do you mean?"

"We are, we are."

"Are you saying we're not?"

"No, no." He smiled. "We're getting out of… that market."

Clearly there was something he was not telling me. "Fuck your mother."

His eyes shifted sideways, he leaned closer. "We are. We're out of… the dust. We're going to be importing pharmaceuticals.

Y'know, for the American market."

At that moment a very complex set of gears, levers, and bolts all operated, and a door opened. "The plastics! The plastics to China! And we're bringing back, what? H?"

He smiled, uncharacteristically bashful. "No, no, nothing like that. Prescription drugs. Y'know, pain pills. Legal stuff, with a prescription."

"But who gives the prescriptions?"

"Doctors, I guess." He smiled.

The door opened, and on the other side, in this new place, was a lawn, like the gardens of Versailles. Green grass and small white bunnies. Candy pops grew on trees. My father had been one step ahead of the law, two steps ahead of the bureaucrats, and a half a kilometer ahead of me. "Opioids!" I whispered. "Oh, God, that's beautiful! I should have known. A crooked furrow never plows straight."

Chapter 34
FRANK

Sunday morning I woke up too early. I was in the comfortable bed in the girl's room, had no real reason to get up, nothing to do, So I used my foolproof method to beat insomnia. When lying down to sleep, or if I wake up in the middle of the night or too early and find I'm not sleepy, I think of all the things I have to do the next day. Not in a general way, but as in at 7:30… at nine… by lunchtime. It doesn't matter if the tasks are large or trivial, the point is to establish a kind of order, think of details. This never fails to relax—or exhaust—me, and I fall right to sleep. Never fails, but now it was failing.

So I got up about seven, made coffee, ate half a banana, and before long Adam came out of his room, already completely dressed, with shoes. I wondered if he had slept with his clothes on again.

He said, "Are you going to church?"

"I don't think so."

"Well, we're going. Mrs. C and us."

So we went. I was just along for the ride, and Cris let us know by action and expression how bored he was, but Adam followed along, with no coaching from Brenda. His whole demeanor was different this morning. Serious, even somber. It gave me hope. I took it as regret over his action and words of last night. In that sense it was almost an unspoken apology to Brenda, and especially to me. I would have preferred a spoken apology. But at this point I would take small victories.

We returned home and Brenda made scrambled eggs and fried potatoes. She's a proficient cook, but we were in this pattern of always seeming to be short of food or short of time for meals. Probably an indicator of two single people trying to adjust to having a family again. There was just enough for the four of us, mainly because Adam didn't eat much at all.

By the time we finished it was past eleven. I asked the boys to help me cut the grass and clean up the back yard. It's a small yard, so it wouldn't take long. When we finished I thought I might go home for the day, take a break from "family life," watch golf on TV, take a nap on my own couch.

Adam took a barrel of clippings out to the dumpster in the alley. I was still raking and needed the barrel to finish the job. I went out to the alley to hurry him up. There the barrel sat, still full. Looking down the alley, I saw Adam for a few seconds before he turned the corner on Forty-Eighth Street.

I looked around. Cris had gone in the house, there was no one else about. I started walking. It was a reaction, not even a thought. There he went, there I went, as I would do to retrieve a baby that might wander out into traffic. By the time I reached the end of the alley he was cutting across the street toward McDowell. He didn't seem in a hurry, and I was resolved to follow him, if at a distance. The afternoon was warm, the sky blue. Unlike last night, I did not feel anxious—as long as I could keep Adam in sight.

When I reached McDowell he was headed up the long, gradual slope to Papago Park. The globular buttes at the top of the rise waited patiently for us, the wind caves on the faces black with shadows. Adam turned and looked back toward me. At first I thought it was a random glance, but then he stopped and turned toward me for a second before plodding on. His pace did not increase, and I continued as before. I had left without water, which would get to be a problem sooner or later, but the work shoes I had on were very good for walking, even walking a long ways. My knee let me know it was there, but seemed content with the strain so far. I even noticed that the slight vertigo I'd been experiencing was gone.

During a lull in traffic, Adam crossed the street in midblock and kept walking. I followed, dodging a couple of cars. That short trot and the continuing slope were now pinching my knee. When he came to the end of the fence which bounds the National Guard station, Adam cut across the open desert toward the south butte and seemed to pick up the pace. I let him go. The loose granite and rolling hillocks of the desert park were tougher walking, and across the open ground he would not escape my sight. As I followed, a cottontail bunny would occasionally move across the edge of my vision, cautious, not frightened. These were city bunnies.

Finally he reached the base of the rock, a solid pile of pinkish-gray stone that rose in a series of rounded boulders maybe a hundred feet in the air. He stopped there, as if waiting for me.

When I finally got there, I said. "Is this where you went last night?"

He pointed up to the top of the rock.

"In the dark?"

"It wasn't dark. There was plenty of light to get all the way to the top. I've made my peace." He was quite calm, his voice firm, almost dull.

"What? Your peace?"

He looked at me—a handsome kid, very calm. From McDowell Road, only a couple hundred yards away, I could hear the whoosh of cars hurrying by on their errands. In the opposite direction, down by the river, planes were taking off and landing at the airport. But it still seemed quiet there on that hill. "They have no idea, do they?"

'Who?"

"Them. Everyone." He swept his arm across the city. "What it's really all about. I'm good now with what I'm going to do." He reached under his shirt and pulled my pistol from the waistband of his pants. He handed it to me. "I don't need this."

"No, you certainly don't." I took the gun.

"I'm going up there." He pointed to the top of the rock again. "But I'll be right down. I've found a good spot where they won't find me for a while. It'll be better than a gun."

"Adam. You're not making sense. Let's talk."

"No reason to talk." He spoke in a low, dull monotone. "You should just go home." A gust of breeze rippled his shirt. "I've made my peace. I'll see my father's murderers in hell. They come in dreams to kill me, so I must get to them the same way."

That was either deeply profound or insane. At this point it hardly mattered. I put my hand on his shoulder. He winced and threw it off with a violence that belied his calm words.

"It's not your fault, Adam."

"Maybe not, but it's got to stop. I saw it all and didn't do anything. I knew it was coming. I could have told him not to go, not to fight those people, that they would kill him, that they would kill all of us. I know them. I know what they do to people to get even. But I did not stop him. And she did not stop him. They said they were doing it for us, but I don't believe it. They were caught up in it. They wanted—" He lifted his hands in a hopeless shrug. "They had to win. What'd they win?"

I felt a rising panic. What do you say when you have no idea what to say and the wrong words might be fatal? "Adam, I know what you're feeling."

"Then you know there's no point in arguing."

"No, of course not. But you have to realize, no one can go through trouble alone. You're not the first one to deal with tragedy and fear in your life. It's not easy to survive. It's fuckin' hard work, the hardest thing you'll ever do. But you have to keep trying."

"I've heard all this before you know. I've seen the movies,

the TV shows. We'll have a serious talk, then we'll hug and cry and all better."

"Don't make it a joke. It's hard. It's very hard, and nothing will make it alright. But just live through today. Go to sleep tonight. Maybe it will be better tomorrow. But even if it's not, you can get through one more day and make it to bed one more time, can't you? That's not so much, is it?"

"You don't know, here in America. I was born in purgatory." A shy smile curled the corner of his mouth. "Heaven doesn't want me, and it never will."

I was speaking from desperation, not logic. "God hates a coward."

"I'm not going to God. I'm going to hell to meet my killers. And to be with my father."

There was a wisp of an opening in those words. "You told me he was a good man. I remember now. You said he was a brave and strong man."

"Shut up! He was, but not smart enough. I should have been there. I should have died. Give me the gun."

I popped the clip out of the gun and handed it to him, grip first. He wasn't expecting that. He took the gun and looked out across the hillside. From where we stood he could see a long way, to downtown Phoenix and clear across the valley to the blue mountains on the other side of the city. It almost seemed like he was taking one last look. If someone died here now, the mountains wouldn't care. The cars and planes would not slow down, the buildings spread out around us would not blink. The bunnies might be momentarily startled, but they'd quickly recover and get on with their day.

He smiled. "Did you remember to check the chamber? There could be a bullet in there. Just one. That's all I need."

"That's right. But you don't want to take that chance. You know, I loved my dad, and he died a terrible death, but I never would have killed myself for him."

His eyes shifted. At least I had got his attention.

"What happened?" he said.

"He drank himself to death."

Adam let out a harsh, surprised laugh.

"Yeah, it sounds like a joke. But it wasn't when he finally got to dying, it took him a week, and I watched it. His organs just quit working, one by one, until only his heart was going, beating and struggling to keep him alive when everything else was already dead. It was the saddest thing I have ever seen. Until today."

I touched his arm. He did not throw it off.

"Let me tell you the lesson I learned." I paused until he met my eyes. "It matters how you go out. It matters what happens at the end. My dad did many fine things. He had a good and productive and fairly happy life. But he was worn out and used up at the end, and he died with a terrible loneliness in his heart. Your father, the way he died was part of his life. It's something for you to build on. He died doing something he believed in. Yes, you mourn him, but you honor him by moving on, by taking the next hill. Wherever he is, heaven, hell, or standing right here, if you do this, you will crush his spirit and his memory more than his own death ever could."

Adam raised the gun to his head with his left hand. Tears streaked his face.

"But go ahead," I said. "You have to do what's right for you."

He stared at me.

I stared straight back. "You want to do those punks' job for them? You want to finish what they couldn't do? Go ahead."

He closed his eyes, swayed a little in the breeze. I fought the urge to grab him. Wherever he was going now, he was going by his own choice. Suddenly he pulled back his arm and threw the gun far down the slope, where it clattered and skittered and came to rest under a bush. I held up the clip, turned, and threw it in the same direction.

The clip that I knew, because I'd glanced at it when removing it from the gun, and then confirmed with my fingertips while talking, was full. It could not hold another bullet, so no bullet could have been released into the chamber.

I thought about telling him that. Maybe some other day. I hugged him as hard as I could, and he hugged me. I thought, you don't choose a family, family chooses you. That's the kind of thing you would hear at the end of a movie or a TV show when they're hugging and crying and all better.

Chapter 35
TEDDIE

Antonio's phone chirped. We went outside.

"We'll take my rental," he said, and started to walk around the back of the car.

"Okay," I said. "Let me drive."

"You don't have to."

I walked over to him and held out my hand for the key. He dropped it in my hand.

"And you have the remote?"

"Yeah—"

"I want you to give it to me," I said. "I want you to walk in there clean, make sure everything looks okay. If it does not, you walk out. I'll be waiting around the corner. If everything looks okay, text me okay. I'll come in with the remote. If everything is not okay, I'll pick you up and we leave."

"You don't have to come in."

"No I want to. I want to be there. If anything goes wrong I want you to be able to walk out free."

"I understand," he said.

Which is funny. Because I didn't understand why I was doing

that. Not completely. A sense of loyalty or protectiveness toward the man who had become, in many ways, a father or brother figure to me. And leftover guilt. I had not been careful enough when Angel got killed. I couldn't just follow along anymore and do what I was told.

A car drove through the parking lot—an Infiniti, driven by a teenager, it looked like.

"That's him," said Antonio.

We drove south, then west, through a desert area where the road rose between two large rocks, and then down again into the broad, flat city of Phoenix. When we got to Thirty-Second Street the Infiniti turned right, went up a couple of blocks, and turned left. I followed into a street of small brick houses, painted different colors: white, yellow, gray. After another left turn, the car stopped next to a long, high hedge of oleanders. Antonio's phone buzzed.

"Yeah." he said to the phone, listened, then tapped off and put it in his pocket. He pointed down the street. "It's right down there, a block and a half on the left. It's a wheel-alignment shop. The last garage door is where we'll be. The closest one to where we are now. Pull up next to it so we don't have to back up to leave. I'll call you when we're ready."

Antonio got out, walked ahead to the other car, leaning away from oleanders that pushed out into the street, and got in on the passenger side. He spoke to the kid for a minute. Neither of them glanced at me. Then they pulled out, drove down the street, and turned left, out of sight. I could just see the corner of the shop. Cars drove past on the busy street just beyond it. The house to my right was blocked from view, but the one on the left, though small in size, had a rail fence and a rusty iron plow in the granite yard, as if it were a tiny cattle ranch.

I did not see any cars or people that attracted notice. Just routine comings and goings. I marked every thirty seconds that passed. After seven and one half minutes, a text came.

OK.

I started the car and drove a block. Now I could see an

asphalt lot behind the shop that opened into the parking lot of a grocery store. That would be the way out. Through that lot and back onto the main road. The Infiniti was parked at the shop, and there were other cars parked in the big lot, but I couldn't see anyone around the shop or inside. I waited for an approaching car to pass, but it turned into the same lot I was going to, and another one drove up from the grocery store lot, quickly. Both cars parked behind the shop. Men with guns were jumping out of the cars and running toward the shop. I made my turn, but kept going on to the supermarket parking lot. I did not look over there. But now I realized there was a car behind me with two men inside, and they were watching me. I drove calmly through the lot and out onto the main road. They followed me.

I realized it had been a mistake to drive Antonio's car, which might have had a tail all morning. Well, it was too late to change that now. I sped ahead as much as possible on the busy street, going back the way I came. On the long rise up between the big rocks, I glanced back down the slope, and did not see the pursuers. When I looked ahead again, I had to swerve to avoid a dark man jaywalking who had come out of nowhere. I drove to the back of the hotel, and hurried through the grounds, trying to seem casual. As I approached my room, I saw the cop car, the unmarked one that had been following me, pulling up at the end of the breezeway.

The question is not was I ignorant or innocent? I was certainly both. I am a little less of each now, already.

When DeTirro disappeared—I don't call him by his first name anymore—after the hijacking, when we thought he was being held by the state police, he actually had been secretly handed over to the DEA, and everything that followed came from that visit. He was willing to give up Abella who, with Angel now gone, was his chief rival for supremacy in the gang.

He was setting up both of us. He didn't care if Abella was killed. Maybe he didn't care if I was killed. Maybe he did.

Abella took the hit for smuggling the drugs in the truck. He was the one the DEA really wanted. And DeTirro walked out of the lockup that same day. They later said he had been mistakenly released, suspected only of being a low-level courier. Once he was out he went back to Mexico, as they surely expected him to do. They had given him a mission there.

The DEA had Abella, so they were happy. But the FBI wanted somebody for the Oakland kidnapping, and Abella gave them my father. DeTirro took the offer to him: he could retire and leave Mexico, or face a probable civil war in the gang, and the threat of arrest and deportation to the U.S. He didn't agonize over it, I gather. He disappeared, and it was over a year before I found out he was living on the Costa del Sol, Spain. The Mangos drug gang ceased to exist. DeTirro took over the remnants of the organization's activities—does anyone care about prostitution, extortion, and larceny? No.

And certainly not about plastics recycling. Apparently law enforcement did not know what the plastic was being traded for. Some future DEA bureau chief, or Mexican federal undersecretary will no doubt make their reputation by burrowing into this operation and busting DeTirro, or whoever is then in charge.

It won't affect my father, and it won't affect me. I pleaded to a money-laundering charge and was sent to Illinois. I'll be out when my three years are up. I'm studying English, discrete mathematics, and programming. It is going to be a challenge, but my brother and sister, who I still have contact with, have been very encouraging, and I see a future in engineering or business. Getting arrested was actually my big break. I'm not really sure what my inner conflict, as she called it, really was. But I think I solved it.

I have heard, through a third party, that DeTirro says that he set up me being arrested to protect me. From being killed, from going to prison in Mexico. While I have for a long time scoffed at this very convenient interpretation by him, I am perhaps coming around to at least grudging respect for it. I am going somewhere else in my life, and maybe that's what he meant by protecting me.

Chapter 36
MALLORY

I was up and dressed by eight thirty and ordered room-service breakfast. Teddie had said we would have to leave by one, so I scheduled a mudpack and massage at ten thirty. I had my own room, so it really did feel like a vacation. While I ate, I watched *The Legend of Zorro*. I'd never seen the end of this movie. I still haven't.

Right about the time when Zorro kisses Catherine Zeta-Jones, there was a knock on the door. Teddie. This time I let him in.

"Hey," I said, keeping it light. "You up and about already? You do hit the road running, I'll say that."

He didn't reply, just shut the door and turned toward me with a sadness on his face like he'd just lost his best friend.

I felt a stab of panic. "What?"

He sighed, and even his breath was shaky. "There's been a change of plans."

I sat down in the chair. Something bad was coming. "You're scaring me."

"No." he walked over to the table where the breakfast tray still sat. He was carrying the gym bag, and he set it on the chair in front of me. "I want you to have this."

"Have what?" I didn't want to look inside.

"This." He spread open the top of the bag, took out the smaller nylon bag, and unzipped it. Inside was a lot of money, neatly stacked. He riffled the bills with his thumb.

"I want you to have it," he said. "It's not going to do me any good. Do you still have the watch? You haven't been wearing it."

I stood up, scared and angry. "Okay, what the fuck's going on?"

He dropped the money back in the gym bag. "I am going to walk out of here and the police are going to arrest me. They don't know anything about you. I want you to have this because otherwise they get it. Just take it and go. When they check the hotel records, they will see that I paid for this room, and they are going to come in here. But there's nothing that has your name on it, and they won't be here for a while, so you have time to get out. There's a shopping center across the street. You can go over there and call a cab and catch a plane home—or whatever you want to do."

"What are you trying to do to me? This is dirty money, and the cops are going to come in here and grab you, me, and the money."

"No. You can believe me or not, but here it is." He picked up the gym bag from the chair and dropped it on the table, on top of the breakfast tray, rattling the dishes and cutlery. "Now, I gotta go. I'm doing you a favor. Because you are a good person. I don't know. I like you"

He reached out and held up his hand in a stop sign. I raised mine and we interlocked fingers. He smiled a brave and emotional smile. He let go, turned, and walked out the door.

Now I remembered how I was scared of him at first. I cursed myself for letting my guard down, for being seduced. And now trouble had found me. I shuddered. Once. I did not have time for more. Since I was already dressed, I stood up and grabbed my small suitcase. That could not be left behind. I packed everything I had brought and, taking the suitcase and Teddy's gym bag, I walked out the door toward what I thought was the back way out of the hotel. I walked out there, past the dumpster near the golf course, and since there was no one around, I tossed my suitcase in the dumpster. Then I continued around toward the front of the hotel, carrying the gym bag. Just before I turned a corner, I dropped the gym bag between the wall and a bush. Then I continued around the corner.

There I saw a sight that scared me even more. Teddie sat in the back of a police car that was parked between three or four other police cars, and a bunch of people were standing around who were not guests of the resort. I picked out one of the cops standing at the edge looking bored. I walked up to him.

"Sir, there's a bag over there, behind that bush. It looks suspicious."

"Really?" He gave me a superior smile.

"Really. Right over there, that bush with the pink flowers."

"Okay, We'll, uh, check it out."

Because he was so superior, because I looked to him like an affirmative action girl on her way to the civic center, he let me walk away. Before too long, I suppose, he went over there and found a gym bag full of money. What he would not know is that the bag was several thousand dollars light. Three thousand, seven hundred, I later counted. And it turned out that the watch was a real Movado. A very nice Movado.

As I walked away, I looked at Teddie in the police car. He was just sitting there. He looked at me, he saw me, he did not react, and he did not look sad. I wonder if he remembered that it's important to have an H.E.A.

Chapter 37
BRENDA

Out of the blue, the FBI guy, Benton, called.

"We found the mother."

When Frank and Adam got back from their walk I told all of them. The boys were excited, and a little while later she called. Both of the boys sang praise of me and Frank—very sweet—but they begged her to come right away. She told them she would arrive the next day, Monday. Emotions were high all around. We played cards that night. We had just discovered that both of them were little card sharks. It was fun, it was nice, and I could already feel the nostalgia of something ending.

Benton would not tell us when she would arrive. He did not want us at the airport, so he would bring her over. Not knowing when that would be, I stayed home from school with the boys. But at four thirty I had to go to the memorial for Kurt, so Matt came over to stay with the boys. Frank came home, changed clothes, and drove us.

The timing of the memorial was for two reasons. First, school let out at three thirty; and second, it was understood, according to Frank, that the formal service would be brief—Kurt had been cremated—and most of the memorializing would be at the patio bar next door to the funeral home. I never thought of it before, but that is probably a great location for a tavern, especially one like this, with a patio and beach umbrellas. The message is: Life Goes On.

Kurt's family, his parents and brother and sister, were grieving. Most of us fellow employees talked to them briefly and formally, but then left them alone in their family circle.

Frank and I sat down near the other teachers in my grade level. They were already in a subdued conversation that sounded very worky. I concentrated on Frank.

It had been a long process, coming to him. Opening up. He showed me much that impressed me, and the best part was, none of it was designed to impress. And I, of course, was completely exposed to him. In all my glory. It has not been easy. Like I told him once, there just wasn't room in my head for any more. But during the confusion, I now saw, we had been circling closer and closer.

I clasped his hand and held it on my knee. His hand bigger than mine, and hard, like wood. We were both thinking as much about Adam and Cris as about Kurt. But it was hard, with his grieving family a few feet away.

"I can't imagine," I said to Frank. "He was just ripped away from them." I was secretly holding on to the idea that we, Frank and I, had avenged his death that same night. That was a small comfort we could not give them. He gave my hand a squeeze. He was thinking the same thing.

We had a drink. The atmosphere in the place seemed to get a little lighter.

"God," I said, "this is so good for the boys, their mom coming. I hope they're going to be alright."

"I hope she can handle it," said Frank.

"Handle what?"

"Everything." After a while he said, "We're about to get out of a lot of responsibility."

Pregnant pause, as they say.

"And," he continued. "We're about to have a lot more time and a lot less stress."

"Yes, it's going to be different." Any intimacy between us had been soaked in drama, buried in crisis. On this rocket-sled ride of what, ten days, eleven days, there had scarcely been time to breathe. We still had worries now, we still had things to think about and precautions to take. But we could handle them, and now it was time to get back to a quiet, normal life.

"What would it be like," I said, "to sit down, have a nice dinner, a long chat, a bottle of wine? Is there anything normal we could possibly talk about?"

"I think so." He smiled. A nice smile, not designed just to impress me.

I stared into his eyes and wondered, *Am I real to you? As a person, as a middle-aged teacher with a grown child? As a woman who could love or even be in love?*

"Let's schedule it." He gave my hand a squeeze. "The bottle of wine, the talk, etcetera."

As I looked at Frank, I saw behind him, by the entrance, a policeman. And another one, and another one, and Benton. The policemen, in their navy blue uniforms, stood by the door, looking at Frank and me. I assumed they would go and pay their respects to the family, but they just stood there as Benton crossed and bent over, speaking quietly with the parents for a moment. He nodded and stood up. The policemen began moving toward us.

Chapter 38
FRANK

As the policemen moved toward us, it punched me in the gut. *They know. They know.*

"I wish there was another way," said Brenda.

A little breeze came up, and for a few minutes, the surrounding silence was broken as waves lapped at the unseen shore below us in the dark. We sat, the two of us, in my truck overlooking the blackness of the water, my boat and trailer attached to the truck, waiting for the first light of dawn. Cowboy and Letterman already lay in the boat like a couple of stiff tuna.

"You want the heater on?"

"No, I'm alright." She stirred in her seat and pulled the hoodie tighter around her. I'd given it to her to wear so she'd look at least a little bit like someone going fishing.

By the time we had arrived at my house from school, I had reworked the plan. The bodies had to disappear completely. I had to drive to the storage yard in south Scottsdale to pick up my boat. Then we'd headed north.

"We'll go over by the dam," I said. "It's deepest there."

"As long as no one can see us."

"That's why I came here. Saguaro's too busy. You couldn't be sure who might see you." Bartlett Lake, farther from Phoenix than Saguaro Lake and less popular, had dirt ramps and no lights.

"You're so smart," she said. "You thought of everything, just like you do this every day. Were you a cop before, or some kind of spy?"

"No," I shrugged. "Nothing like that. Just a lifetime of doing a job. Making do with what you have."

That was why we needed the Yucca Flats story. And we needed to be sure no one followed us, which was impossible in town, but once we got on the dark, single-lane to Bartlett, it was easy to tell we were traveling alone.

"You don't have to go on the boat, I can—"

"I'm going." That was her teacher voice. Firm.

A single point of light from a night fisherman shone out on the lake. The glow of Phoenix grayed the southern horizon, but the sky above us was still black and covered with stars that outlined the mountains to the east.

We had to wait because my boat had no lights. It had them, they just weren't working at that time. While we waited we slept, a little. I woke over and over again, until finally I could spot the first glimmer of dawn I didn't need a lot of daylight, just enough to make out the shoreline and any obstructions in the water. Going out there, I wanted as much darkness as we could get.

She snugged the point of her chin down into the collar of the sweatshirt. "Natalie called and left a message on my cell phone."

The social worker. "I had forgotten—"

"At six thirty. I got it when I went back to my room."

"Jesus. Six thirty? That's right when—"

Brenda nodded. "I texted her that the kids had gone home

with a family member. I was thinking of you, as an uncle."

I almost laughed. But I had something else on my mind. Weighing heavily. "I have to say, I'm not sure this is the right thing to do. Or the smart thing."

"We decided. We can't change now. We have to make the bodies disappear and hope no one knows they ever got to the school."

"They might already know."

Her eyes teared up. In the light from the dashboard radio her face appeared hard and pale. "They might."

"Well, there is another way."

She reached over and laid her hand on my shoulder. "No."

I said it anyway. "I'm the one who killed them. I'll take the rap and take my chances. I was going to retire in a few years anyway. I'll go away."

She squeezed my shoulder. "You didn't kill anybody. It was self-defense."

"It's wrong to hide it," I told her. "And it makes it look worse. After all, once the other one died, we're off the hook for not taking him to the hospital. The cover-up has no chance. Their bosses will figure out what happened. And when they do, we're going to need the police on our side. We've got to change up. I'll take the rap. Put it all on me. You go up there to California, whatever, find a safe place for the kids. And you stay there, too."

Above the mountains the sky had definitely begun to color.

"No. I'm not leaving. I have a job." There was the teacher voice again.

"But can we just leave the boys there with your brother?" She had called him before we left the house.

"Well, I think so," she said. "He volunteered. He's that kind of guy. I explained we had to turn around and come right back."

"We're making life-changing decisions here. They can get a sub for you for the last month."

"It's two months. I'll take my chances. The boys will be alright, Willy and Gemma will take good care of them. And it's a lot safer than here."

I said, "But if the police know the truth, the police can protect us. Look, if we hide it, then you're liable, too. If I own it, then it's just me to face whatever, and I think I'll be alright."

Her chin sank deeper into her collar. "But once the truth begins to be told, it all has to be told."

The first morning birds called in the brush at the edge of the parking area. "So I'll tell the truth," I said. "I don't care."

"But I do. You didn't kill both those guys."

"Exactly. It was self-defense."

"No, the second one, the heavy one, was deliberate." She took a breath and straightened up. "Premeditated. I smothered him with a trash bag. Wrapped it around his head and stuffed it in his mouth. That's why I left the boys in the classroom. There was no way we could let him live. He was too dangerous."

She looked at me for my reaction. It took me a minute to hear and understand. Then I felt an inexplicable joy. I was not alone with this... thing. Guilt, accomplishment, heroic deed, incredible stupidity—whatever it was, I shared it fully with another person. I reached across and wrapped her in my arms.

"They came here to kill children," she said, in a small, muffled voice. "They came from a world where that's okay. They were going to kill those two boys. They were going to take pictures, and spread them around. As a warning."

"A warning to who?" I asked.

"To us, to kids, to Mexicans, to Americans." She straightened up. "I wish we could send a message back to their masters, that they can't bring this violence to our school, our town. I know we can't do that..."

"They were evil and I killed them. That's enough."

"We."

I nodded. "We."

We got the boat out in the first bare light. They were in big black plastic bags, one bag pulled on from the top, the other from the feet. There was a volleyball net tightly wrapped around the bags, and a twenty-five-pound stanchion weight tied to each net. The first one I eased slowly over the side, and he went vertically down into the water. Then I lowered the weight down to the surface and released it. The body was already under water, and it slipped out of sight immediately. The second one I did the same, except this one—I didn't know which was which—floated. Why one would sink and the other float I did not know. But a wave of revulsion swept over me looking at the floating bag of human there on the motionless surface of the lake. When I released the weight he went down with a glumph, and I shivered at the sound, or the sight, or the horrible act I had just completed. I didn't exactly say a prayer for them, but I did pause a moment, caught up with some deep, unidentified emotion. I had asked Brenda to sit on the opposite side, to balance the weight somewhat, and to watch the shore. Not really necessary, but it kept her eyes off the disposal process. Someone had to do the dirty work, and that was me, but there was no need for her to see it.

When we were back on the ramp I slipped while cranking the boat up onto the trailer, and scraped my jaw on the winch. It gave me a bruise and a scratch that was painful for a day, but it's almost completely healed now.

As the policemen walked up and surrounded me, I reaffirmed to myself the goal: Protect her. And the story: Both of those guys died in the rollaway; we were trying to throw their bosses off, etc. Tell as much of the truth as you have to, and even give them a little extra. But they both died accidentally.

And then they will say—Benton will be the one— "No. He was suffocated. You can easily tell. And we found the trash bags with the blood, the rags."

The trash bags in the cans I forgot to empty, to hide

somewhere. That were still, I now remembered for the first time, in the school dumpster until the following Monday.

If they do it as a state trial, maybe I can plead self-defense, but more likely some kind of accidental manslaughter, and I can get off with a couple of years or even probation. After all, I was a hero and a victim, they were drug-gang killers.

No. Three years at least. Not that I will last that long. Mexican cartels have assassins and lackeys and bosses in every prison, everywhere. And there will be no one there to protect me. I will be going in as a marked man. Marked by the Mexican mafia or some such thing—members or cousins of the Mongos or whatever they call them. So they will probably come after me, and the cops or the guards may not do much to help me because I lied, tried to hide evidence, and publicly questioned whether they could protect the boys and us. In other words, I had questioned their integrity. They won't be sympathetic.

How long will it take? Hours? Weeks? But the moment will come when one, or two, or twelve of them corner me, when I will see in their eyes that they have no problem killing me, and they *want* me to see that it's no problem.

The officers now stood in a half-circle behind us. Everyone in the place was staring at Brenda and me in silence. We stood up. Benton was standing at Brenda's other shoulder. A Phoenix policeman with captain's bars on his collar was now on my left. Very close. Brenda and I were holding hands. Her half-smile told me she wondered what the hell was going on.

I was not wondering.

In a clear, slightly raised voice, Benton announced, "I apologize for interrupting this solemn occasion. But I have information that I think everyone needs to know."

Absolute silence and stillness.

"We have made an arrest in Kurt's killing."

At *arrest*, a whoop let out, followed by an intense buzz of explanations, questions, cackles, and sobs, such that what Benton said after that was largely unheard. I felt a hand clamp on my arm. One of the policemen behind me.

I was very confused. In Kurt's killing? How could they have made an arrest in Kurt's killing? I looked at the police officer next to me, whom I had never seen before. He gave me a dead-eyed, no-bullshit stare. Like he has no problem arresting me for a crime I did not commit, and he *wants* me to see that he has no problem with that. And I understood that they were going to pin this on me. Despite my years of disciplined righteousness, of steely self-assertion, of standing up to every man who needed standing up to, for just that moment I was a scared black boy about to face harsh white justice. Benton was going to tell all of Kurt's family and friends that I killed him. And he's the FBI, so they'll believe him, of course. They might rip me to pieces right here.

This could not be happening. I couldn't feel the ground under my feet. I struggled to speak, to raise my hand, but I was immobilized. Brenda looked at me, wanting to join in the happiness, but also confused.

Benton waited until the noise died down. "His name is Nacio Figueroa. He has been detained in California and will be brought back here for trial. He also had a hand in the kidnapping and terrorizing of these two fine people, and two innocent children there in California. And this man—" he beamed at me "—had a hand in his capture."

The place erupted again. Now my hand was being shaken and people were patting my shoulder and my back, and policemen's faces and badges and blue shirts swam in and out of my vision, as chortles and chuckles of approval washed over me. Nothing was making sense. How had I captured anyone? And who was Nacio Fig—

"No!" I hissed at Benton.

"We'll talk," he said. "Wait 'til you hear the whole story!"

Brenda gave me a squeeze and a kiss. "Isn't that good news?"

The traffic stop. It had to be the traffic stop. At which I was nothing but a clueless passenger. But that was also the informant, who was outside that night, who followed us home. He had killed Kurt?

Benton left after a few minutes, and the cops, who I now noticed were all high-ranking types, not the detectives and patrolmen we'd been dealing with, were right on his heels. We followed them out. The policemen were moving off toward their cars, but Benton saw us and turned back. "I'm on the way to pick up the mother at the airport. We'll come over to Brenda's, I would say, about seven."

"We'll go home and get them ready," said Brenda. "Where are they going?"

He smiled. "I don't know. Can she stay with you?"

I almost laughed, but Brenda said, "Sure. We'll make it work." She smiled at me. "Right?"

"Yeah, I suppose we will."

"Okay." Benton seemed to gather his thoughts. "We thought we had him on a string, but he double-crossed us. Nacio. You were right. In fact he was probably in charge of the two guys who came into the school. He only called his handler after everything went wrong. So he's just as much the killer."

"And he's the one who followed us home. What was to keep him from killing us?"

"I suppose nothing, but he had already contacted his DEA handler around seven thirty. And from there on they were aware of his movements. We don't know who actually clubbed Kurt. But it doesn't matter. He's on the hook for it. But we'll keep after the other two. That's one thing about Nacio: He's a real gut-spiller. I'm very sure he'll spill on them."

I was very sure he wouldn't. I really wondered if they had set up this informant just to have somebody in jail. But it was not my job to sort that out. My job was to be glad that they were now focusing on him, not the other two, not me.

"And don't worry. We're going to try to keep the spotlight away from you both and the school as much as possible. That little thing in there," he flicked his head toward the entrance of the bar. "Pointing you out. I won't be repeating that. I just couldn't resist. Both of you have done extraordinary and honorable work, with the boys, with us. I just thought it needed at least a moment of acknowledgement."

"And that's not all." He leaned toward us. "Yesterday we arrested two of the Mangos kingpins. I think it is safe to say they are now out of business. The gang, not just those two. What's left of the gang will have no further interest in revenge against the Padillas—the boys."

"Are you sure?" I asked.

"Well," he said, "again, nothing is ever one hundred percent, but they really don't have the means to strike at anyone right now. Especially here in the U.S."

I still felt a sort of gloomy hangover from my moment of terror. "What about in prison?"

Benton laughed, not understanding the question. "Well, most of them are going to be in prison for quite a while."

As he walked away, the first thing I said to Brenda was, "I think the guy got set up."

"Benton?"

"Yeah, maybe him too."

She nodded toward the bar. "Do you want to go back in?"

No way, now. Not as a hero. "Let's just go home and get ready."

As we walked to the car she said, "I wonder if they will stay in Phoenix? Will they stay at our school?"

"Well, I hope so. But aren't they actually rich?"

"I don't know."

We climbed in the car.

I looked at her, sitting there, smiling in the seat next to me, in the car in the cool dusk. Beautiful, happy, certain. And it came to me with sudden and absolute clarity, what we would do, how it would work, every step of the way. Getting to know each other, falling in love, lasting forever. It was there all at once, clear as a road map or a slide show. I didn't have to look ahead, because the next step would appear when needed. I had absolute confidence in that. This clarity brought with it joy.

"She's going to stay with us?" I said. "Guess it's back to the couch for me."

"Oh." Her smile became a laugh, her eyes sparkled, her arms enfolded me. "We'll make it work."

The End

AUTHOR'S NOTE

This is a work of fiction, but it was inspired by reading non-fiction and memoirs of gangsters, their families, and drug cops, as well as histories of Mexico. The following may be of interest.

- *90 Church: The true story of the narcotics squad from Hell*, by Dean Unkefer.

- *Honor Thy Father*, by Gay Talese.

- *This Family of Mine: What it was like growing up Gotti*, by Victoria Gotti.

- *God's Middle Finger: Into the lawless heart of the Sierra Madre*, by Richard Grant.

- *Labyrinth of Solitude*, by Octavio Paz.

ABOUT THE AUTHOR

Fred Andersen is an author of fiction and history who lives in Arizona.

To read more, visit fxandersen.com or the author page of your online bookstore.